INSATIABLE

A Sydney Rye Mystery, #3

EMILY KIMELMAN

Heading illustration by Autumn Whitehurst

For Nana and Poppy

There are new words now that excuse everybody. Give me the good old days of heroes and villains. The people you can bravo or hiss. There was a truth to them that all the slick credulity of today cannot touch.

-Bette Davis, *The Lonely Life*, 1962

1

Sunshine on a Sunny Day

CARLOS WAS THE ONE WHO FELT MY PHONE VIBRATING; IT WAS under one of the napkins we'd used for our picnic lunch. I found it, and glancing quickly at the "UNKNOWN" on the caller ID, picked it up. While used to calls from unknown places, I was not used to calls from this guy.

"Sydney, how are you?"

I didn't actually recognize his voice right away. I rolled away from Carlos, sitting up. "I'm sorry, but I don't know who this is." It was when he laughed that I recognized him. "Bobby?"

He laughed again. "I'm glad you remember me. My heart would be broken if I could be so easily forgotten."

I stood up, Carlos looked up at me, a question in his eyes. I shook my head and stepped away from our blanket. My dog, Blue, a huge wolf-like creature with one blue eye and one brown followed me, keeping at a heel. "Forget you, Bobby Maxim? In order to do that I'd need a lobotomy."

"With your penchant for revenge, I half expect to see you bursting through my closet doors some day, guns blazing."

I laughed. "Who says I'm not in there right now?"

"I know exactly where you are. I've been keeping very good track of you."

I looked around the park. Gentle green hills spotted with couples and groups of friends lounging on blankets dominated the landscape. On a field below me a soccer match was beginning to form. A woman ran by in a skin-tight suit, nothing on her jiggled.

"Are you here now?"

"No, no. I'm calling to ask a favor."

"That's rich."

Someone tapped me on the shoulder. I spun around and stepped back. Blue let out a growl. Carlos stood behind me, his hands out, palms forward in a sign of peace. "I just wanted to let you know I'm going to join some mates for a game of football."

"Sorry, that's great. I'll see you in a bit," I said, covering the mouth piece. Carlos smiled and jogged off down the hill.

"Does he know about you?" Bobby asked. I didn't answer as I watched Carlos join a group of other men on the field below. "Sydney, are you there?"

"I'm not doing you any favors. I don't know if you're totally clear on the fact that you took something from me."

"Sydney, I don't understand this animosity. I was just doing you a favor."

"A favor!" I heard myself yelling. Looking around I saw that I'd attracted the attention of several of the groups of Londoners trying to enjoy their first day of sun. "You bastard," I hissed quietly. "I hope you rot in hell."

"I'm sorry I didn't do it sooner, darling."

"Call me darling again and I will make it my life's mission to take your ball sack. Are we clear?"

"Anything you'd do with my ball sack would be very welcome."

"I forgot what a sick fuck you are."

"A sick fuck who did you a favor and is now looking for one in return."

"You're insane!" I heard myself yelling again. I took a deep

2

breath. In through my nose, out through my mouth. Blue tapped his muzzle against my hip to let me know he was still there.

"Sydney, I didn't know what you two had planned. I would have killed Kurt long before you showed up. Remember, I'm not the one who left my fingerprints behind; whose blood was spilled all over the floor. You took yourself down, it had nothing to do with me." He said it in an off-hand way. Like I was being petty and missing the big picture.

"You killed him," I whispered, trying to control my anger, but I could feel myself shaking. "That was my right. Kurt Jessup murdered my brother and I should have been the one to end him."

"At the time I had no idea about that. Mulberry didn't tell me what you were planning, just that we had a problem. I had no intention of stifling your little revenge act. If anyone should be pissed it's me. At least you got the treasure."

I stood on the green feeling lightheaded. It was like Bobby Maxim was taking the world and flipping it upside down. "What are you talking about? Mulberry told you that?"

"Oh Cher, you didn't know?" Maxim's voice rose an octave, teasing and dripping with syrup. A cold knowledge traveled from my toes right up to my brain, my best friend betrayed me, our relationship was built on a lie. I walked toward the shade of a tree, reaching out to rest a hand against the rough trunk. "Mulberry called me, told me about Kurt. About him killing Tate and Joseph," Bobby paused, "about how he killed your brother, James." I picked at the tree in front of me, breaking off a piece of the bark. I looked at the white underneath, the exposed inner branch. "Now don't get all upset and quiet on me, dear. He only did it to save you."

"Save me?"

"From becoming a killer."

"You think someone can be saved from that?" I heard sadness in my voice and hated myself for it.

"No, I don't. I think you are what you are, Sydney. And I think it's amazing. I want you on my team." He sounded upbeat and excited about our future together.

I didn't answer.

"Aren't you even curious about the case?" Bobby continued.

"No."

"It's a good friend of mine in Mexico, his daughter has disappeared. The reason I'm hoping you'll help is she's a fan of yours."

"What?"

"She's on that site about Joy." I felt nausea creep up my throat. Mulberry told me about the website but I had yet to visit it. I couldn't face whatever kind of madness I had spawned. The basic principle, that Joy Humbolt murdered the Mayor of New York to revenge her brother's killing, was off by a couple of heartbeats. The member's fanatical agreement that Joy was a hero was just sick. "You had a real effect on that Jackie," Bobby continued. "Starting that site about you really turned her life around. She's a serious nut bag. You should be proud."

"Jacquelyn Saperstein is suffering under a false impression of who I was. All the people on that site are deluded. I'm not a god damn hero."

"Come work for me."

"No."

"What if I could pardon you?"

I realized I should hang up the phone. This guy was so deep under my skin I practically felt like a puppet. "Ha," I said, "you're going to pardon me for something you did?"

"I could make the charges go away. You could be Joy Humbolt again."

I hung up the phone. Turned it off. Sat back down on my blanket, refilled my wine glass and spent the rest of the afternoon watching Carlos play a hot game of soccer while Blue napped peacefully by my side.

Carlos was surprised when I said I wanted to spend the night at his place. He didn't say anything but I saw the jump of his eyebrows and a sweet smile cross his lips. I felt a stab of guilt. He thought I wanted to get closer but I was just using him to avoid my place.

I woke up around 3 a.m. in Carlos's darkened bedroom. I lay there and watched shadows cast by the curtains move across the ceiling as car's headlights passed by. The shadows looked like opaque, transforming African masks.

When I stood, Blue raised his head and then followed me out into the living room. Wrapping myself in a blanket I found on the couch, I wandered into the kitchen. The fridge was full but I didn't want anything.

My phone was in my bag, still turned off. A deep, sharp pain in my chest stopped me from calling Mulberry. If it was true that he had conspired with Bobby Maxim, I didn't know what to say. And I didn't want to lose him.

Mulberry helped me when no one else would. I never could have made it out of New York alive, let alone a millionaire, without him. If he hadn't come to Mexico and pulled me out of my self-pitying spiral of alcoholism, I'd probably still be there. He gave me the name Sydney Rye. More than a name, he gave me a purpose. I'd always thought his help came from friendship. But now it all had a shadow over it. What did Mulberry really want from me?

Blue hopped up on the couch and rested his massive head between his paws. He watched me pace around the living room, eventually closing his eyes and snoring softly. Over the last three years, Blue had changed as much as me. When I first adopted Blue he was underweight, a chronic chewer with separation anxiety, and a penchant for trying to attack strangers on the street.

Now he was thick and strong; besides the slight limp where Kurt Jessup's bullet ripped through him, Blue was the picture of canine health. His coat would have looked at home on a wolf; it was glossy and shone in the gentle light from the street lamps that filtered through the living room windows. Blue was gigantic, the height of a Great Dane, the long snout of a Collie, and he took up most of the couch.

The bullet that shattered Blue's shoulder blade left a scar, thick and pink, hidden under his fur. My scars from that fight included a streak of ruined skin under my left eye that tingles with damaged nerves. Above that same eye the ghost of another wound lingers. Not as deep, it is a gentle reminder that runs above my eyebrow fading into my hairline, of what madmen will do if you don't stop them.

I grew bangs to cover the damage I could and cut the rest of my long blonde hair into a neat bob, the ends just grazing my shoulders. Being a fugitive you'd think I would need more of a disguise but there are no pictures of me with the scars and besides, I know how to disappear. Most people don't want to see a killer so they don't see me.

Carlos's computer sat in the corner of the living room on a white desk whispering to me. I pulled up the chair and woke it up.

I stared at the blank Google page for a moment and then typed in "Joy Humbolt." Jackie's site was the first to pop up. Amazing to think that my history was being told by a woman I barely knew. True, I'd proven her innocence and chased away the specter of incarceration. She said I'd saved her life. What had she done for me? Turned me into a goddamn folk hero.

I clicked on the link and held my breath while the page loaded. I didn't know what to expect but I was shocked to see a scanned copy of the letter I wrote Jackie three years ago on the landing page. It was written on hotel stationery from the Excelsior where I'd exiled myself. It was written in Joy's neat, angry, black letters. I remembered writing that letter in sudden vivid detail. I thought I knew everything that had happened and everything that would happen. I had a plan; God must have been laughing his ass off.

In the letter I explained that Jackie's husband, Joseph Saperstein, was murdered by Kurt Jessup. I explained the reason Kurt killed Joseph was that Joseph planned on stealing a lot of money from Kurt and running off with his mistress. I didn't mention that I was going to steal that money. The letter was full of bold sentences full of fact: "Mayor Kurt Jessup shot your husband in the face without remorse. He thought setting you up for it was appropriate because you should have kept your husband at home."

I wondered at Jackie's reaction to this letter. To make it public, what was she thinking?

The letter went on to describe how Kurt killed my brother, James Humbolt. I paused at the sentence that read "I clearly misunderstood my place in this game and Kurt Jessup took advantage of my ignorance. But don't worry, Mrs. Saperstein, I'm going to kill him."

When I wrote that letter it was like a promise to myself that I would do something right in all the wrong. I knew I couldn't bring my brother back, but I thought I could do something meaningful. I was not afraid to run from my life and leave everything behind. However, you cannot, as most of us know, leave everything behind.

But none of that mattered. Kurt Jessup was dead when I found him. And Joy Humbolt was guilty of a crime she didn't commit. But I was the only who knew that. Well, me and Bobby Maxim.

I pounded on the desk next to the keyboard in frustration. Blue raised his head and looked over at me, his ears alert. I shook my head at him but he slipped off the couch and came to my side just the same. I rested a hand on his head and tried to calm down.

It felt like a lifetime ago that I'd worked as a dog walker on the Upper East Side of Manhattan. It was Bobby's dog, Tobby, an out of control, spoiled Golden Retriever who ran down the alley where I found Joseph Saperstein's body. That discovery changed my life, embroiling me in the complicated and unsavory world of Manhattan's elite.

It was at a private club with low lighting and lush furnishings that I first met Bobby Maxim. I was on the arm of his friend but that didn't stop Mr. Maxim from hitting on me. He wanted to do some very nasty things to me. Judging from our conversation, he still did. But I bet there wasn't a blonde on the planet Bobby didn't want to spank or be spanked by. His sexual proclivities aside, the fact remained that he was not to be trifled with.

Even if Maxim didn't know Kurt Jessup was a killer he must have suspected; how could you be the head of one of the biggest P.I. agencies in the world and lack the ability to sniff out a murderer? But he still made him Mayor of New York. Nobody becomes the king puppet of that city without Bobby's say so.

As I looked at the letter, I marveled at what a fool I'd been and how clear that was to me now, only three years later. The question was how would I look back on this moment, was I sabotaging my life again? Should I accept the pardon? End this game?

With a sigh, I read the last paragraph of Joy's letter. "I know that Joseph and you were not at your best but at one time you did love one another. Even in the face of betrayal and loss of identity we cannot give up. Don't let this stop you. Don't let anything stop you. There can never be enough."

The last paragraph's script deteriorated until the last sentence was barely legible. It looked like the letter of an insane person. I laughed out loud. It looked like a split personality.

I scrolled past the letter to people's comments.

Where ever you are Joy, I'm thinking of you and I hope you have found peace.

I can't believe you are all praising this woman for murdering someone! Does no one care about the rule of law!

Joy Humbolt suffered a severe trauma and clearly needs to be treated in a secure psychiatric facility.

And then half of them were pleas for help.

I don't know what to do. I wish I had Joy's strength. If you're out there please help me.

My daughter has been missing for two years. Please help me find her.

The comments went on and on. I hovered over the tab for the forum but turned away, sickened by all of their opinions and needs. Who were they to judge me? Ask me for help? Why had Jackie exposed me in this way? And then it occurred to me that they were talking about Joy Humbolt, who really didn't exist at all anymore. I was Sydney Rye, my new identity suited me just fine. I worked for a small detective agency and lived in Central London. Joy Humbolt was gone.

But all these people didn't know that. They thought Joy was still out there just waiting for the right invitation to come back. I didn't want to pardon Joy Humbolt, I realized. I wanted to kill her. That would end the manhunt, end the website, and free me once and for all.

I turned my phone back on and waited for it to come back to life. Mulberry was at the top of my list of favorites and I touched his name. The phone began to ring.

"Sydney? Is something wrong?" A beat of silence passed while I wondered what to say. *You bastard, you sold me out to Bobby Maxim. You were my friend. You're the only one I have left, how could you do this?* I thought, staying silent. "Syd?" Mulberry asked, making sure I was still there.

"I got a phone call from Bobby Maxim this afternoon," I said.

Mulberry sighed. "I know."

"You know?" Of course he knew, I realized. They were in this together from the beginning right up until this moment. "I don't even have a choice, do I?"

"You always have a choice, Sydney."

"Shut the fuck up." I heard Carlos move in the bedroom and retreated toward the kitchen lowering my voice. "I trusted you."

"I know, look, I thought I was doing what was best at the time. There was no other way."

"No other way? How about just let it happen the way I wanted."

"You did get what you wanted. He's dead. You killed him. Without Bobby I never could have gotten you where you are now."

"What?"

"Wait, what are you talking about?"

Mulberry didn't know that Jessup was dead when I got there which meant that... "Do you work for Bobby Maxim? Is our agency affiliated with Fortress Global Investigations?"

"He didn't tell you."

"I guess he figured that was your job."

"Sydney, I'm sorry. I wish there was some way to say I was sorry enough for you to understand." I didn't answer him. There was no point. "I love you, Sydney, you're my best friend."

"Friends don't do this Mulberry." I felt tears burning in my eyes. "Friends do not-" I cut myself off knowing I couldn't make it through without crying. Deep breath in and then out.

"Sydney-"

I hung up. Holding the phone in my hand I squeezed my eyes shut and focused on what I needed to do. There was a text from Bobby Maxim with a phone number telling me to call when I was ready. I touched the number.

"Took longer than I thought," Bobby said.

"I don't want a pardon," I told him. "I want Joy dead."

"Dead?" I could hear a smile on his lips. "But why?"

"You don't need to know anything more than what I want. If I get this girl back for you, I want Joy's body to end up somewhere. I want the manhunt to end and I want those idiots on that site to know that she's not coming. Joy Humbolt is dead."

"Long live Sydney Rye."

2

A Game of Sorts

WITHIN 24 HOURS I WAS AT THE AIRPORT WAITING FOR A MAN. We were flying to Mexico pretending to be husband and wife. The missing girl, Ana Maria Hernandez Vargas, was the daughter of a senator and a very successful businessman. They didn't want anyone knowing they'd lost their precious little bundle so my new partner and I were playing a game of sorts.

People moved between the rows of seats under a soaring ceiling of metal beams and glass. Outside, planes taxied, took off and landed. The bright sun glinted off their wings making me squint.

Several times I saw tall men with sandy blonde hair and sat forward, but as they approached I realized it wasn't my new partner. Blue sat on the floor, his head hovering above my knee. He kept his one blue eye and one brown focused on me. Every move I made he calculated if it was a request of him.

"Hello, darling," a man said behind me. A light kiss brushed my neck. Blue stood and raised his hackles. With a small wave I told him to lie down. What kind of a wife has a dog that doesn't trust her husband's touch?

"I missed you, Peter," I said, and smiled as the man stepped to my side.

"I missed you, too, Melanie," he smiled at the alias. Peter Franks was really Blane Nichols, head of all operations in Mexico for Fortress Global Investigations. Blane was tall and well-built, his eyes were a murky green, the same shade as well-worn money. He was young for his position and I wondered what working with such an ambitious man would be like. I crossed my legs and he watched the slit in my skirt open and close.

"It's good to see you, too, Fluffy," Blane said to Blue, then reached out to pat his side. I laughed. No one but Melanie Franks, wife of almost billionaire Peter Franks, would name a dog like Blue "Fluffy." Fluffy was an "emotional support animal" allowing him to fly in the cabin with us. According to the file Bobby Maxim sent me, Melanie had anxiety that only Fluffy could ease.

Usually when I travelled with Blue, I flew private. That's one of the upsides of stealing millions of dollars worth of treasure, you get to fly on whatever kind of plane you want. However, for this trip, Bobby wanted our arrival to be obvious so we were flying commercial. First class, of course.

A petite brunette wearing a blue and white scarf around her neck stepped behind the desk marking the gate and picked up the phone to announce the boarding of our flight. First class passengers were invited to join the elderly and disabled on deck. Blane kept his hand on my lower back as the three of us headed down the gangway. He carried a light brown attaché case made of a very soft leather and I noticed a gold watch peek out from under his French cuff. This close to him, I smelled a mix of clean soap and light aftershave.

I ordered champagne because, why not? It did more to ease my anxiety than Blue's hot breath on my knee. The champagne helped me fall asleep, and though restless (I kept waking up realizing my jaw was hanging open), it was better than spending the flight analyzing whether each noise the plane made was normal or the last sound I'd hear before plummeting to my death.

When I woke it was dawn and we were descending into the Mexican capital. Blane leaned over me to look out the window as we crossed the mountains and were suddenly above the city. It filled the valley, buildings pressed together, a regular bowl of humanity. Communities of shacks spread like tendrils out of the mass of urbanity up the hillside. None of them crested the top. There are some things Mother Nature will not allow.

As the plane lowered I could make out individual streets lined with bright purple flowering trees. The traffic moved quickly on the highways we cruised over. As the plane bumped down on the runway I held my breath and squeezed the armrest. An image of the wind picking up, the plane tipping until its wing scraped the tarmac in a shower of sparks then tumbling wing over wing and finally exploding in a mushroom cloud of orange and black raced across my brain. A round of applause broke out as the plane taxied safely toward our gate. I joined in. Blane shot me a look. Melanie would never clap at being alive.

A man wearing a driver's cap and holding a sign with 'Franks' printed on it was waiting for us. He smiled when Blane nodded to him and immediately took our luggage. Blane started to speak in very quick Spanish as we moved through the crowd. I struggled to understand. My Spanish, never great, spent the last two and a half years being forgotten. Blane on the other hand, conversed easily.

My experience with Mexico was limited to less than a year spent on the Sea of Cortez. And most of that time was wasted drinking and feeling sorry for myself. That is until Mulberry came and offered me a new life, a new identity. Another couple of months of training and one murderous blood bath later, I was shipped to London where Mulberry hoped the only blood baths I'd be involved in would be at his direction.

Our driver, a man named Tito, led us to a limo that was blocking traffic. He had a quick, heated discussion with a parking cop. A couple of crumpled bills and a minute later we were on our way. The tinted windows shielded us from the bright sun as we headed into the heart of the city. I leaned back against the black leather seat and watched the city pass underneath the elevated highway. It's hard to grasp the size of this place from within it. I tried to equate the image I'd seen from the sky with the sprawl outside my window.

Graffitied walls and crumbling structures gave way to meticulously maintained parks and soaring skyrises as we entered the center of the city. I pictured it as the center of the valley with the rest of the city radiating out toward the mountains. The beauty of it surprised me.

Puerto Penasco, the town I'd lived near, was a dusty place with broken bottles lining the sandy streets. There was nothing of Mexico City's aesthetic there. This city was thoughtful. Everywhere I looked was a detail to be admired. Complicated topiaries lined the boulevard and delicate flowers were planted in the median. The sky was clear and blue as we moved through the thickening rush hour traffic.

Continuing into older neighborhoods the buildings became private. From the street all I could see were the tops of flowering trees peeking over tall stuccoed walls covered in bright green vines. Soon we were in Planco where the stout buildings housed Gucci and Hermes. We arrived in front of a four-story adobe building covered in a vine that blossomed with bright pink flowers.

A man in uniform waited for us. He opened my door and gave me a big friendly smile. "Welcome to Casa Vieja." I smiled and accepted his hand. Blue followed me out. He stopped on the cobblestone drive to take a deep stretch. Blane took my arm leading us into the lobby. The floor was a complex mosaic made of small, smooth brown stones in a circular pattern. I could feel the rounded top of the stones through Melanie's thin-soled shoes. The walls were a deep terra cotta. The desk, which a friendly woman with almost black eyes and matching hair that fell far past her shoulders stood behind, was carved wood. I ran my hand over the texture, letting my fingers linger in the deep grooves, as Blane made arrangements.

We walked up adobe steps open to the elements. I heard the flap of bird wings and a loud squawk which was answered by another. It was hard to believe that one of the largest cities in the world surrounded us. The same man who opened my car door opened our room. We walked into a living room with a curved ceiling painted turquoise. The couch, upholstered in a striped fabric of grey and blue, was deep and its cushions freshly puffed. The carpet was so soft it felt like what I imagine walking on clouds must be like. A full kitchen with traditional patterned tiles was open to the living room. Its windows faced the street.

Once the bell boy was gone and the door closed, Blue explored the room. His long snout and its perceptive nose grazed over the plush carpeting, investigating every corner. Blue's ears twitched back and forth picking up sounds that not even the most complicated of human instruments can perceive.

I moved into the bedroom, dragging my suitcase with me. Melanie's suitcase I should say; I travel light, Melanie could teach the circus a thing or two. I hefted it onto a luggage rack and unzipped. Blane leaned lazily in the doorway, his top button unhooked. "I'm going to call our clients and arrange a meeting for this evening. Most likely cocktails. Do you have anything to wear?" He was smiling.

"I'm sure I can find something," I smiled back at him. The suitcase was delivered to my apartment along with my plane ticket and a file on the case within 12 hours after I'd hung up on Bobby Maxim. I'd thrown in a couple of personal belongings, taken a shower, napped and headed to the airport. Blane walked back into the living room and Blue joined me in the bedroom. Blue did a quick tour of the room, checking the perimeter and under the bed, then with a sigh he laid down, resting his face between his paws. I pulled out a gown so long that without heels I'd step on its hem. I admired the bold pattern of lavender, cream, black and yellow. It is not something I would ever wear but Melanie...

The pitter patter of a light rain began as I pulled out socks and underwear placing them into drawers. A flash of lightning filled the room with the deep rumble of thunder on its heels. The rain was coming down harder now. I walked over to the open window. A strong wind that carried the scent of wet cement, played with my hair.

"They want to meet at seven. They'll send a car," Blane said, walking into the room. "So we've got the whole day." He took his jacket off and hung it next to my dress. "What will you do with it?" He turned to look at me.

"I think I'll take a bath and then review the file." He smiled. "Maybe take a run around the neighborhood if this storm passes."

"Sounds like a plan." Blane, holding a manila folder, laid on the bed. He grabbed the pillow off my side and propped himself up higher. Leaving him flipping through papers, I went into the bathroom. With the door closed, I turned on the tap to fill the bath. After finding just the right temperature, I faced the mirror.

Thunder clapped and my lips trembled at the intense sound. My lips give me away. I've learned to lie with my eyes: to smile with them when I feel disgust; to make them sparkle when I feel dread. My lips though, they curl at those I distrust and sneer at those who repulse me. They cling to an older version of me. They still think they belong to Joy Humbolt.

The rest of me is entirely Sydney Rye. Sydney's arms are strengthened from endless hours of pushups and tricep presses, her stomach is hard from crunches and side bends. And my legs, I use my legs to run. I don't know who Sydney Rye would be if she didn't run.

I tested the water in the tub, and finding it almost unbearably hot, eased into it. Water lapped at my clavicles. I let my eyelids close til my lashes kissed.

They started as a buzzing, like the sound of bugs against a window screen at night. The noise grew louder and I could make out individual words in the din. Joy, joy, joy, joy, joy, joy it seemed to be twerping.

I sat up with a start in the cold bath. Water sloshed over the edge and I looked around wildly for a moment trying to recollect where I was. The honey and cream colored marble, the gold faucet, and my toenails painted sweet salmon pink. Mexico City, pretending to be Sydney Rye, pretending to be Melanie Franks.

I sat back in the tub but it was too cold so I climbed out. Wrapping myself in a big fluffy robe I walked back into the bedroom. Blane was where I left him, engrossed in paperwork. He glanced up at me and then back down at his notes. Blue lifted his head off the carpet and tracked me as I got underwear, socks and a sports bra out of a drawer and then walked to my suitcase to pull out jogging shorts, a tank top and my running shoes. Seeing the shoes Blue stood and came over to me. His tail wagging, he tried to follow me into the bathroom but I closed the door.

I changed quickly while preparing myself mentally for the physical challenge ahead. I loved to run but had trouble taking that first step. Blue was a great help with this as he had no problem getting out the door. Blue did not have half the problems I did. He woke up in the morning without an alarm, he ate perfectly balanced meals; Blue's life was filled with easy discipline. Mine came at more of a price.

Out on the street the rain had stopped. I walked a couple of blocks just letting my body warm up to the idea of movement. It didn't take long before I wanted to run. I started going a little faster, jogging gently past shop windows filled with pencil-thin, faceless mannequins posing in extraordinary fabrics. A woman teetering on stiletto heels while jabbering into her cell phone walked a small, white, curly-haired dog. The little dog strained against its pink halter, yapping at us. Blue's head stayed straight and even with my hip. The little dog's bark faded as we turned onto a side street filled with shade, the sticky sweet scent of flowers, and the soft whoosh of a breeze. My pace picked up as I tread on fallen bright purple petals. I felt my heart quickening as Chapultepec Park rose up ahead.

Crossing into the park, I began a sprint. A line of families waiting to enter the zoo watched us pass. Little arms shot out to point at Blue, whispers of "lobo" followed us.

I felt like I was flying. Not a thought entered my head only the joy of speed as I raced down an empty path. When my chest felt like it was on the verge of explosion and my legs were no longer communicating I slowed down. The path under my feet was a light sand. The trees around me bent and swayed in the gentle wind. I relished the shade and mild temperature, the occasional gust that helped cool me.

My body recovered quickly and I picked up my pace again. My first trainer, a man named Merl who Mulberry sent to me in Puerto Penasco, taught me not to, as he put it, "blow my load" at the beginning of a jog. I tried to keep my pace steady as Blue and I wandered down paths that wound past lakes, families picnicking on large green fields, and shrubs pruned into abstract shapes.

Coming off a shaded trail into an opening, I looked up against the sun and saw six columns in a semi-circle at the top of a platform. I raced up the steps, taking them two at a time (not thinking about Rocky, or at least trying to avoid the comparison). At the top I stopped to catch my breath. Turning away from the columns toward the city, I looked out over a large boulevard. It appeared to go on forever. I felt that the whole of the metropolis lay before me.

Juanita Vargas Llosa de Hernandez was a tall woman with tight skin and a strong jaw. She had a well-practiced smile and a firm hand shake. Her husband, Pedro Hernandez Gonzalez, was shorter than her. He was soft everywhere but his eyes. They were one of the most powerful couples in Mexico. She was a Senator and he owned hotels that dotted the capital, lined the Caribbean Sea, and hugged the Oaxacan coast. They had a daughter, Ana Maria Hernandez Vargas, who was missing.

Blane leaned back in his chair and smiled at the small group. He'd known Pedro for years. "No one does business in Mexico unless they know each other," Blane told me on the drive over. Pedro stood next to the bar holding his glass. He filled it with ice and then poured tequila over it. His wife sat on the couch watching her husband with narrowed eyes and clenched fists. She did not have a drink. I wished she would.

The ice in my glass clinked against the sides as I swirled the tequila, cooling it. It was a smoky blend, almost like a cognac. Tequila, known to Americans as a drink to shoot or mix in a margarita, is a different animal in Mexico. It is aged as carefully as an Irish whiskey, its flavors as delicate as a French wine. I sipped my drink and smiled at the subtle layers of flavor and smoky overtone.

A crystal chandelier dangled from the towering ceiling. On the walls, painted a soft yellow, hung an array of paintings. One showed an Aztec city surrounded by never-ending corn fields. Another portrayed a family with an overloaded donkey walking along a road to somewhere. The one right above the couch that Juanita sat on depicted Jesus in the arms of his mother. Mary's face was a passive gentle mask as she admired the child in her lap who wore a halo around his head. The mother on the couch under the painting was wound so tight I feared she might explode right there in front of us.

"My daughter," she said with just a hint of accent, "is hiding, not missing." Her husband looked over at her, anxiety written across his face. "She has money, she has friends. If someone took her they'd want something and no one has requested a thing. She is doing this because we had a fight and she wants to remind us that she is important."

"She is important," Pedro jumped in.

"Of course she is." Juanita waved a hand of dismissal at him.

"Do you agree with your wife that your daughter is in no danger?" Blane asked Pedro.

The man looked into his tequila, his brow furrowed and he took his time when speaking. "I think she is safe right now, but I worry that out on her own our enemies may find her."

"Who are those enemies, Pedro? Tell me about them," Blane said.

Pedro crossed the room to look out one of the long narrow windows covering the south wall. His glass almost empty, he finished off the last sip before answering. "My wife and I make lots of people angry." He turned to Juanita who was watching him, her face taut. "Juanita pushes for women's rights and that is something that many in this nation resent." Her face softened as her husband continued. "My wife is a very strong woman and she does not back down from those who aim to keep women without rights or protections." He stopped speaking and looked into his empty glass.

"And I am a businessman who over the years," he paused as if looking back over those long years. His eyes looked tired. "I have angered competition, former employees, local activist groups." He waved his hand at each enemy on his list.

"What was the fight about?" I asked. All eyes in the room moved to me. I didn't realize how invisible I was until I spoke. Juanita smiled at me and shook her head.

"I will let my husband explain that. I prefer not to be in the room." She stood up and straightened her pencil skirt so that you'd never know she'd been sitting. With her head held high Juanita left the room, closing the large wooden door behind her.

Silence filled the space. A door somewhere else in the house closed with an audible thump. The honk of a car horn, dulled by the thick walls and shut windows, reached us as barely a toot. Ice clinked in Pedro's empty glass. Facing the window he started to talk, "The fight was over a young lady I have been..." He faltered for a moment, not sure of which word to use. "A woman I've been seeing."

He was quick to add, "In most Mexican families this would not be an issue but our family is different." Pedro turned back into the room and crossed to the bar. "I am a man who was raised to be *the* man." He filled his glass with more tequila, not bothering to add ice. He swigged from the glass and I saw a line of sweat forming on his brow. "I love my daughter very much. And my wife." He paused, his words hanging in the air.

Blane and I didn't speak. This guy had stuff to say and we didn't want to interrupt.

"My wife is incredible, you know," he continued, rushing through the sentence, pushing it out in almost a gasp. "She has done more to bring women's issues to the forefront of this nation than any other figure in its history. But you cannot change a country overnight. It is not possible." He slammed his drink onto the bar and looked over at the painting of Mother Mary and then quickly away.

"I think that Juanita's work is very important. I want my daughter to live in a world where she has all the rights of her male counterparts but..." He was looking for an excuse, something reasonable to tell us about how fucking some other woman was really OK but he couldn't think of one. He filled his glass again and took a seat near Blane. He lifted the glass to his forehead and held it there with his eyes closed. "I do not know what I have done."

Blane looked over at me and with just the slightest movement of his head gestured that I should leave. I stood up, almost steady on my heels, and left the room. As I closed the door I heard Blane begin to speak in a steady voice.

Once in the hall I didn't really know what to do with myself. My heels clicked on the tile floors as I looked around, hoping to find a bathroom or something interesting. I jumped and sucked in my breath when out of the corner of my eye I saw Juanita sitting in a straight-backed wooden chair pushed into a dark corner of the hall.

"I did not mean to frighten you," she said. My hand over my heart, I nodded. She stood up and came towards me. "Did he tell you?"

"Yes," I answered.

She smiled. "And what do you think? As an American woman, what do you think about that?"

"It happens all the time," I answered.

"Would you stand for it?"

"It depends on the relationship."

Juanita nodded. "My daughter does not understand. She thinks that it is hypocritical." She laughed and it echoed in the empty hall, bouncing off the cool tile, coming back to us sounding almost not like a laugh at all.

"She is very young," I said.

"Yes, she is." Juanita's eyes unfocused and a small smile spread across her face. It was amazing how it softened her hard features. "I'd like to show you something."

Juanita led me down the hall back toward the main entrance and up the grand staircase that faced the front door. We went left and followed a carpeted hall past several rooms until we came to a door marked "STAY OUT!" We went in.

There was no doubt that the owner of the room was a teenage girl. Her childhood and the beginning of her adult life clashed everywhere. Taped over the delicate pink rose wallpaper were posters of men just out of puberty wearing tight pants and scarves over bare, hairless chests. Small ceramic horses shared space on the mantel with a mess of earrings, necklaces and the occasional cosmetic. The girl's bed, obviously made by a maid as no one going through such emotional upheaval could produce hospital corners like that, was covered in teddy bears.

Juanita sat on the edge of the bed. "Maria is a modern woman. She believes that she is equal to men."

"Isn't she?" I asked.

Juanita pulled a pink bear over to her and looked into its empty plastic eyes. "Yes, of course, but most men don't know it." Pushing the bear aside she turned to look at me. "You know women are equal according to our laws, but in practice, they are not. When a woman is raped or murdered, it does not matter unless she has a wealthy, powerful family. Poor women in this country are treated as dogs."

"I know," I said. Along the Mexican/American border, girls are murdered as if they were cattle. They are raped, mutilated, shot and then their bodies dumped on the road without even the barest of graves. The girls work at the many factories that line the border. Their killers are impossible to punish because he is not one man but an attitude. An attitude that it is OK for police, who are also the drug runners, to celebrate successful smuggling trips by killing women without connections or family. I knew a girl who died that way. Her killers suffered a similar fate... though I didn't rape them.

"Most women do know," she said simply. "But my daughter

does not understand. If I left Pedro it would not help anything. I would not be happier, he certainly would not, and my career…" she paused and her eyes shone brightly in that little girl's room. "How can I be a mother to the state if I cannot even help my own daughter?" She looked away from me and her chin wrinkled.

Pulling herself together she continued, "This is one of the reasons she is mad, because she says I care more about my career than my family, but what she does not understand is that I am fighting for my family, not just for her, but for her daughters and their daughters. I am fighting for the daughters of Mexico." It was a good line, one I guessed she used before.

"Ana Maria is right in some ways," she continued. "I am very afraid of what other people will think." She let out a snort of a laugh. "That is why you are here as Melanie Franks and not whatever your real name is." I smiled at the idea that I had a real name. "I don't want anyone to find out that I have lost my daughter."

"Do you have any idea where she is?"

Juanita looked up at me. "I think it is possible she is with her cousin Alejandro. We called him and he says she is not there, but he would happily lie for her."

"Where is Alejandro?"

"In Playa del Carmen. He manages Pedro's hotels on the Yucatan." She smiled and it didn't look like it was for joy.

"Ana Maria and Alejandro are close?"

"They have always cared for each other deeply. He is Pedro's sister's son." She looked back over at the pile of teddy bears. "He is adopted." She reached out and took another stuffed animal from the pile. This one was brown and raggedy. "We got her this in New York at FAO Schwartz. She was only eight, a little more than ten years ago. It is amazing the way things change so fast." She pulled the bear closer to her and toyed with one of its little paws. "She rode on Pedro's shoulders and she would cover his eyes and laugh." A tear dropped onto the stomach of the bear. Juanita ran a well-manicured hand across her eyes and sniffled back a sob.

She stood up and faced me, her eyes streaked with red. "I trust that you will find my daughter and that you will bring her home. Bobby said that you had insight that would be invaluable. I believe him."

"We will do our best," I promised. Juanita Vargas Llosa de Hernandez nodded and then walked out of the room, leaving me alone with her memories.

4

Strangers in Paradise

THE NEXT MORNING WE LEFT FOR PLAYA DEL CARMEN. AFTER landing in Cancun we travelled on a highway with barely a curve which ran parallel to the Caribbean Sea. The road, a single lane in each direction, brings tourists from Cancun south to Playa del Carmen and Tulum. Unair- conditioned buses passed each other wildly, swerving into oncoming traffic and then veering at the last possible second back into the correct lane. Natural growth of ratty trees and thirsty scrub hugged the roadway interrupted only by the hotel entrances that explained the reason for the road at all.

Our car turned and passed through the gates of The Paradise Hotel. On the hotel grounds the natural vegetation that lived by the road was gone. A long stretch of blacktop carried us through manicured grounds forced into order by a team of invisible gardeners and one hell of an irrigation system.

The hotel rose before us, surrounded by palm trees swaying in the breeze. We pulled into its circular drive and could see the azure blue of the Caribbean Sea through the open lobby. A uniformed employee opened my door and welcomed me to Paradise. I squinted against the bright sun and smiled. A warm breeze played with my hair as my luggage was unloaded.

Blue sat on the sidewalk, his neck stretched out toward the sky, his nose sniffing the scents that floated by on the passing air. I felt Blane's hand curl around my waist and he led me into the lobby. It opened to the driveway on one side and the Caribbean Sea on the other. Couches faced the crystal blue water that rose and fell in small swells. Some people sat enjoying drinks as large fans provided an artificial breeze to the space.

Blane checked us in and our luggage was loaded onto a cart. A bell boy led us past the elevators, through an arched doorway and out to a shaded path where a golf cart waited for us. The man behind the wheel invited us to step aboard. I turned to look at Blane who smiled. "Pedro made special arrangements for his good old friends the Franks."

The small electric cart carried us down a path that ran by the beach. Some people were laid out on chaise lounges baking themselves in the bright sun while others read books under umbrellas. The water was dotted with the heads of swimmers and the occasional happy cry of a child carried across the waves to us. The blue of the sea met the blue of the sky in a barely perceptible horizon.

As we continued, the crowd thinned, and when we stopped in front of a large cabana with its own private patio, the shore was sparsely populated. Blane tipped our driver who then pulled a u-turn and headed back the way we'd come.

The bungalow had a name. It was painted on a wooden sign next to the front door: "Luna de Miel." Next to the sign, an iguana missing half his tail soaked up the warmth of the sun. Blue's ears perked and his head cocked when he noticed the giant lizard. "I wouldn't mess with him," I said. Blue turned to look at me. I waved him into the cabana before he could start any trouble.

The bungalow was one large space. A king size bed shrouded in mosquito netting faced a flat screen TV. A small sitting area took up one corner and a small kitchen the other. A ceiling fan meant to resemble palm fronds circulated the air. Blane pushed open the doors and let the sea breezes toy with the long white curtains.

Our luggage arrived and so did a fruit basket with a note from

Pedro's nephew Alejandro. "Welcome to Paradise! I hope that everything is to your liking. Please join me for dinner this evening at eight. I very much want to help." Blane held the card in his fingers, wiggling it up and down.

"What do you think?" he asked.

"She's here," I said, looking out at the sea. The blue of the water and its never-ending movement filled me with a sense of well-being and calm. "Wouldn't you be?" I asked, turning to face Blane.

He smiled. "I guess you're right. If I had a loyal cousin who would hide me from my parents, I would come to him for help."

"What do you think of Ana Maria, just a spoiled rich kid?"

"I don't know," Blane answered, pulling his laptop out of his bag and placing it on the coffee table.

"You've know Pedro a long time. Have you met the girl?"

"Sure, a couple of times," he said, looking at the laptop's screen.

"So what's she like?"

Blane looked up at me. "I don't know her really. She seems silly enough for a girl."

"Silly enough for a girl?"

He sighed and looked at me like maybe I was going to make something out of nothing. "I just meant that she seems like a normal teenage girl. Nothing special."

"I wish we could have talked to some of her friends. I don't know, gotten a sense of her before we came here."

Blane shrugged and returned his gaze to the computer. "I think we'll find her."

"Yes," I agreed. "But how will we bring her back? If she doesn't want to come?"

Blue whined at me and I looked over to see him sitting in the kitchen next to the sink. He looked up at it then back at me. I headed into the kitchen and found a white bowl in the cabinet. Filling it with chilled water from the fridge I placed it on the ground for Blue. He lapped at it, spilling droplets onto the tiles.

"Check the safe in the closet," Blane said. "Should be two guns according to this." He was reading something on the screen of his laptop.

I headed into the closet and found the safe. "What's the code?"

"2568"

I punched in the number, the lock turned with an electric whirl and I opened it up. Inside were two guns and couple of boxes of bullets. "They're here," I called into the bedroom. I closed the door and reset the code.

"Good," Blane said, as I came back into the room. "Don't think we'll need them but you never know."

I eyed the bottle of champagne nestled in our fruit basket. It was dripping with condensation. I pulled it out on the pretense of putting it in the fridge but made sure that Blane noticed me carrying it. "Why don't you pop that?" he said, looking up from the computer. "Do it on the patio where people can see you. After all, we are a loving couple on vacation." He smiled. I smiled back.

Out on the balcony I eyed the iguana with only half his tail. He appraised me from under sleepy lids and then returned his stare to the sea. Blue settled himself near the steps. Laying his head between his paws, he closed his eyes and set about the all-important job of boiling his brains in the hot sun.

I removed the champagne foil and then its protective metal cage. The cork popped with a satisfying bang. I yelped in mock surprise and then laughed as Blane stepped out onto the patio. Foam spilled over the lip of the bottle and onto my hand. Blane laughed and took the bottle from me. I glanced at the few people who dotted the beach and guessed that none of them cared.

Blane poured the champagne into two flutes he'd carried out with him. Handing me a glass he asked, "Anyone out there look like they are looking?"

I shook my head laughing. "No, this all seems rather ridiculous, doesn't it?"

He shrugged. "I don't mind pretending I'm married to a beautiful woman like you." Blane stepped closer to me and I cast my eyes back to the iguana. I could feel Blane looking at me and for a moment I thought he might touch me. My skin felt alive at the prospect, super-sensitive waiting for the contact.

Clearing my throat, I stepped back. The last thing I needed was clouding my head with this guy. He worked for Bobby Maxim so obviously he could not be trusted, not in bed, not in my head; no, I should not trust this man.

"I'm going to get ready for dinner," I said, moving past him into our honeymoon suite.

He smiled as I slipped by. "Sounds like a plan, Sydney." He let my name roll off his tongue and I turned to look at him. There was something in his eyes, something joking, or knowing. Something that wasn't there a moment ago.

At ten to eight a golf cart arrived driven by a man dressed in the hotel's uniform with a smile on his face. We climbed aboard and the machine's engine hummed as it carried us through the winding paths of the property.

We passed the main building of the hotel. The sounds of clinking glasses, cutlery against plates, and voices straining to rise above it all reached us. Couples stood on the balconies. Backlit by the hotel's bright and welcoming lights, they look like silhouettes putting on a play. We continued under a star-filled sky past empty beaches and breaking waves until we reached a mansion that was lit up for the night. It was a modern building, all glass and concrete. The landscaping was minimalist and a pool glowed deep ocean blue, its surface shimmered as a soft breeze passed by.

Our driver stepped out of the golf cart and offered me his hand. I heard a door slide open as I stepped onto the paved path and looked up to see a short, squat figure silhouetted against the house's light. As he came down the steps to greet us, the moon came out from behind a passing cloud and illuminated his face. He was smiling at us; his teeth were so straight and white that only an orthodontist with the help of a skilled dentist could maintain such perfection. His hair was thick, wild and as black as the sea that fronted his home, yet his eyebrows were perfect arches above deep-set eyes.

"I am Alejandro. Welcome," he said, offering Blane his hand. They shook and then he turned to me. "Welcome." I put my hand out. Instead of shaking it Alejandro cupped it softly and lifted it to his lips. He lightly kissed right above my knuckles then lowered my hand and released it. I smiled, pleasantly surprised by the antiquated gesture. "It is a pleasure to meet you both. Please come in." He waved toward the house. We followed him along a paved path cut through the sand to the patio surrounding the pool. It was made of a cement-like material with chunks of something in it that caught the moonlight and twinkled.

"Glass-fault," Alejandro said. I looked at him. "The pavement, it's glass-fault. It is made of recycled bottles from the hotel."

"Oh, neat," I said, sounding like a simpleton.

"I am trying to make my carbon foot print as small as possible." He laughed. "My feet are not very big, why leave a huge mark on the planet?" He laughed some more. Blane and I joined him. Alejandro led us up several steps to the patio where a man waited. He was unusually tall, seeming even more so when compared to Alejandro. "Cocktails?" Alejandro asked.

Blane ordered a vodka martini and I asked for a tequila gimlet with just a splash of cranberry juice. Alejandro decided to have the same and the tall man turned on his heel in a military manner and walked into the house. Alejandro gestured to a table and chairs facing the sea. A woman wearing a blue maid's uniform and a white apron brought us a plate of cheese, fruit and nuts.

The three of us sat out on the deck listening to the lapping of the sea at the shore and the rustle of the wind in the palms fronds. The silent man returned with our drinks and after he was gone Blane said, "I suppose we should cut to the chase."

Alejandro smiled and nodded. "I like a man who is direct."

"Do you know where she is?"

"Ana Maria," Alejandro sighed, and looked out over his pool, past his beach, beyond the Caribbean, to the horizon, the thin line marking the end of what humans can see. "She is so young."

"Far too young to leave her parent's house," Blane said.

Alejandro laughed softly and turned to look at Blane. "You know my mother, my birth mother, probably had me when she was younger than Ana Maria is now. Do you know much about the Mayan culture?" he asked, turning to me.

"Not much," I admitted.

"It is a fascinating history."

"Most peoples are," I said.

He laughed. "You're right. I suppose because my blood is Mayan I find it more interesting than others."

The maid came to the door and announced that dinner was ready. We followed Alejandro into a large room with cream walls. A modern dark wood dining table with matching chairs was set for three. Alejandro offered me a seat to the left of his. The place setting was beautiful in its simplicity. The glasses - one for water, one for wine - were clear with long stems and no pattern. White soup bowls sat on white plates. The cutlery had soft edges and modern lines. The texture of the placemat and napkin reminded me of a tightly woven basket.

Soup arrived, green and creamy. "It's asparagus," Alejandro told us, as it was ladled into our bowls. When the staff left, the soup tasted and complimented, Blane brought up the girl again. Alejandro lifted his spoon to his mouth and swallowed before answering. "I am afraid I am in an uncomfortable situation here." He put down his utensil and leaned back in his chair. "As you know, my uncle is my employer, and beyond that I respect him greatly. But, I do not know if I can help him."

"Do you know where she is?" Blane asked. Alejandro closed his eyes and laced his fingers together. We waited. The tall, statue-like man came into the room to clear our plates. Alejandro stayed in his meditative state

"Alejandro?" Blane said. Alejandro's eyes opened and he looked at Blane but did not answer. "You know you can't keep her."

Alejandro smiled and nodded. "I don't think anyone can. She has her own mind. I've never met a stronger one." Alejandro sighed. "She is here."

"Where?"

"Ana Maria," Alejandro said quietly, almost to himself.

"Yes, where is she?" A blush of red started to creep up Blane's neck.

"You will not find her unless she wants to be found. Ana Maria is very much in charge of her own destiny."

"She is only a child."

Alejandro's eyes jumped to Blane's face. "You underestimate her at your own peril."

"What are you talking about? She's a kid."

Alejandro pushed back his chair and stood up. He was not tall or big, but there was something set in his face that made him frightening.

"Don't," came a soft voice from the patio. We all turned to look. Ana Maria stood in the doorway wearing a dress that made her look much more like a woman than a girl. Alejandro's face softened at the sight of her. She crossed the room to his side. Ana Maria was only slightly taller than our host. Alejandro looked up at her. "Mrs. Franks, Mr. Franks," she nodded at us each in turn. "You look a lot like my father's friend, Blane," she said. "And you," she continued, turning to me, "I recognize your face." I felt uncomfortable sitting down while they both stood. Blane rose out of his chair and I followed.

"Ana Maria," Blane said, "Your parents are very worried about you."

She smiled down at her feet. "I find it hard to believe that it is me they worry about."

"Your mother is very upset," I told her.

She looked into my eyes and said, "You have been deceived." It was a creepy thing to say and I felt a chill run through me. Ana Maria turned away, the hem of her long, open-backed dress swished across the glass-fault floor as she crossed to the bar. I watched her shoulder blade shift as she lifted ice cubes out of a silver bucket and dropped them into her glass. Ana Maria's movements were elegant and I imagined she must have taken ballet. She picked up a decanter of light brown liquor and poured it over the ice which cracked loudly in response.

"Anyone else want a drink?" she asked.

"Look Ana, you've got to come home," Blane said.

She laughed as she crossed the room. "I don't have to do anything." She walked past us and out onto the patio. Blane went after her as she floated down the steps onto the beach. She turned toward the hotel and disappeared from view. Blane reached the sand and looked after her. He turned to me, "She's gone," he said.

"I told you that you could not find her if she did not want to be found," Alejandro said, behind me. Blane was standing in the moonlight alone. He twisted one more time to check the beach but clearly he saw nothing. Blane came back up onto the patio and rushed at Alejandro.

"Do you know how pissed Pedro is going to be when he hears that you've been hiding her?" Blane asked. Alejandro did not answer. "Are you sleeping with her, is that what this is about?"

Alejandro's face reddened. "I am not," he said.

"Well, you certainly look like you'd like to," Blane said. Even in the soft light I could see that Blane's face was red with anger. He turned away from Alejandro and focused on me. He threw up his hands and stormed back toward the beach.

"Shall I arrange transportation?" Alejandro asked me as we watched Blane disappear down the path. I thought about following him, walking all the way back to our bungalow and then I looked down at my shoes. "Or perhaps we could have one more drink?" Alejandro suggested. I smiled at him. "I cannot help you find her, but I will certainly offer you my hospitality."

"As long as you help me to a drink I think we'll get along just fine," I said.

"Certainly." He held his arm out toward the house and I stepped back inside.

5

Drunk For a Reason This Time

"YOU'RE DRUNK," BLANE SAID, WHEN I STUMBLED OVER THE doorframe into our cabana.

I laughed. "Doesn't take much."

"What?" He was lying on the bed but when I knocked into the coffee table and nearly went down he stood up. "I can't believe you're drunk."

I waved him away with a big, sweeping arm gesture that sent me off-balance, but luckily I landed on the couch. "I'm surprised you're not," I said. His forehead wrinkled into a look of disgust. I smiled. "Who do you think I got drunk with?"

"What?" He only looked confused for a second and then understanding bloomed across his face. "Alejandro."

"Of course. I'm going out on his boat tomorrow. I understand him."

"What do you understand?"

"His love for her. It's not sexual, you must understand. You must understand. He kept insisting that I understand. Guy can't hold his liquor." Blane came and sat next to me. There were two of him for a second but then they merged into one very handsome man. I smiled and blushed and leaned back, which turned out to be sideways and fell off the couch.

Blane picked me up and I remember laughing as we both tipped back onto the couch. "Did he say where she was?" he asked, his voice strained with the weight of lifting me.

I shook my head. "He doesn't know. He has no control over her. She is apparently a very powerful little girl. She has her own agenda, he said." I curled up into a little ball and felt very tired and very comfortable.

The morning light filtering through our white curtains woke me. I blinked against the sun and rolled away from it; closing my eyes, I buried my head into the pillow. I heard the shower running and smelled soap. I stretched, pushing my feet out from under the covers and over the edge of the couch. Blue licked my toe. I yelped and then laughed. Sitting up I realized my hangover wasn't that bad.

I needed to go for a run. It would help dissipate any remaining alcohol in my system and give me time to think. I hurried, wanting to be gone before Blane got out of the shower. He was going to ask me a lot of questions about my drunken night with Alejandro and I needed to clear my head. I pulled on my jogging shorts, a sports bra and white tank top. Grabbing my iPod shuffle and headphones, I attached Blue to a leash and slipped out the door in my bare feet.

It was a gorgeous day, the sun was bright, the sky that incredible blue and the Caribbean, well, it's the Caribbean, isn't it? I walked away from the bungalow toward the main building of the hotel letting my body get used to the idea of moving rather than drinking. I hit play on my shuffle and White Snake's "Here I Go Again" filled my ears. I started to pick up my pace, jogging right at the line of the sea, avoiding the water but taking advantage of the hard-packed earth. Blue kept pace with me, my slow jog equivalent to his walk.

I've had a lot of drinking partners, I thought, as the song made me run faster. But none quite like Alejandro. Firstly, I've never sipped tequila on a suede couch with a Mayan. Let alone a Mayan who admits, but only in the strictest of confidence that his cousin is "not like other girls." He seemed to believe that there was something unnatural about her.

Before I could finish my thought the music picked up and I stopped thinking about Alejandro, the tequila, his couch, the case and my life. I raced past the main building of the hotel, my heart pounding against my chest as I maneuvered around children building sand castles and overweight tourists lying out, scorching their skin in an attempt to get that healthy glow.

Blue and I were past the hotel and the crowds when my breath gave out and I had to slow down. I jogged slowly, trying to keep running but looking down at Blue, I knew that I wasn't going any faster than a slow walk. I took huge, heaving breaths as the song faded away.

Before the next one began I looked up and saw that I was passing Alejandro's house. There was no one out on the patio and all of the glass doors were closed. I wondered if he was out jogging like me or if he slept in. Perhaps he was already at work. We'd arranged to meet for cocktails on his sailboat at sunset. He'd asked me toward the end of the night. And as I remembered it, looking up at his empty house, I thought there might have been a note of desperation in his voice, a plea in his eyes.

My lungs recovered and George Michael and Queen started to play *Somebody to Love*. This song is hard for me to hear but I listen to it anyway. I picked up my pace leaving Alejandro's house behind. The beach ahead of me was deserted as my feet pushed through the sand. Blue picked up his pace to keep up with me. And then the beat started and I could hear the crowd clapping. It starts soft but then builds. This version was recorded live soon after Freddy Mercurey's death and you can hear the desperation in Michael's voice. And the crowd responds, yelling back at him. All of them are pleading to find love.

I dropped to the sand and started doing pushups, feeling the sweat dripping down my face. The burn in my arms makes it easier not to cry. It's not that I'm so desperate to find somebody to love or that I'm so lonely I'll start crying on the beach. It's that prison cell he talks about. Mine is filled with images of my murdered brother and although I spend most of my time out of the cell, it still owns me and no matter how far I run or how many pushups I do, I can't ever seem to escape.

I rolled onto my back and started doing crunches. The sun was bright and I could feel its heat on my face. My abdominal muscles burned as I brought my chest and knees together over and over again. When I could not stand it one second longer, I ripped my headphones out of my ears, and standing up, raced toward the sea. Blue followed, his tail high with excitement. I ran through the shallows, my feet splashing water up into the air. Reaching the breakers, I dove headfirst into a wave.

The cold water felt amazing on my hot face. I rose back to the surface and filled my lungs with air. Another wave came and I jumped up, letting my natural buoyancy carry me to the top of it. Blue swam around me, his legs pumping underneath him, his tail swishing from side to side.

Back at the cabana, Blane was eating a breakfast of egg whites, toast and tea. He smiled when I came in. I showered and then joined him. "I ordered for you, I hope that's OK."

"Sure." He lifted a silver top off my plate to reveal egg whites and toast. I smiled. "Thanks, looks great," I lied. Blane's breakfast was bland but I cleaned my plate.

"So," he said, "what happened last night?"

I cleared my throat and was about to tell him everything when an instinct told me not to. It was a weird feeling, but I suddenly didn't want to give him everything I had. Looking across the table at Blane, at the look on his face, I just didn't trust him. "I think," I started, "that she came to him because she was so upset." I was lying. I actually thought, based on Alejandro's cryptic drunk-talk, that she might have made up the whole fight with her family so they wouldn't know her real reason for leaving. I was hoping he would reveal said reason this evening. "I think she's just a confused girl. We need to convince Alejandro to tell her to go back to her parents and I think she will."

Blane was looking at me with no expression in his eyes and I started to sweat despite the cool breeze from the fan above my head. "Really?" he asked.

"She's just pissed at her parents. She's probably going through that phase when you realize that your parents aren't perfect and it makes it you angry. She'll come home with us if we make it clear that her parents want her to."

"It's that simple?"

"Don't you think?" What was going on, I thought. Why are we talking to each other like this? Why do I feel like we are on different sides?

The fan spun, the curtains swayed, the sea lapped at the shore and we watched each other. Blane turned away first, he picked up the newspaper that lay sprawled on the couch and pretended to be reading when he asked, "So what time are we going out on the boat?"

"Alejandro invited me for sunset drinks."

"I assume he meant for your husband to come as well." He didn't look out from behind the paper.

"I think he knows we're not really married."

"You told him?"

I bristled at the accusation. "He's not an idiot. I didn't have to tell him we are detectives, I'm pretty sure that Pedro did, or Ana Maria, or maybe he figured it out on his own, but I really don't think he fell for it. Besides, is he not supposed to know? Isn't this," I waved my hand around the cabana to encompass our fake matrimony, "just for show anyway?"

Blane brought the paper down and looked at me. "So you didn't tell him?"

"No, I didn't." I stood up and walked over to the closet but had nothing to do there so turned back to him. "What is going on?"

Blane raised the paper, covering his face and said, "What?"

"Seriously, what is going on? What is this really about? Something is not right."

"I have no idea what you are talking about."

"I know there is something besides a missing girl going on here I just don't know what."

He lowered the paper again, a smile on his face. "You have a reputation for going on your instincts; it appears that they have let you down this time." I stared at him. "Should we go to the beach today, dear, keep up appearances as the happy vacationing couple?" He raised his eyebrows.

"Don't you think we should be looking for Ana Maria?"

"I think she'll be on the boat this evening. Besides," he laughed, "apparently she is so strong we have no chance of forcing her home. We won't be able to find her unless she wants to be found. I'll be sure to put that in my report." He laughed again as he raised the paper back over his face. I suddenly wondered if this was what real marriage was like.

6

A Surprise Guest

WE SPENT THE DAY ON THE BEACH. IT WAS WEIRD. BLANE PLAYED Frisbee with Blue, and I sat under an umbrella pretending to read a paperback about a woman who happens to be a virgin who meets a bull rider on a farm and they fall in love but he loses a leg, and well, I couldn't really follow the rest because I was too busy thinking.

Several things were bothering me as I watched Blane flick the Frisbee through the air. I suspected that there was something else going on here. Alejandro talked about Ana Maria as though she was much more than just a young girl angry at her parents, but I didn't know what he meant. And the whole pretending to be married thing was so ridiculous. I knew so little about Mexican politics that it made the book in my hand that much more frustrating. It was a part of my cover. Apparently Melanie Franks liked bad books. Maybe her husband wasn't satisfying her sexually. I smiled at that thought as I watched Blane run into the ocean, Blue on his heels. They jumped through the waves together until they were on the other side swimming casually through the swells.

Another thing that kept tickling the back of my brain was the feeling in my gut that Blane was hiding something from me. I knew it was impossible to trust Bobby Maxim or any of his employees, but what did they want from me? There was a perfect little picture in front of me that showed an angry girl, a handsome detective, a devoted cousin, and a simple solution. Convince the girl to go home. Why couldn't I just believe it?

Blane and Blue came out of the water. Blue raced passed Blane and barreled toward me, his tongue lolling out of his mouth, his ears flat to his head. His limp was no longer pronounced, but I could tell that his left shoulder didn't take quite as much weight as his right. Blue stopped and shook, sending water and sand all over me. I laughed and yelled for him to stop in the same breath.

Blane came up laughing and flopped onto a chaise lounge. He smiled up at me, his eyes squinting against the sun. He looked so handsome and nice that I wondered if I was paranoid. Maybe we were just here to bring home a missing girl.

The day passed and we returned to the cabana to get ready for our sail. "I think you should go alone," Blane called to me from the bathroom. I was in a robe freshly showered and looking at all the silk in my closet.

"What?" I called back.

"You should go alone. He trusts you and I think you'll have better luck without me." I walked to the bathroom door. Blane was shaving, his chin in the air and his cheeks covered in foamy white cream. He brought a straight razor from the top of his neck to the point of his chin then dipped it into the water-filled sink.

"Really?" I said. I was suspicious of his motives, but maybe the day on the beach had built some trust between us.

"Sure." He left it at that. I watched him for a moment as he carved the shaving cream off his face and then I turned back to my closet. I didn't know what was going to happen on the boat and I wanted to be prepared. I ended up with a pair of very low heels designed by Chanel that looked like they would be easy to kick off if nothing else. I chose a pair of light cotton white pants. I put on a lacy bra (the only kind Melanie wore) and buttoned a silk top over it. I decided against earrings and wore a simple gold chain instead.

"You look nice," Blane told me, as I rummaged around in my purse making sure I had everything I needed. I looked up at him and decided I really wanted a weapon.

"I want to take a gun," I said.

Blane laughed. "That's not very friendly; you're just going for a cocktail cruise. What could you possibly need a gun for?"

"You never know," I said, a smile creeping onto my lips.

"I don't think it's appropriate." He turned away from me, ending the conversation. I went into the bathroom and put his straight razor in my purse. Then again, maybe our day on the beach together didn't mean shit.

When the golf cart arrived, I climbed into it and Blue jumped up next to me. Blane waved from the patio as we drove away. The marina was a 15 minute ride through lush gardens. We drove through the gates and down the first dock. We passed yachts bobbing gently in their slips. A couple waved from their deck, I waved back. The sounds of water slapping against hulls and the wind jingling rigging filled the air.

Alejandro's boat was the last one and it was the biggest. I'd never seen a sailboat like his before. The sides of the boat were black and sleek; it reflected the glinting of the sea in bright star-like dots of light. He waved to me from the deck and held out his hand as I crossed over the gang plank. The floor beneath my feet was a light wood. Two computer consoles flanked a large wheel. The mast towered above our heads.

"This boat is amazing," I said, craning my neck to look up the length of it.

"I would say the same thing about your dog," Alejandro said. I looked over to see Blue sitting on Alejandro's foot.

I laughed. "He likes you."

"And I like him." Alejandro pet the top of Blue's head which came up past the man's waist.

"Alejandro!" a woman's voice called from the dock.

He leaned over the rail, smiled and waved. "Hola," he called. I stepped to the edge and saw a very tan, very beautiful woman standing beneath us.

"Alejandro, you must come and see," she called up. "Antonio has caught the biggest fish." She laughed.

Alejandro turned to me, "What do you say?"

"I love a big fish," I answered.

The woman's husband, Antonio, was standing next to a giant fish. Antonio was wearing white shorts and a collared shirt. His legs were skinny and his belly huge. His wife, Isabella, looked at him with such pride that it was hard for me to think she was just in it for the money. Even though her thin frame was weighted down with gold, it looked like she really loved this guy. This Fisherman king.

Antonio made us both touch the giant creature. It was wet, cold, and slippery. The fish hung next to his boat. It was as tall as him. Antonio shook our hands after we touched the fish. We walked back to Alejandro's ship after refusing a drink from the enthusiastic Italians.

We motored out of the harbor and as we cleared the last buoy, Alejandro's fingers worked over one of the computer screens and the sails raised. I smiled, amazed at the technology allowing one man to control such a large vessel. The wind filled the sails and the boat cut through the crystal clear water with barely a sound.

"I'll make us some drinks," Alejandro said, as he headed toward the interior.

"What? You're just going to leave it?" I asked.

He laughed. "Don't worry. It's on autopilot." He disappeared into the cabin. I looked back at the shore. Lights were starting to blink on in the hotel rooms that lined the coast. I turned to the sun and watched its color intensify as it neared the horizon.

Alejandro returned with our drinks. I sipped at mine and smiled. "This is a great mojito," I said.

Alejandro sat across from me. "I thought you would like it."

We were silent for awhile enjoying Mother Nature's light show. "I have to tell you," I said, "Ana Maria's got to go home."

Alejandro looked over at me and sighed. "I'm afraid she is far too important."

"Where is she?"

"I'm right here." I turned to see her standing in the doorway leading to the cabin. Blue stood.

"You do that a lot?" I asked.

She smiled. Ana Maria looked her age this evening. She was wearing white boat shoes, blue jeans and a white cotton long sleeved shirt. Her long, brown hair was pulled back into a pony tail that danced in the wind. "Recently," she answered me. Ana Maria crossed the deck to join us. She sat next to her cousin and he looked over at her. She nodded.

"Do you know anything about the Zapatista?" Alejandro asked me.

"A little," I answered. "They are a revolutionary group of indigenous people, right?"

Alejandro smiled without humor and leaned towards me. "You are right that the Zapatista represent indigenous people but also more than that. You see the Zapatista want justice and equality. We have been fighting the corruption of the Mexican government for years and we are slowly winning." There was a light in his eyes that wasn't coming from the setting sun.

"I don't see what that has to do with me or Ana Maria." I turned to her.

She frowned. "I don't think you understand how important this is. How corrupt our government is. How desperately we need to change things."

"But my job is to bring you home."

"Do you know about the protests in Texcoco?" I shook my head. "Flower vendors protested being removed from their land so that a Wal-Mart could be built. Do you know what happened to them?" She leaned closer to me. "The Zapatista came to help and the police," she swallowed and her eyes filled with tears, "beat them, raped them. They shot a 14-year-old boy. A boy only 4 years younger than me. How can I be too young to try and save my country when he was not too young to be killed by it?"

I didn't have an answer for that. I looked over at Alejandro. "You see, she cannot go home. She wants to stay here and fight," he said.

I looked around at the luxurious sail boat we were sitting on; the white sails filled with wind, the computer consuls that guided our journey. "I don't understand how you're fighting a revolution from here."

Alejandro opened his mouth to speak but Ana Maria was first. "Alejandro is a very important man. He is going to lead us into the future. Right now he has to play along but when the time comes he will change the world. We will get rid of private property. Everyone will be equal. We have already accomplished this in several rural regions. We do not need the corrupt politicians or hotels or condos. Mexicans can live in peace with one another and the land."

"That sounds really great," I said, because it did. Just like the idea of a flying horse sounds awesome. "But you belong at home with your parents."

She snorted in disgust and leaned away from me. "I expected more from you."

"Why?" It was my turn to lean towards her. "Your parents hired me to find you and bring you home. What made you think I would join your revolution instead?"

She looked at me and said: "Because you are Joy."

"My name's Sydney."

Her eyes narrowed and she said it again. "You're Joy. You killed the Mayor of New York, a corrupt politician, to avenge your brother. I know who you are. At least I thought I did. And I'm not the only one-" She was interrupted by a soft laugh on the wind. Blue raised his hackles and began to sniff the air.

I looked around but didn't see anyone. "Did you hear that?" I asked. They both nodded. Alejandro stood up and approached one of his consoles.

"I'm taking us home," he said.

"Great idea," the voice answered. Alejandro didn't look up. The boat began to turn, the boom swung over our heads and we were facing the other direction. The wind died out of the sails and we slowed to a stop. It was so quiet that I had to strain to hear above my own quickening heart beat. Blue stood and with his nose to the ground, headed toward the mast. Alejandro powered up the engines and with a rumble we began to move again. The sun had almost set and everything was casting long shadows.

I was looking at Ana Maria when her pupils dilated and she made a small gasp of surprise. Turning around I saw Blane. Blue watched him closely as he began to cross the boat.

"How did you get on here?" Alejandro asked.

Blane laughed. "For revolutionaries you guys really don't know what you're doing. I climbed on board when you were off looking at that big fish. On your next voyage you might want to think about slightly better security." He looked like he was enjoying himself.

"Ana Maria you're coming home with me. And Alejandro," he paused to let the smile on his face turn into a grin, "I think you might have to die."

"What!" Ana Maria yelled.

"Blane," I said, "you don't need to frighten her like that. I'm sure she'll come home with us." I turned to her. "Don't worry, we aren't going to kill anyone."

"Sydney, what makes you so sure?" I wasn't sure at all. "You think I should just let this revolutionary live?" He said 'revolutionary' in a mocking tone. Blue was right behind him, but Blane hadn't noticed.

"Blane," I laughed. "What are you talking about? The Zapatista? Come on."

Blane turned to me. "The Zapatista are trying to bring down the government. They have wide-spread support in rural areas and they cannot be allowed to continue."

"Are you kidding me?" I stood up. "We are supposed to bring this girl home and that's it. If you want to go on some government-saving killing spree you can do it without me." He pushed me hard and I fell back onto my seat, knocking over my drink and smashing my elbow into the wood. Blane whipped a gun out from under his jacket and pointed it into my face. A low rumbling growl came from Blue.

"Sydney, I am your superior and you will do exactly what I say."

"Didn't anyone tell you I don't like guns in my face?" I said, with pure ice in my eyes.

He turned away from me and grabbed Ana Maria by the hair. She screamed. Alejandro made a move to intervene, but Blane leveled his gun at the man's chest. Alejandro stopped, his hands out by his side, his eyes trained on the gun. Blue looked over at me where I was still sprawled on the seat. He wanted to know what to do. He could, with little danger to himself, but a lot to Alejandro, take out Blane's gun arm.

"Blane!" I yelled. "What are you doing?"

"I'm doing what the client wanted."

"To pull their daughter's hair?"

"No." He didn't take his eyes off Alejandro. "To end a revolution." A shot rang out. Alejandro crumpled to the deck. I made a small hand motion. Gripping onto Blane's arm with his powerful jaws, Blue took him to the ground. The gun skittered across the deck and fell overboard. Blane let go of Ana Maria who stumbled to the ground after him. Blane began to hit Blue with his free hand. Ana Maria launched herself on top of Blane and scratched at his face while Blue shook his arm loose from its socket.

The boat was alive with the sounds of violence. Alejandro moaned while clutching his stomach. Ana Maria grunted with effort. Blane yelled part in pain and the rest in rage.

"What the fuck are you doing?" Blane yelled. "Get the fuck off me!"

I pulled the straight razor out of my purse giving myself an advantage over everyone else on the boat. "Ana Maria!" I yelled. "Get off him!"

She looked over from her position, straddling Blane, and I waved for her to get off. She looked back at Blane who was doing his best to punch Blue in the head, then back at me.

"Seriously, get the fuck off him."

"Get your fucking dog off me!" Blane yelled. Ana Maria crawled away from him, and I called for Blue to release. He released his jaw but only stepped back a couple of feet, never taking his eyes off Blane.

"Ana Maria, check on Alejandro," I said. She looked at me, her hair was half out of its pony tail, a flush colored her cheeks. Her eyes were bright. Then she looked over at her fallen cousin and started to cry. Blane gripped his arm, blood oozed from between his fingers. Splotches of blood mingled with sweat on his brow.

"You're in some serious trouble," he told me.

"I've been in worse." I walked over to where he lay and frisked him looking for another weapon. He didn't have one. "You only brought one gun?"

"I thought I had a partner," he said, staring straight ahead at Ana and Alejandro.

"Bullshit," I said.

"This is your job."

"What are you talking about? I was told we were going out to get the girl. Not kill someone."

"We do what the client wants." He clenched his jaw in either pain or anger.

"Yeah, well I didn't hear him ask us to murder anyone." Electric lights came on illuminating the deck. It was slick with blood. The sky was dark and the sea black but the coast was bright with the twinkling of humanity.

"What are we going to do?" Ana Maria asked me.

I looked up at her. She had a streak of blood across her cheek and the bottom left corner of her white shirt was drenched with it. I clenched the straight razor in my hand.

"How's Alejandro?"

"He needs a doctor."

"Watch him," I told Blue, pointing at Blane. Alejandro leaned against the base of one of the computer consoles. His face, drained of color, was set in a grimace. He clenched at his stomach with both arms. Alejandro looked up at me but didn't say anything. A trickle of blood seeped out of the side of his mouth. When a person gets shot in the abdomen they can live for hours or even days without medical attention. Or they can bleed out in a matter of seconds. Only time would tell us Alejandro's fate.

"Do you know how to drive this thing?" I asked Ana Maria.

"I think so," she said. I turned to look at her. Ana Maria's eyes were wide and bright. She looked at me waiting for direction.

"All right, get us home now." I crossed to one of the consoles.

She joined me at the computer. "It's already set to get us back to the dock," she said.

I knew there had to be a radio on the boat, but I didn't know how I wanted to do this. Getting the police involved seemed inevitable but was bad for everyone involved. Except Alejandro. I looked over at him. His breathing was uneven and rasping. He was probably going to die. That sound, the noise that blood makes when your body is trying to breathe it, isn't known as the death rattle for nothing.

I went over to Blane. He was still lying on the ground being as still as possible while Blue watched him. "What do you want to do?" I asked.

He shifted his gaze from Blue to me. "What are you talking about?"

"How do you see this ending?" A rogue wave hit the boat and I stumbled a little but quickly regained my balance. Ana Maria screamed. I turned to see Alejandro slumped to the side, his arms still wrapped around his belly, his eyes open but unseeing. Ana Maria ran to his side and was trying to sit him up while she sobbed uncontrollably.

Basically what I had here was a fucked situation. Blane, my so-called boss, was injured but alive and there was no way he was going to just let this go. What I didn't know was whether this was his personal plan or if we were really supposed to kill Alejandro. I couldn't imagine that Ana Maria's parents, any parents, would want their daughter to witness her cousin's murder. And what would be in it for Fortress Global Investigations?

"Was this your idea?" I asked Blane.

He laughed. "Are you crazy? This was so not my plan."

"I don't mean the way things went down, I mean killing Alejandro. Did the Vargas's really want us to murder him in front of their daughter?"

Blane laughed again. "I'm not telling you shit."

"If you want to live you've got to."

"Please, you're not going to kill me." He smiled up at me and I knew he was right. But I wasn't going to let him know that. I dropped to my knees and pushed his razor up under his chin. His eyes got wide but he didn't really look afraid.

"Don't you know about me?" I asked. He didn't answer. I pushed the blade harder into his neck. He leaned his head back trying to get away from it. "I'll kill you. And I'll sleep like a baby afterwards." I pushed harder and felt the blade cut into his skin.

"She's the reason you're on this case. We were using you as bait."

"For what?"

"For her, for him. We wanted to find out if it was true. That they were plotting to take down the government. We knew she'd tell you."

"Her parents are in on this?"

He smiled. "It was her mother's idea." I couldn't tell if Blane was lying. "The Zapatista are dangerous. They have to be stopped."

I leaned back on my haunches taking the blade with me. Blane took his hand off his injured arm and used his sleeve to wipe away the thin line of blood under his chin.

"Why didn't you just tell me?"

"We had a feeling you wouldn't go along. I guess I underestimated you." He smiled.

"Does Mulberry know?"

"Sure. He's a partner, isn't he?" Blane watched my face. "Or didn't you know that?" He smiled.

I chewed on my lip. This could all be lies; it was possible that Blane was acting alone but why? He could be working with Pedro without his agency's knowledge but again, why? A man this ambitious, who had come this far, why would he throw it away?

"What about the girl?" I asked. "Were you going to kill her too?"

"I'm going to take her home to her parents. They will deal with her."

"What does that mean?"

Blane smiled. "I don't know what they plan on doing with her, but I wouldn't trade places with her."

I left him lying there on the deck with Blue watching. Ana Maria was holding Alejandro in her arms and crying. He wasn't breathing anymore. I looked down at the young girl. Less than an hour ago she'd been so full of hope for her country, for the ability of man to change his place in this world. And now she was holding a corpse in her arms.

If we went back to shore I'd have to explain a dead body and an injured man. I could hide the body, drop it in the ocean, but what about Blane? I couldn't keep him captive forever. Eventually I'd have to let him go and he would come after me. The lights from the land closed in on me as I surveyed the bloody deck.

"Drop the anchor," I said to Ana Maria. She looked up at me. Tear streaks lined her face. "Drop it." I pulled Alejandro off of her. He was still warm. If I didn't know better, I could almost believe he was alive. I grabbed Ana Maria by the arm and hauled her up. She didn't fight me. I pulled her over to the console and repeated my demand. She sniffled back tears as she pushed the buttons. The engines died, the slow whirl of the anchor dropping started. When it stopped, there was no sound except the lapping of the ocean against the hull, the wind playing in the rigging above our heads, and the thump of my heart beating in my chest.

7

Dumping a Body is Never Easy

THERE IS SOMETHING ABOUT THE AIR THAT BLOWS OFF THE Caribbean. It is salty, but not like the ocean. It is fresh, but not like the breeze that flows over a lake or river. It's like the little bear's porridge; just right. And at night, when your whole life has just been flipped, it's comforting in its consistency.

"What are we going to do?" Ana Maria asked me. I was sitting on the back of the boat with my feet dangling in the water. They looked incredibly white and slightly misshapen. Ana Maria was standing above me on the deck, holding onto the ladder to steady herself against the gentle rocking of the boat. Her brow was deeply furrowed and the blood that covered her was starting to dry and crack. I thought about telling her to go take a shower but then realized we needed to deal with Alejandro's body before she bothered to clean up.

"Joy?" she said.

"My name is Sydney," I answered, glancing over my shoulder at her.

"OK, Sydney. Will you..." She shook her head and her chin wobbled slightly. I thought she might start to cry but instead she cleared her throat and said, "Take me with you?"

I turned back to the sea. The sky above was filled with stars and a giant, bright white moon. It made the water into a high contrast black and white print. I looked back down at my legs and a thrill of fear ran through me as I imagined a giant silver barracuda coming to eat them. Pulling my calves out of the water, I hugged them to my chest.

"Please," she said behind me, "I'll help you, really I will." Ana Maria started to cry. At first it was softly enough that I could pretend I didn't hear it but soon it turned into deep sobs. When I finally looked over at her she was hugging the ladder, shaking. I stood up and faced her. She looked terrible. Red eyes and puffy lids, her nose was running and she wiped at it with the back of her hand which left a streak of blood there.

"They will come after us," I told her. She nodded, a flicker of hope behind her eyes. "Ana, you've never had to run from anything. It's not fun. It's scary and dangerous and to be honest, we are unlikely to survive." But in my mind I was already planning how we would. I could see ten steps ahead of where we sat anchored now. In my mind we were already safe. And I couldn't do it without her. Someone had to drive the damn boat.

"I can handle it, anything you need," Ana Maria said, her voice was strong and while the whites of her eyes were red there wasn't a tear in sight.

"Fine," I said, "lower a lifeboat." Walking over to Blane, I said, "All right. This is where you get off." I helped him to his feet. He didn't struggle as I hauled him off the deck. Ana Maria lowered one of the two dinghies into the water.

Blane laughed when he saw it. "You're putting me in there. And then what?" He turned to Ana Maria, "You two are going to head off into the sunset." I pushed him toward the little boat. "Seriously, Sydney, this is insane. You can't really be considering-" I cut him off by shoving him off the edge. Blane landed with a thud and a yelp at the bottom of his tiny ship. Blue let out a bark of excitement and paced the edge of the deck looking down at his prisoner.

"Bon voyage."

"Sydney! Sydney!"

Ana Maria stood next to me looking down at him. Her fingers tapped against each other in nervous excitement.

"Pull up the anchor, let's get back to the marina," I said. Ana Maria did as she was told and we were under way. The yells of my former superior died out in the wind. I wasn't quite sure, but I thought I heard him say something about ruing the day. I laughed out loud at the thought. Ana Maria looked over at me and I stopped. "Sorry," I said.

She shook her head. "You have to laugh when life is at its worst."

"Right." I smiled at her.

"What about Alejandro?" she asked, looking over at his slumped form.

"I think we need to give him a burial at sea," I said. I watched her closely, waiting for a protest or a look of horror. But she didn't get upset, not even a flicker of anger crossed her face. Ana Maria walked over to her cousin's corpse, kissed him gently on the forehead and then with a grunt of effort began to drag him to the edge. I watched her and so did Blue. Neither of us made a move. She positioned him parallel with the side of the deck and whispered softly, crossed herself and then with a push that was almost a shove, he fell. A short silence was followed by a loud splash and then nothing. Ana Maria sat crouched at the edge of the deck.

"Ana," I said. She didn't turn. "Ana, it's time for you to take a shower." Silently she stood up, passed me without a glance and disappeared below deck. I looked at the trail of blood that Alejandro left in his wake. A large pool marked where he died, a thick line as wide as his body showed the path his corpse took overboard, and a smaller but deeper river slithered toward the helm.

I pulled my phone out of my bag and place a call. "Sydney Rye account 0054624," I told the operator. The two short rings of European phones rang in my ear. "Darcy Milligan, Private Jet Charters, consider it done," was how Darcy always answered the phone. "Ms. Rye, how can I help you today?" Here was a woman who could solve at least one of my problems. Darcy set up my account when I first moved to London and had been my loyal Private Jet rep since then. Mulberry actually gave me her info, but I thought I could trust her. Part of Darcy's job was discretion.

"I need a flight as soon as possible, Darcy. I'm in a bit of a rush."

"Of course, Ms. Rye. Where are you?"

"I'm in Playa del Carmen, at the marina attached to the Paradise hotel."

I heard her nails clicking on her keyboard. "Of course, Ms. Rye, I'm happy to set that up for you. What is the closest airport?"

"I'm not sure."

"OK, how many people are traveling with you today?"

"Just me and one other person and Blue."

"Where would you like to go?"

"The Caymans."

"Certainly, would you like me to set up your usual apartments there?"

"No, Darcy, I don't want anyone to know I'm there."

"Yes?"

"I want the flight to continue after dropping me off in the Caymans and I don't want anyone to know I got off." Darcy didn't answer for a moment but I heard the tapping of her keyboard.

"Ms. Rye, I have a plane that can be ready in 60 minutes. You're booked for a trip to Jamaica with a layover in the Caymans to refuel."

"Darcy, I love you."

"Thank you, Ms. Rye. A car will meet you at the marina in 20 minutes."

"Perfect, Darcy."

I hung up with Darcy and looked down at my phone. I wanted to call Mulberry, but I didn't fully trust him. Either he knew about this set up or was complacent in it. I needed to get rid of my phone before Blane reached land. After one more moment of contemplation, I dropped it over the side and watched the phone disappear beneath the water with barely a sound.

I went below deck for the first time. It was luxury. There was a full kitchen with stainless steel appliances just a little smaller than normal. The counters were shining black granite and the cabinets a light wood. The kitchen was open to a salon with an L-shaped couch in navy blue that surrounded a table large enough for eight to eat comfortably.

I heard the shower turn off and hurried down the hall toward the state rooms. Opening the first door on my right, I found neatly made bunk beds. The door across the hall opened onto a small state room with a single bed. An open leather duffel bag was on the floor. I picked it up and quickly established that it belonged to Ana Maria judging by the clothing. I rifled through it looking for her phone. It wasn't there. Casting my eyes around the room I searched for a purse but didn't see one.

Ana Maria walked in wearing a towel wrapped around her body and one over her hair. "What are you doing?" she asked, anger flaring in her eyes.

"Looking for your phone," I said, cocking my head. "Is that a problem?"

"Why?"

"To get rid of it. I don't want them using our mobiles to track us."

"Oh, right," she said, smiling. "That makes sense." Opening one of the drawers in a built-in bureau she handed me an iPhone. I clicked the button and a lock screen glowed. It was a picture of Alejandro and Ana Maria on the boat, their arms around each other, grinning while wind whipped through their hair. Ana Maria turned away from the image toward her bag.

"Thanks," I said.

"We should be docking soon. I'll need your help," Ana Maria said.

"I'll jump in the shower, then," I said.

She nodded. "It's right down the hall."

I found the bathroom and pulling off my bloodied clothing, climbed into the shower. I stood under the spray and closed my eyes. Using a washcloth I scrubbed at my body, leaving it feeling raw but clean. I turned off the tap and finding a towel, wrapped myself in it. I tried avoiding the mirror but the bathroom wasn't that big. It was definitely me looking out of the glass. Melanie Franks was gone. I pulled my hair back and tied it in a loose bun, put on a robe that was hanging on the back of the door, then headed out to find some clean clothing.

Ana Maria was smaller than me and her clothing was never going to fit so I checked Alejandro's closets. His state room was twice the size of the others. A large bed took up most of it. Small windows ran right next to the ceiling. As we bobbed along the view shifted from sky to sea. Alejandro's closet was big for a boat and filled with clean, pressed clothing.

I found a pair of khaki pants that were too short and too big, but in conjunction with a belt, fit enough. A white cotton shirt, just a little too broad, completed my look. I felt better in his clothes than Melanie's. They might be the clothing of a dead man, but I preferred that to the duds of a fictional character. I grabbed an extra pair of pants, two pairs of boxers and two t-shirts. I rummaged around a bit more hoping to find a backpack. Melanie's huge purse, which was already very full, was now bursting with the addition of the clothing.

"Sydney!" Ana Maria called down to me. I dropped what I was doing and hurried above. The marina was very close. "You'll need to jump," Ana Maria said, standing behind the wheel. "I'll throw you the ropes."

"Great," I said.

"Have you ever done this before?" she asked.

I shook my head. "No, but I think I can handle it."

Ana Maria laughed. "I'm sure."

She was an expert captain and brought the large vessel right next to the dock making it easy for me to jump off. She hurried from behind the wheel and threw me the stern line. I tied it off on a nearby cleat the best I could. Using the bow thruster she brought the nose of the ship against the dock and threw me the second line. I wrapped it around another cleat and then Ana Maria was by my side. Looking down at my work she kneeled and quickly retied the line.

"I've just got to put the springers on," she said, climbing back aboard.

"OK, I'll grab our stuff."

I hurried back below decks and picked up my over-stuffed purse and Ana Maria's duffel bag which she'd left closed and ready to go on the table in the galley. I stopped for a moment before joining Ana Maria. I pulled her phone out of my bag and looked down at the picture on its lock screen again. I wished that I could break into the phone. There was so much I didn't know about this girl. Unfortunately, I had no idea what she'd use as her password.

I climbed back onto deck and saw Ana Maria tying more lines on the dock. Taking her phone to the edge I lit up the screen one more time before dropping it off the side.

Throwing Ana Maria's duffel onto the dock, I followed with Blue on my heels. "A car is meeting us," I told her.

"Won't someone wonder about the blood?" she asked, looking back at the stained deck.

"We'll be gone by then. Come on," I pulled on her arm. Ana followed, picking up her duffel.

The car was waiting as promised. We climbed into the back and I leaned my head against the seat. It felt good to be out on my own. I'd spent the last three years training and learning and working methodically towards specific goals designed for me. Now I was the one in charge. In charge while on the run was not quite as empowering as in charge while not hiding from homicidal mani-acs, the law, and one Bobby Maxim but it would have to do.

I wondered where Bobby fit into all of this. He sent me down to find his friend's daughter. Or did he send me down here to set me up for another assassination? Why not use the same patsy twice? If that was the case, I really needed to kill that guy.

"Do you think my father hired Blane to kill Alejandro?" Ana Maria asked, breaking into my thoughts.

I hoped her father hired Blane, that it was a private deal and not through the agency, that Bobby and Mulberry weren't tied up in this mess. I prayed that when I'd left the room, when I'd been looking at the posters on Ana Maria's walls and listening to her mother's plea for help, Pedro had been plotting Alejandro's murder. That way Mulberry was still on my side. "I don't know," I said.

She turned away, looking out the window. "I think he did," she said.

8

Rich and Easy

THE STEWARDESS, WHOSE NAME TAG READ NICOLE, HANDED ME A Bloody Mary without even asking. Darcy left nothing to chance. "I need to make a phone call," I said.

Nicole nodded and gestured toward a handset at the front of the plane.

"Who are you calling?" Ana Maria asked me.

"An old friend," I said, getting up.

I took a long sip of my Bloody Mary before picking up the phone. I needed to call Mulberry. I didn't know if I could trust him, but I at least owed him the opportunity to explain. Additionally, it felt safe to call from a plane. Try tracing this one, ha.

"Mulberry, it's Sydney."

"Jesus, what's going on?" he sounded worried.

"I was going to ask you the same."

"Where are you?"

"I need some questions answered first."

"What?" He was remaining calm and I tried to do the same.

"What were Blane and I supposed to do?"

"Bring the girl home." I paused, it sounded rehearsed. Or was that my imagination?

"What about Alejandro?"

"I was going to ask you the same thing."

"What?"

"Blane says you killed him," he whispered, as if saying it out loud made it true.

"Jesus," I said.

"What happened?"

I looked over at Ana Maria. She was sipping her Coke and looking at the clouds outside the window. "Blane killed Alejandro," I said.

"Where are you?"

"I can't trust you, Mulberry."

"Sydney, why? I believe you."

I laughed. "A lot of good that does me."

He sighed. "I can't tell you how sorry I am about all of this."

"I'm getting sick of you apologizing."

"Then let me make it up to you. Let me help."

I chewed on the straw that came with my drink. "I'll think about it," I said, and then hung up before he got the chance to respond.

None of this made any sense. I didn't know what side Mulberry was on or why there were suddenly sides. A couple of days ago my life made sense. I laughed at that thought because it was so stupid. My life never made sense.

"What's going on?" Ana Maria asked.

I chewed on my straw some more. "Blane is saying that I killed Alejandro."

Her eyebrows pushed together in conference over her dark eyes. "I don't understand."

"Me either," I admitted.

She sipped her Coke looking over the edge of her glass at me with wide eyes. I picked up a newspaper and tried to read it but my mind was too full. I could risk trusting Mulberry which might work out, but with Bobby Maxim involved I needed to be very careful. Of course, it was possible that both Mulberry and Maxim were out of the loop. Maybe, as I hoped, Blane and Pedro had their own thing going on. It wouldn't be the first time Bobby misjudged the maniacal nature of one of his associates.

I glanced over at Ana Maria again. She was picking at a hang nail, looking almost bored. Blue sat next to me and leaned his weight against my side. It felt good. I slung an arm over his shoulder and looked over at him. "Here we go again, boy," I said, kissing the crown of his head.

When we landed "to refuel," Nicole asked if we wanted to stretch our legs. We stepped out onto the tarmac into a hot night. The wind was up and clouds moved across the sky quickly. It looked like rain was on its way.

"There is a lovely view of the ocean just on the other side of that fence," Nicole told me. "The gate is rarely locked," she said, pointing to a nearby exit. "Town is not far from here. There is a hotel not even a mile down the road if you can believe it. You could walk or catch a cab. If you weren't headed to Jamaica, that is."

"Thanks," I said, with a smile.

"What is going on?" Ana Maria asked as we headed for the gate. "I thought we were going to Jamaica."

"Not really," I said, as I pushed open the gate. It let us out onto a road lined by lush tropical foliage. Within minutes, a safari truck half-filled with tourists appeared. I waved to the driver who stopped but was hesitant to let us aboard with Blue in tow. "He's a gentle giant," I told him.

The driver bit his lip and looked over his shoulder at the half-full truck. "I don't know," he said, shaking his head. He had short, cropped hair that was sprayed with gray, a small paunch around his belly, and worry lines across his forehead that put him in his late 50s to my calculations.

I reached into my bag and pulled out a $50 bill. "Would this help make up your mind?"

The driver's eyes narrowed but he nodded. He took the money. As Ana Maria and Blue headed for seats in the back, a shadow of suspicion crossed his face. I hurried aboard before the driver could change his mind.

The other tourists got off at a Hilton and we followed suit. Getting a room was simple enough. Though a manager had to be called in when I explained that I didn't want to use a credit card but would gladly give them a cash deposit. The manager was happy to accept my money and Melanie Frank's passport without question. I threw in a tip for both the manager and her suspicious underling.

Once in the room (ocean view, two queen-sized beds, pet friendly, rack rate of $340 a night) Ana Maria and I climbed into our respective beds and slept heavily.

The next morning as sun shone in through our windows, I looked over at Ana Maria sleeping peacefully. For someone who just saw her cousin murdered, the girl seemed unusually restful.

I ordered us breakfast and she blinked her eyes open as I replaced the phone onto its receiver. After our coffee and eggs, I told Ana Maria, "I think we've come far enough together. While I appreciate your help, it does not make sense for us to stick together anymore."

"What do you mean?" she asked.

"I think maybe you should go home." While I'd needed her to dock the boat and having her escort me out of the country helped, now I'd be better off on my own.

"I can't go home," she said, "my parents don't want me. They killed my cousin. They might kill me." I wondered if that was true. Would the man and woman I met in Mexico City really kill their own daughter? And for what? I didn't even really understand the explanation Blane had given me for Alejandro's death. The Zapatista seemed like little threat to the democratically- elected government of Mexico. And Ana Maria, a threat?

"Do you really think your parents would kill you?" I walked over to check out the view. The hotel was U-shaped and we could see not only the ocean but also several pools and their respective bars.

"My mother," she spat out the words, "is only concerned with her own power."

"But isn't she fighting for women's rights?" I asked.

Ana Maria let out a jaded laugh that belonged to a much older woman. "She cares as much for the poor women of Mexico as I care for the rich. My parents are criminals," Ana Maria said. "They should be in prison."

"Any chance of that?" I watched a little boy on the pool deck running across the wet surface, his father following with his arms outstretched trying to catch the child before he fell.

"I don't see how."

"Don't you have friends? What about the Zapatista? Can't you stay with them?"

She snorted a laugh. "They can't even take care of their own let alone someone as important as me."

"OK, well Ana Maria, I don't get any of this." I turned back into the room to face her. "Why would your parents want to kill Alejandro?"

"Alejandro was adopted. You know this." She was standing in front of the TV, her fist clenched by her sides. "My aunt was sterile and a Catholic." I moved away from the window and sat on a bed. "Do you know about the Pope and his connection to indigenous people?"

"No."

"The church supports their rights and believes they should be shown respect. My aunt is a very religious woman and so when she decided to adopt she wanted an indigenous baby." Ana Maria paced in front of the TV which showed a schedule of the hotel's events over a soundtrack of Muzak.

"What did your father think about that?" I asked.

She laughed. "I'm sure you can imagine."

"Not really."

She glanced at me, then continued pacing, her fingers starting up their nervous tapping I'd noticed on the sailboat. "The coast of Cancun, the Yucatan Peninsula, was once the land of indigenous people. My father was on the front lines of turning it into a destination for the world. He does not care if he destroys the delicate ecosystems. Or if he pollutes the drinking water and the sea."

"Go back to Alejandro. I don't get what any of this has to do with him."

She took a deep breath and closed her eyes for a moment. "Let me start again. It is important that you understand. Alejandro started working for my father when he was sixteen. It was at my aunt's urging that my father even hired him but Alejandro was a hard worker, and smart. My father saw that he could use him. He thought that if he put him in charge of his hotels on the Yucatan that the indigenous people would not fight against his hotels the way they did against the others. He thought that if he put a Mayan in charge, the Mayans would stop fighting him."

"Did it work?"

She shrugged her shoulders. "In a way. Alejandro was smart, as I said. He was very young when my father put him in charge. Only twenty years old when he became General Manager." Ana Maria stopped pacing and Blue went and sat by her side looking up at her calmly. Ana Maria didn't notice him.

"Alejandro was made General Manager in 1997. Does that year mean anything to you?" I shook my head. "It was three years after the free trade agreement with Canada and the US. The agreement that started the Zapatista war." Ana Maria walked over to the window and looked down at the pools below.

"One of the refugees was Alejandro's brother. Alejandro did not know about him because my aunt did not tell him that he had an older brother. Maybe she didn't know. But he knew about Alejandro and when he had nowhere else to turn, he came to him."

"You can imagine Alejandro's surprise. Here he is managing a chain of hotels that run along the most expensive coast in Mexico and his brother, a poor farmer without a farm, comes wandering out of the jungle looking for help."

"Alejandro's brother, Miguel, explained to Alejandro what the government was doing to him and their people. Alejandro knew about the conflict in Chiapas. Everyone did but he did not know, or perhaps he did not want to know, it had anything to do with him."

"Of course, he took his brother in. He began to make changes to the hotels. Making them as green as possible. He wanted their impact to be not only the lowest in Cancun but in the world. My father let him because unlike the other hotels in the area where crowds of local people marched with signs letting the tourists know where their shit was ending up, his hotels were beacons of environmental health. You see, it was not my father, it was all Alejandro. My father just took the credit." She turned to me, her mouth was turned down at the ends and her eyes were cold.

I shrugged. "If you say so."

"It's the truth," she said, "I'm not a liar."

"I didn't say you were."

She turned back to the view. "Alejandro began to help the Zapatista. He helped build their websites. He organized meetings for their leaders with political figures. He did all this, of course, with a mask; no one knew that he was who he was. It would be too dangerous."

"How long have your parents known?"

"I do not know."

"When did you become involved?"

"Alejandro and I have always been close. I would follow Alejandro around and he didn't mind. Two years ago, I heard him on the phone talking to his brother. He respected me enough not to lie. Alejandro told me the whole story."

"Why did you run away from your parents now?" She bit her lip and her chin wobbled. "Your parents said that you left because you found out about your father's affair."

"That was just an excuse," she said, "I didn't want them to know the real reason I was going to Alejandro. I didn't want them to know what he was doing because I was afraid." Her voice caught in her throat. She hastily wiped her hand across her eyes. "They didn't even start looking for me until I'd been gone for two weeks. What does that tell you?"

"You left home two weeks ago? I was told it was-" I counted back in my head. When we got to Mexico City, I thought she'd been missing for two days. Then we got to Playa del Carmen, that's another day. The night on the sailboat makes four and today would be five. "Five days."

Ana Maria's eyes widened. "That's when Alejandro made contact with Luis Sanchez Zedillo."

"Who?"

"My mother's opponent in the next election."

"Seriously?"

"Yes."

"Why would he do that?"

"Alejandro agreed with the Zapatista that they should fight for their rights but he thought that they should try using the pre-existing system."

"But Blane said he was trying to overthrow the government."

"The Zapatista would love to see the corrupt political system thrown out and in its place a form of democracy much closer to the people. They would like political terms to be only two weeks so that everyone in the community has a chance to lead. However, Alejandro thought this was impractical. He wanted to work on electing politicians who supported the indigenous cause."

"Does Luis Zedillo?"

"Alejandro thought he did."

"So Alejandro believed that he could help the people of Chiapas by turning to your mother's opponent?"

"He hoped."

"And this was on the day that your parents called Blane for help."

"Yes, it appears so." Ana Maria dropped to her knees. "Please," she said, clasping her hands together. "Don't force me to go out on my own. I'll never survive without you."

I looked down at her. "I don't know..."

"Please, I know I can help you. I just know it. Give me a couple more days."

"I'll think about it," I said, standing up. "I'm going out for a bit. I'll be back in a couple of hours."

"I'll come with you." She stood, smiling.

"No, stay here. I don't want anyone to see you."

"What?"

"For all we know, your parents reported you as kidnapped." She started to speak, but I cut her off. "Look, I'm in enough shit as it is, getting caught for kidnapping is not on my 'to do list' so if you want to stick with me, you've got to do what I say."

Her mouth was a tight line of discontent. "Blue will keep you company," I said. She didn't smile. "You can leave any time you want, just not with me."

"No, I want to stay with you." She grabbed my hand. "Please don't make me go back to them. Please." She started to cry. Ana Maria bowed her head and her whole body shook. What was I supposed to do? I put an arm around her.

"It's OK," I told her. "Everything is OK."

She hiccupped and looked up at me."You won't leave me, will you?"

"We will see," I said.

Her face crumpled and she leaned against me. "I'll die if you leave me. My parents will kill me."

"Shh," I said. "I'm not going to let anyone kill you."

"You won't?" she said, looking up at me again.

"I promise."

She smiled. "Thank you, Sydney. Thank you."

I left her and Blue in the room and headed down to the lobby. I got a cab right out front that dropped me off at my bank. Mulberry set up my account with me soon after I joined his agency. The thing I loved about my bank was it didn't care where my money came from or where it was going. After pleasantries with a teller, the manager, a tall woman with long hair piled into a bun at the nape of her neck, appeared with a big smile on her face.

"Ms. Rye, we are very happy to see you again," she said leading me to her office. "Can I get you a drink?"

"Sure, a glass of water would be great," I said. "It's hot out there."

She smiled, stark white teeth against her pitch black skin made a gorgeous contrast. "Certainly, have a seat and I'll be back in just a moment."

She was gone just long enough for me to check out the photos of two cute as button kids on her desk. "Yours?" I asked, when she came back in holding a glass of chilled water.

Handing it to me she answered in the affirmative. "4 and 6."

"A handful, I'm sure."

She laughed. "Yes. Do you have kids?"

"No," I shook my head.

She nodded, "Smart," she said with a laugh. "And you are still young."

"Sure."

"What can I do for you today?" she asked.

"I need a new checkbook, I've lost mine."

"No problem," she wrote a note on a pad. "Anything else?"

"I'm going to need some traveler's checks and some cash."

"No problem. How much?"

"Let's say $20,000 in traveler's checks and another $10,000 in cash."

She wrote on her pad for another second then turning to the computer, started typing. "I'll get those brought in for you. Are you on the island for a couple of days? We can have the checks rushed if necessary."

"The quicker the better please." While not positive where I was headed next, I knew that staying in the Caymans didn't make sense. Mulberry knew I banked here and Bobby Maxim wouldn't have to be a genius to figure out where I stashed my cash.

"Tomorrow morning then?" she asked.

"Perfect."

A knock on the door announced the arrival of my traveler's checks and cash. The manager counted them in front of me to double check and within 15 minutes I was back out on the street.

9

The Bar and the Ballroom

THAT EVENING AS I WALKED ACROSS THE HOTEL'S DECK, THE SUN rolled down the west side of the world and darkness crawled toward the top. A translucent moon hung on the horizon waiting for the light to leave.

The hotel was big and filled with people eating, drinking, and nursing their sunburns. Mostly Americans and Brits, I blended in enough. I found the buffet by following the flow of the crowd. A large ballroom that long ago might have been used for dancing now housed a table the length of a basketball court. The food, hidden behind sneeze guards, glowed under florescent lights. Men, women, and children lined both sides. What started out as clean white plates at the front of the room ended as the bottom of a questionable balancing act by the end. I passed a small girl with pale white skin, stringy brown hair, and a plate filled with donuts.

A high-pitched wail came from a nearby table and I turned to see a child forcing a fistful of broccoli into another kid's mouth while their dad dug into a juicy hamburger. I was looking for the kitchen door, but I was thinking about how I was on the run from something I didn't quite understand, I had no friends or family to turn to, and the fact that I was completely alone in this world except for a mutt with a slight limp and a teenage girl on the edge of hysteria. Looking around at all the families, at the couples sharing a third plate of food, the groups of girls in bikinis giggling, I felt my loneliness like a pointed blade in my gut.

I ran back the way I came. Racing through the lobby, out into the driveway, and past a line of taxis, I stopped in a quiet grove of palm trees. I started crying, which I hadn't done in a long time. It was one of those cries where you're not thinking about anything in particular, it's just that the emptiness inside you becomes overwhelming. My stomach tightened and I sobbed. The last three years I'd worked so hard to become a detective. I pushed my body to the limits of its physical strength. Lies became second nature. The truth a beacon of hope. And here I was, leaning against a tree in paradise alone and without a plan.

Even before I was on the run I'd been alone, so very fucking solitary since James's death. I laughed through the taste of tears in my mouth. I spent all my time trying to solve mysteries for other people. Trying to make the world fair and right. What did it get me? There was no solution to this problem. Pedro and Juanita controlled too much. I was just one woman. And I didn't even know if any of it mattered.

I sat down resting against a tree. It was dark now. The stars hung low in the sky and the moon shone brightly. The Caribbean dipped up and down turning the sky's reflection into a blurry mess of black and white. I wiped my face with the hem of my shirt. I looked down at my hands, turning them palm up and then palm down. My nails, unpainted and kept short, matched the rest of my hands: utilitarian. When I was eighteen I painted my nails burgundy. Six months in New York City, my nails long and red, I remember looking at them gripping a silver pole on the subway. I thought they looked like the hands of an adult woman.

Looking down at my hands now I decided they needed a drink. It wasn't hard to find a bar. Never is in Paradise. The bartender was a guy with curly hair and a slight slur in his speech who intro-duced himself as "Scotty". He was pale and sweating. I ordered a shot of tequila and a beer. He asked if I wanted to buy him a shot, too. I smiled and quickly agreed.

We clinked glasses and I threw the shot into my mouth, using my tongue to force it down my throat. A shiver ran through my body and tears welled in my already swollen eyes. Scotty swiped the empty glass away and replaced it with a beer so cold condensation poured off it, soaking the bar. I sipped it long and hard before saying, "thanks."

Scotty smiled. "Anytime." Then he laughed. The laugh of a man who laughs for a living. "Here on vacation?" I wondered how many times in a day he asked that same question and then got the same answer.

"No," I said. A thought ran across my brain. I wanted to tell him everything. Shock the hell out of him. Then again, watching him wash dishes, taking each glass and rubbing it first in one sink, then a second, finally a third then shaking it out in the air and placing it on the side-board I thought maybe he'd heard it all. Then again, maybe he just heard the same thing over and over again.

"Business then?" He looked over at me. His eyes were a light green framed by blonde lashes the same colors as his curls. I shook my head. A large man bellied up to the bar a couple of stools away from me and yelled for a Mai Thai.

I looked over at him and was filled with loathing. I hate guys like that. The ones who think they should order people around without even a hello or any modicum of human interaction. I felt like taking my beer bottle and smashing it on the bar. In my head I started to play out my revenge on this fat fuck. I'd smash the bottle, which would shock the hell out of him, and I'm thinking Scotty might be surprised by that too. Then it would be two steps, maybe three to get right up in the guy's face. Grabbing him by the collar, I'd take the sharpest corner and lay it right next to his eye then watch his pupil grow to take it all in.

I shook my head banishing the violent image from my brain as the man waddled away carrying a plastic cup full of liquor and cheap juice. "Another shot?"

"Yeah, Scotty. I think that's a good idea."

As he poured the tequila he asked, "Here on your own?"

"At this bar, yeah, all alone, Scotty."

He smiled, the tequila kissed the edge of the glass and he stopped pouring. "I meant at the hotel. I can see you're alone here."

"I'm not staying at the hotel."

"Just heard about my fine drinks, then?"

He slid the shot down the bar, not spilling a drop. "Can I get one for you, too?"

Scotty smiled. "Always."

"Guess I'm not alone now."

"Never."

We clinked glasses and some of the tequila spilled onto my hand. The second shot never hurts as much as the first. I slammed the empty glass onto the bar. I felt more awake, more able to laugh. And Scotty was a funny guy. He told me about this one night when he was doing body shots off this chick when her husband showed up and tried to kick Scotty's ass. But Scotty's tended bar a long time and he used his spray gun on him. Scotty pulled it out of its holster next to the ice bucket and showed it to me. He showed me how he sprayed the guy right in the face with a stream of Pepsi by shooting Pepsi out onto the bar. I was rolling.

On the way back to the room, I was unsteady on my feet. I was humming Bon Jovi's "She's a Little Runaway" because it was the last song that Scotty played. I was smiling, feeling like maybe there was a solution to this problem. I had enough money I could just do this forever, get myself a nice boat and hop from island to island drinking with the likes of Scotty. God knows they made good company.

I stumbled over a curb that came out of nowhere and landed on my knees and hands. I rolled onto my back and looked up at the sky twinkling up there. I breathed in the clean air and thought about that girl on the subway who took pride in her long red nails; I tried to remember what it was like to be her.

She, so unlike me, was scared of physical confrontations. When a man looked at her, it made her nervous. She thought that he might try and take her bag, or worse, force himself on her. But she wasn't afraid to make mistakes. She was scared but she was filled with hope and an insatiable urge to do. Do anything, something. "Well, I do do," I said out loud. The last three years I'd been listening to other people tell me what to do.

My decision to follow orders was a simple one based on the fact that I could not control myself. Last time I was on my own, I killed several men. Granted, they were murderers who deserved it, but that wasn't a side of me I liked to explore.

"Off the reservation" was how Mulberry put it. I came out on top but that might have been luck. There was a general consensus that I was not the best at making plans where everyone survived.

But what plan would get me out of this one? There was nothing to do. And I was alone. I laid there listening to my heart beat, the breeze rustle nearby palm trees, and the sea lap at the shore. "Alone, alone, alone," I muttered under my breath, staring up at the never-ending space above my face. Then I felt a flicker in my chest. "Alone?"

10

I've Been Living on the Edge of a Broken Heart

"ANA! ANA!" I CALLED, AS I PUSHED INTO THE HOTEL ROOM. Blue greeted me at the door and followed me into the bedroom pushing his head against my hand looking to be pet. Ana Maria was on one of the beds , the TV controller in her hand.

"What?" she said. "Did you bring dinner?"

"Ana, you're on that website about Joy, right?" She nodded. "How many people are on there?"

"I'm not sure," she said sitting up and muting the TV. "There's at least a thousand members in Mexico."

"Jesus Christ. Any in the Caymans?"

"I could check."

"Do they have profiles or something? I mean can you find out who the people are?"

"Yeah, it's all online. We have chat-boards and stuff. I'm a forum monitor so I can access that kind of stuff." Ana Maria blushed and looked away from me.

"What do you guys talk about?"

"Just, like, you know, your philosophy."

"Philosophy." I couldn't help but let out a snort of a laugh. "What philosophy?"

She looked up at me. "You stood up for yourself and for your brother. You didn't let the machine roll you over. Don't you know there are a lot of people out there who wish they could do the same?" A pause. "I do." Her eyes were serious and I felt strange under her gaze, almost ashamed of myself. I do too, I thought.

"Ana Maria, I want to see the site."

She shrugged. "Sure."

We went downstairs to the lobby where a complimentary computer was provided for the guests. Ana Maria pulled up the site and there was that letter again, my childish handwriting and arrogant prose. I swallowed, steeling myself against the anger, pain, and humiliation I felt when I looked at it. Ana Maria clicked on the forums then signed in and started scrolling through names.

"It's all women," I said.

"There are some men," she said, and then after a pause, "not many, but some."

"I want to find anyone who lives in your parent's neighborhood or nearby, any police?" A loud squeal distracted me; I looked up to see a teenage girl being tickled by a male counterpart as they passed through the lobby. They looked kinda drunk and like they were having a lot of fun. That's what Ana Maria should be doing, I thought, not hanging out with a depressing fuck up like myself.

"Here is someone in customs," Ana Maria said.

"Great," I said, watching the kids head out to the pool deck. "We need to find as many people as possible." Would any of them really help us? How much could I ask them to risk?

Ana Maria turned away from the computer screen. She was smiling at me. "This is awesome," she said.

"Maybe," I said. Leaning over her shoulder I saw a familiar face. "Malina," I said.

"What?" Ana turned to the screen. "She is very pretty. Says she owns an entertainment facility what do you think that is?"

I closed my eyes. Malina. "We met in Juarez," I said. Just a couple of months after James's death.

Ana Maria looked up at me. "You were friends?"

"We shared a common purpose."

"What?" I shook my head, not willing to share with Ana Maria the journey Malina and I bore together. Malina saw me at my worst, my most out of control, and here she was on Joy Humbolt's site singing her praises. Obviously, she figured out who I was and didn't reveal me. I did give her enough money to last a short life-time. A gift for a woman I admired. "What?" Ana asked again.

"Where is she?" I asked.

Ana Maria turned back to the screen. "Mexico City."

"I'll have to give her a call," I said with a smile. Malina changed the way I felt about everyone on that site. Maybe they weren't all nut bags. Malina was one of the smartest, quickest, most ruthless women I'd ever met.

Later Ana Maria and I enjoyed sandwiches sitting on our respective queen-size beds. I perused the pages of member's profiles we'd printed. I was surprised by the number of female police officers on my side. I flipped through seeing a general theme. Women were sick of being stepped on. They wanted to change the world and men wouldn't let them help.

A 28-year-old lawyer who worked near Pedro and Juanita's neighborhood complained about the treatment she received not only from her clients but also her employers. Over the past two years, she was passed over for promotion seven times. Her male counterparts, and even her underlings, got promoted right past her. Her latest post announced her intention to quit and go to work for a non-profit fighting for women's rights.

I was going to ask this woman to help me. Would she do it? I wondered. Would she take it as an opportunity to live out her princi-ples or would she ignore me? How many of them would listen to me?

Looking back down at the young attorney's profile, at her angry posts over the last six months, her increasing urge to do something building up until she decided to quit her job, I thought she would help.

I was going to offer her much more than new employment. The thought spread a smile across my face. Ana Maria chewed on a bite of turkey and flipped through another pile of profiles. "What about finding a woman to seduce my father?" she asked.

"Doesn't he have a girlfriend?" I asked.

"He was tiring of her. Let's find him someone new. That will be the best way to learn what he is doing. Man can't keep his mouth shut or his pants zipped." Ana Maria wiped some crumbs off a sheet of paper and passed the profile to me.

I looked down at a photograph of a pretty woman living in Mexico City. I turned to look at Ana Maria. Her brow was creased in concentration. Ana Maria's eyes exuded intelligence but no emotions as she questioned whether the exotic dancer described on the piece of paper in my hands was the right one to help spy on her father. I just had to ask, "Ana, are you sure you want to do this?"

She cocked her head. "Of course." Ana Maria looked back down at the pile of possible supporters. I kept looking at her until she continued, "Don't you understand? They killed..." her chin wobbled and tears appeared at the edges of her eyes. She sucked in a big breath of air and continued, "They killed Alejandro. I can't let them get away with that."

"But they are your parents."

"That does not make them above the law." She looked up at me with fire in her eyes. Her chin crinkled but she didn't look like she was going to cry. For a moment I thought she might hit me. Then the flame died down and she turned back to her work.

I held up the picture of the beautiful girl Ana Maria suggested we sic on her father and said, "I don't feel right asking anyone to do that." I put her profile to the side.

"Don't be afraid, Sydney. We have to be bold if we want to win."

I looked over at Ana Maria. "I'm not going to ask someone to prostitute themselves for me, no matter what the ultimate goal."

Ana Maria bit her lip. "You're right. I'm sorry." She turned back to her pile of profiles. They would be our ground force. Our eyes and ears in Mexico City. I wanted to know not only what Pedro and Juanita were doing, but also if Blane was still there. How his arm was doing? I smiled at the thought of Blue's teeth marks in that perfect forearm.

"Computer programmer," Ana Maria said, handing me another profile. "And a man, see I told you there were men." I took it from her. He loved me because 'she is like a wild animal with a moral compass that no amount of magnetic pull can effect'. "I don't know what that means," Ana said, "but he lists his occupation as Computer Specialist. I think he might be able to help."

I wanted to know what Pedro was saying to his friends. What Juanita's assistant was emailing her. But most of all I wanted into Mulberry's computer. I didn't know if it was possible but I wanted to know what was buzzing around in his email account.

As I laid on my bed that night I thought about Mulberry for a long time. I verged on getting out of bed to call him. It was almost impossible to believe he set me up. Then again I never would have believed he told Robert "Bobby" Maxim about Kurt Jessup. And even if Mulberry wasn't setting me up, someone close to him was.

When I started working for Mulberry three years earlier he'd offered me a new identity and a job, two things I needed. The identity for obvious reasons but the job was a more subtle gift. I didn't need the money but the training he'd provided and the distraction were priceless. When he pulled me off the beach, I was on the verge of drinking myself to death. Being a detective was large enough to block bad memories and help make new good ones.

I never asked who I was working for beyond Mulberry. I assumed he was the big boss man. I'd only dealt with him. But now I was coming to understand that Mulberry was full of shit and that Bobby Maxim owned a piece of the business. I wouldn't be surprised to find out that he was the one behind all this mayhem.

He probably got me my name; it's possible there would be no Sydney Rye without Robert "Bobby" Maxim.

In the morning we left when the sun was just peeking over the edge of the sea. It turned the world a soft pink and left the air moist as we climbed into a cab. We were going to see Easy Robbins, a woman who flew a small charter plane anywhere you wanted to go in the Caribbean. She was based in Grand Cayman and I wanted a ride to St. Thomas where a woman who worked for US customs claimed I was her hero.

11

Ms. Easy Robbins

THE CAB RIDE WAS LONG. I SPENT MOST OF THE TRIP WATCHING clouds get pushed around. They were wispy little things; the innocent cousins of storm clouds. They flew across the blue backdrop of the sky, sometimes bunching up on each other to form little mountains of whipped cream. Then they'd spread out so thin it looked like a spider web was stretched across the sun. From the clouds I'd look down at the picture of Easy Robbins. She was the first one I was going to ask for help. Asking a complete stranger to risk her livelihood and who knows what else for me, for an idea, made my stomach feel like shit (I don't like to blame alcohol for my hangovers).

The nausea reminded me how scary this was. If I mis-stepped, if I fucked this up, I could end up dead, Ana Marie with me. I looked over at Blue, his snout in the air taking in every scent that the open window offered. He might make it, I thought. Ana Maria sat in the front seat, her gaze focused on the horizon. She was barely a woman but at least she had something personal at stake. What would motivate Easy to join me? And who the fuck names their daughter Easy?

I looked down at her profile. Ms. Easy Robbins owned her own plane. She loved to fly. Loved to take risks. Loved life. What did she like about me? According to Easy, Kurt Jessup attempted to rape her while vacationing in Jamaica. She wished she had the guts to "blow his fucking brains out."

Palm trees gave way to the never-ending sea and before long we stopped in front of a marina. I handed our cabby a big chunk of change. He showed me crooked, yellowed teeth in appreciation.

The marina was all boats except for one plane. We headed toward it. Two men stood on the dock watching a woman in cut-off jeans lean over and struggle to pull something out of the hold. They laughed when the woman stumbled back holding an insanely large suitcase. I stopped at the top of the dock to watch.

The woman was tall and lean with brown shaggy hair; she wore a collared blue shirt and a wry smile. She dropped the bag and leaned back into the plane again. The two men looked at each other and then back to her butt. One of the guys pretended like he was going to slap her ass and the other laughed. They wore matching Hawaiian T-shirts. Both their stomachs were too large for their khaki pants and hung over their waist lines. One had blonde hair, the other black.

The blonde reached over and was about to pinch the woman but when she pulled out another bag, it sent her a little off balance and the guy cupped her butt. In a faux attempt to help her, he placed his other hand on her breast. Even from all the way down the dock, Ana Maria and I could both see her face turn red and her mouth become a deep frown. She used the suitcase to knock the guy down. The other man yelled something we couldn't quite hear and started to help his friend up.

The woman said something low and deep. The blonde man looked up, shocked by the words. The dark haired man scrambled to his feet. They grabbed at their overweight luggage and dragged it toward us. The woman stood with her arms crossed watching them walk away. Then she spotted us.

I waved and started toward her. As we passed the men, Ana

Maria stuck out a foot tripping the blonde. He fell hard, scraping his elbow. "Hey!" he yelled. "What the fuck?"

"Yeah," his friend said. "What the fuck?"

"Fuck you," Ana Maria replied. The dark haired man puffed out his chest and started toward her. Blue growled and the man paused.

"Forget about it," I said, and taking Ana Maria by the arm, led her away.

Easy watched the whole thing with her arms crossed and when we got close enough, I put my hand out. She looked down at it but kept hers locked into her elbows. "Hi," I said. She nodded. "You Easy?" She nodded again.

"I'm Sydney Rye." She looked at my face and furrowed her brow deeply. I pushed my sunglasses up onto my forehead showing her my grey eyes and deep scars. Easy took a sharp breath. She looked over at Blue and suddenly it made sense.

"You're-"

"Sydney Rye," I finished the sentence for her. "I wanted to talk to you about a job."

She smiled. "Yeah, sure. Of course. How about my office?"

"Perfect." Easy led the way to a small freestanding building not far from her slip. She unlocked the door and flicked on an overhead fluorescent that came to life with a whirl of electric current. She motioned for Ana Maria and me to sit down in two white rattan chairs that faced a small desk. Framed posters of aerial views of the Caribbean hung on the walls. Brochures for charter flights sat next to ads for day trips to private islands. Easy closed the door behind us and locked it. She turned on a fan to move the stuffy air around and then sat at her desk.

She was in her mid-thirties, pretty in a rough and tough kind of way. For some reason I liked her instantly. Whether it was watching her knock that guy down on the dock or the special attention she was showing me, I couldn't say. But I was feeling at ease with this woman. It suddenly made perfect sense for me to say, "I need your help."

"For the woman who took out Kurt," she leaned back in her chair, "anything."

I smiled, now was not the time to come clean that I'd actually missed my chance to kill that fucktard. "That's nice to hear." I put my elbows on her desk and she shifted toward me. "This is Ana Maria," I said, nodding my head in Ana's direction. "Her parents just murdered her cousin." Easy maintained eye contact. "They're not very nice people, but they are powerful. They hired a guy named Blane to shoot Alejandro in front of Ana Maria and me."

"Why?"

"He was trying to change things."

"That's a dangerous hobby."

"One I've decided to get into."

"How dangerous are we talking here?"

"If you have to ask, you shouldn't do it." Easy leaned back. She chewed on the inside of her lip. I waited for an answer. We all sat there while Easy Robbins thought. The hum of the fluorescent light, the clicking of the fan, filled the space. My chair wheezed when I repositioned myself.

Easy opened a drawer in her desk and pulled out a bottle of rum followed by two shot glasses. She looked over at Ana Maria and brought out a third. "I like to think that you did me a favor," Easy said, unscrewing the top of her bottle. She poured the first shot, without lifting the bottle, the second, and as the third filled she said, "I'd be happy to do one for you." She smiled. The fan blew strands of her sandy brown hair around her face. "What do you need?"

"A ride."

Easy raised her eyebrows. "Where we going?"

"St. Thomas." Easy put a shot in front of me, moved one over to Ana and then raised her own. She looked at me to say something. I raised my glass. "To new friends."

Easy smiled. "And old enemies."

We all brought our glasses to the center of the desk, clicked them together and then poured the rum down our throats.

12

Fast Times

WITH A DEAFENING ROAR EASY ROBBINS'S PLANE LIFTED OFF into the sky. The sun glinted against the windshield and my stomach lurched. The sea was suddenly far below us. The sky seemed like a dome fitted to the flat platter of the earth. I had the sensation that I was in a snow globe.

I turned to check on Blue and Ana Maria. Blue looked out the window with his ears perked and his tail twitching. Ana Maria's hand was pressed against the glass of her window. She looked down at the water, her mouth a tight line.

To take my mind off the fact that we were floating thousands of feet above the earth, I prepared myself for the next meeting. Was it possible that Maude Flemington was going to be as willing as Easy Robbins to help me? I thought back over her profile. Her picture showed a small black woman smiling at the camera, a disembodied hand hung over her shoulder and part of her hair was also cropped. Was it possible that the nicest photo Maude Flemington had of herself was taken while embraced by someone she felt the need to cut out?

I looked over at Easy. She was wearing aviator shades and a calm expression. I saw her eyes behind the sunglasses switch from looking at the horizon down to her instruments and then back to the world below. "How long?" I asked into the microphone that curled in front of my face.

"About an hour left," Easy told me.

"You know a Maude Flemington?" I asked.

Easy didn't answer right away. She looked over at me for just a second and then back to the sky. Easy nodded curtly.

"Yeah?"

Easy took a deep breath. She cleared her throat. "We used to date," Easy said.

I laughed. Easy didn't think it was funny. "Sorry. Sorry," I said, gaining control. "For a second I thought you were gonna tell me something like she wouldn't help me or she was dead or something."

Easy looked over at me. "You're going to ask her for help?"

I nodded. "I want to stay on an island for awhile. I need a base camp for at least a week and I can't do that without a little help from authorities." Easy turned back to the sea. "Do you think she'll help me?"

Easy didn't answer for a minute and the butterflies in my stomach started their steady circling again. The left wing dipped toward the earth and we veered in its direction. In the distance a dark green mound of land rose out of the crystal water. "I guess she might," Easy said.

"Why wouldn't she?" I asked.

Easy shrugged. "I don't know. She's just..." The sentence hung in the air, Easy's voice was replaced by the incessant hum of the propellers.

"What?" Easy shrugged again. "When did you guys break up?" I asked.

"Look," Easy sounded suddenly angry, "she's kind of a coward. Actually she's a big coward. We broke up because she wouldn't admit to anyone that I was more than a friend. You know? And that just sucks. How are we supposed to build a relationship if she won't even tell her friends, let alone her family, that I'm her girlfriend?"

"I'm sorry," I said.

"Yeah, well. We'll see what she's really made of."

"She wouldn't turn us in would she?"

"I don't know."

An island was right under us now. It looked like the head of a broccoli. It was small and very soon it was behind us. We spent the rest of the flight with just the sound of the engines.

Landing in St. Thomas harbor was an exceptional experience. It was my first time in a seaplane and it brought my heart into my throat to head toward the water with the purpose of landing on it. But Easy was a subtle pilot and despite the voice screaming in my head that we'd sink, crash, light on fire, die horribly, we didn't do any of those things. We landed lightly on the surface of the sea and motored by fishing boats and giant cruise ships to dock in a hangar.

I climbed out of the plane, feeling a little unsteady. Blue and Ana Maria joined me on the dock and we all looked around. The shore was lined with warehouses. To our left loomed a huge cruise ship.

"That thing is enormous," Ana Maria said.

"It looks even bigger next to Frenchtown," Easy replied.

"Frenchtown?"

"This neighborhood is called Frenchtown. Behind these industrial buildings are small residences that have been in the same family for generations. It's also one of the main restaurant districts on the island."

"Where's Maude?" I asked. Easy rolled her head in the direction of a small rectangular structure labeled Immigration and Customs. "Do you want to come with me?"

"I think it'd be best if you went alone."

"All right." Blue followed me as I crossed to the building that held a bit of my fate in its four walls. I lifted my chin and held my head high as I crossed the empty space. Talking to Easy was one thing. It was unlikely she would turn me in, it wasn't her job and she didn't seem the type to help out the law. Maude, on the other hand, worked for the government. It was possible that beyond refusing to help, Maude would report me to authorities. That thought gave me a moment of pause and my foot hung in the air refusing to take a step. I forced myself to keep walking. It was a risk but so was crossing a street, flying in a plane, and drinking as heavily as I enjoyed. Life wouldn't be much without risks.

Blue sat next to me and I knocked. A moment of listening to shuffling on the other side of the door followed by a "just a minute" passed before Maude and I were face to face.

"Hello?" she said.

"Hi," I held out my hand and she shook it.

"May we come inside?"

Maude looked down at Blue. "OK."

Inside I slid my sunglasses up onto my forehead taking my bangs with them. Maude looked at my scars and then away not wanting to be rude.

The small office was tidy. A poster reading "Hang in there" illustrated by a big-eyed kitten swinging from a string hung above her chair. I sat down across from her white desk. Blue sat next to me, his snout hovering above the desk by about an inch. The desk had two piles of paper on it. One labeled in, the other out. A calendar with a daily affirmation sat next to a clock that ticked away the seconds. Maude's pens were all the same and they lived in a mug at the top of her desk. A window that looked out onto the marina was lined with healthy houseplants all leaning toward the sun.

"Maude, my name is Sydney Rye."

"Nice to meet you, how can I help?"

"I'm going to ask you a big favor. You, of course, have the option to refuse but I hope that you won't."

She nodded, waiting for me to continue. Her hair was pulled back into a tight bun at the back of her head. The round collar of her white blouse was freshly starched. I looked down to the pin on her breast of a fish that looked a like the one on the bumpers of trucks for Jesus. I faltered for a second wondering if this was a different Maude. I just couldn't see anyone loving kittens, doilies, Jesus and me.

"You probably don't recognize me."

"I don't think we've met," she said in a mild West Indian accent.

"No, we haven't, but you belong to a site about Joy Humbolt."

Suspicion crept into her eyes. "I don't see-"

"Look at me again, Maude," I said, leaning toward her.

"You are-" her voice faltered.

"Yes. I was."

"My God."

She leaned back in her chair and stared at me.

"I need to stay on St. Thomas for a little while, about a week, maybe more. I don't want anyone to know I'm here. I don't want any record that I was ever here. Do you understand?"

She nodded her head and then asked, "Are you in trouble?"

I smiled and raised an eyebrow. "Always. Can you help me?"

"I don't know," she said. "It's complicated and I could lose my job." She looked up but didn't make eye contact. She looked out the window, her brow furrowed in thought. "I guess I could make up names for you or I could-" she stopped speaking but turning away from the window continued. "I could just forget I ever saw you."

I looked out the window and saw Easy by her plane with Ana Maria. They were unloading our luggage. Ana said something and Easy laughed. When I turned back to Maude she was looking at me. "Can I rent a room without a passport or any paperwork from you?"

"You'll need ID but that is all." Maude wanted to help me. I could tell from the deep wrinkle in her forehead that she was hiding in this office. That deep down inside she didn't want to be wearing a skirt that cut her off at the calves. That the poster of the kitten drove her as nuts as it was driving me. The affirmation for

90

the day suggested taking a deep breath and smiling. I think Maude wanted to do something else.

I stood up. "I guess I'm all set then. I didn't realize it was this easy."

"Yes," Maude smiled. "I will forget I ever saw any of you." She stood up and we shook hands. I walked out of the small office and she followed. Easy was watching us. She tried to lean casually against the plane's wing but didn't quite pull it off. Maude looked over at her and some of the color drained from her cheeks. "Easy's helping, too."

"Yeah."

"Did she tell you I would?"

"Nah, I found you myself. I thought I could depend on you." She looked up at me and smiled. Maude had a high brow and large brown eyes with long, thick lashes. Her nose was wide and set above thick lips. Her teeth were white and her smile infectious.

Easy found us a hotel in Frenchtown. The owners, an American couple originally from Philadelphia, were more than happy to let us stay. They thought it was really sweet I was taking my new half-sister on a vacation to get to know her. What with our parents getting married, we should bond. They thought Blue was a real treat and didn't even bother to ask for his paperwork. I used my Melanie Franks ID, paid in cash and everyone was happy. Especially me when I saw that they were writing my information down in a giant notebook rather than a computer.

I sat on the balcony of our room watching the waves slap against the flood wall in front of the hotel and sipped on a beer. Ana Maria was showering and Blue snored happily on one of the single beds. The beer was cold, the sun was warm, and I was feeling pretty great about myself, my plan, and the future.

Easy went out to buy a laptop from one of the duty free shops on Main Street. The hotel had free wireless internet and I was looking forward to making more contacts, to recruiting more soldiers.

I heard the shower turn off and moments later Ana joined me

on the deck wrapped in a white terry cloth robe. Using a towel to dry her hair she asked, "You hungry?"

"I could eat."

"I'll order up some food."

"Get a burger for Blue."

Blue's head popped up at the sound of his name. He stretched out on the bed, extending all his limbs, then with a slight shudder relaxed and closed his eyes again. Ana walked back into the room and I returned my gaze to the sea. A small island, which looked uninhabited, faced the hotel. Every time a boat passed, its wake would send sprays of foam up the seawall.

A knock on the door pulled me away from the view. I passed Ana. She was sitting on the bed next to Blue petting one of his ears. She held the phone with her other hand. "And one rare burger. Really rare," she said. I opened the door to Easy. She was carrying a single shopping bag.

Once the food was ordered we all gathered around the computer. Ana's face glowed blue as she leaned over the screen. "Here we go," she said. "I've got her email and her phone number how do you want to do this?"

"I'll call. I think an email might seem like a prank."

Easy handed me the phone. It reminded me of the kind of phone Sean Connery's James Bond would use to take out an enemy. I lifted the receiver and listened to the tone at the other end. I dialed the numbers slowly and practiced in my head what I would say.

"Hola," a voice said. I hung up.

"What'd you do that for?" Ana asked.

"She was speaking Spanish."

"You speak Spanish."

I stared at her. "Not well."

"I'll do it." She took the phone away from me and gave me another one of those teenage looks. I tried to make my face look like hers but I didn't believe that she was the dumbest person in the whole wide world so it was hard. Ana redialed.

The first words out of Ana Maria's mouth were: "Do you speak English?"

Then she handed me the phone and said, "She speaks English."

I cleared my throat. "Who is this?" the woman asked.

I'd rehearsed this in my head. "My name is Sydney Rye but I was once called Joy Humbolt." That came out great, I thought. I can do this.

"Who?" she asked. Shit.

"Wait, is this Izel?"

"You have the wrong number." Click.

I handed the phone back to Ana Maria. "That was the wrong number."

Ana blushed. "Oops."

"Let's try again."

I dialed the number this time and used Ana's method by first asking if the woman spoke English. She did, so I then asked the second logical question: "Is this Izel?"

"Yes, who is this?"

"My name is Sydney Rye, but I used to be called Joy."

"Humbolt?"

"Yes," before she had a chance to say anything, I continued, "I want to offer you a job. I need you to help me."

"How?"

"I need you to watch a house. I want you to tell me who goes in and who goes out."

"You mean spy on somebody?"

"Yes."

Another silence. I played with the cord that attached the handset to the phone. I wrapped it around my finger making the skin rise between the lines. The ridges of skin went white while I waited for her to speak. "Who's house?"

"Pedro Hernandez Gonzales and Juanita Vargas Llosa de Hernandez."

She swallowed audibly. "Are you crazy?"

"Izel. Here's the thing. Pedro and Juanita hired an assassin to kill their nephew because he was trying to help indigenous people find representation in the Mexican government. Now maybe the rights of native Mexicans are of little interest to you, but I'm sure that you can agree the cold-blooded murder of family is just plain fucked up. Now I want to stop them. I want to make them pay. I'm not sure how I'll do it yet, but right now I need to know what they are doing. Is this something you can help me with?"

"They killed their own nephew? I can't believe it."

"Try."

"Are you going to kill them?"

"No."

"OK."

"Do you want time to think about it?"

"I do not need time to think. I will work with you. But watching a house takes many hours."

"Hire whoever you need but don't tell them who you are working for. Let me know who they are and I will arrange payment."

"Yes."

"Call me at this number," I read the number off the phone.

"Thank you," Izel said, and we hung up.

Both Easy and Ana were looking at me. "How'd I do?"

"Great," Ana said.

I looked to Easy. She nodded. "I thought you were very convincing."

"All right, who's next?"

"Didn't you want to call your friend Malina?" Ana said, handing me her profile. I looked down at Malina's beautiful face. "Maybe she will spy on my father," Ana Maria suggested.

"Can I have a moment alone?" I said. Ana Maria and Easy nodded then headed down to the pool taking Blue with them.

I picked up the phone and dialed the number. It rang three times, I took a deep breath. "Hola!" Malina answered her phone.

"Malina?" I asked.

"Si?"

"It's Sydney Rye."

"My God." I heard Malina cup her hand over the receiver and then the muffled sound of her speaking to someone in the room. She came back on the line. "Hello? Are you there?"

"Yes."

"My God, Sydney, how are you? I'm so glad you called. Where are you?"

"I'm in some trouble."

"How can I help? Anything."

I took a deep breath. "I need some information about Juanita and Pedro Hernandez Gonzales."

Malina started laughing. "This is so wonderful. I know Pedro very well. He is a great customer of mine."

"Really?"

"Yes, yes, I see him all the time. Less so in the last six months but just in the last week he has started to visit again."

"What kind of business do you have, Malina?"

She laughed again, sounding older and happier than I remembered her. "I would have no business without you. I'm sure I would still be in that horrible city. You, Sydney Rye, saved me."

"You saved yourself, Malina."

"Do not be so modest! Without the money you gave me I would be somewhere else, somewhere terrible."

"So what kind of a business is it?"

"Similar to the work I was doing when I met you only now I am the boss."

I was pretty sure that was a nice way of saying she owned a brothel. It appeared Ana Maria knew her father well. "It's good to be the boss," I said.

Malina laughed again. "Si, very good. Now, what can I tell you about Pedro?"

I bit my lip and thought for a moment. "I guess I'm trying to understand his mental state. Is he very upset?"

"I will ask the girl who he is seeing. When I saw him he was all smiles but who knows what is really in his heart. We will find out for you."

"Thanks."

"How do I reach you? Once I have some information."

I read her the number off the phone. "And Malina, I don't think I even have to say this but please don't tell anyone I called."

"Of course not, you know my business is discretion."

There was a knock on the door. "I've got to go Malina. We'll talk again soon."

At the door was a bellboy with our food. "Where do you want it?" he asked.

"You know what? I think we should eat it by the pool. Do you mind?"

He smiled. "Of course not. This is your paradise vacation and we want to make it perfect for you."

I smiled. "That's great."

13

Sleep

I WOKE UP WITH A START. DUSK CREPT INTO THE ROOM CASTING a haze over the space. Blue was awake, too. He stood by the door to the balcony watching. I threw the covers back and felt the air turn the sweat on my body cold. I sat on the edge of my bed and thought about what I was doing. Building an army. What was I thinking? Who the fuck did I think I was?

I wrapped a sheet around myself and stepped out onto the balcony. The trade winds blew steadily, pushing my hair around my face. I sat down and looked out to the little island across the way. It was dark, not a sign of life. Close by, I heard a car door slam, two women laughing and then silence.

Leaning my head against the back of the chair I looked up at the sky. No clouds broke up the perfect arc of dusty blue. I closed my eyes and enjoyed the darkness behind my lids. I had one big contact left to make. A guy who was good with computers. Someone who I hoped could tell me about Mulberry. Tell me if I could trust him. I wondered what Mulberry would say to this. To me on this hotel balcony. For a second I thought he might be proud.

A smile spread across my face. Mulberry would love it. I had the feeling over the past year or so that he was sick of running a company. That he wanted back in the action. Maybe I'd find out he didn't know about any of this. Maybe he'd come out here and join me. We could be working together again soon enough.

I thought back to when we were plotting together in New York. Mulberry didn't want to help at first, but I convinced him to. He chose to join me. Sure, some of it was the treasure but it was also, I suddenly realized, me. I convinced Mulberry to change his life and I could do it with others.

But he betrayed me. In the end he told Bobby Maxim to take what was mine.

I opened my eyes and looked back up at the sky. I could do it. This guy I was going to call today, I was going to call him and convince him to throw it all away. To forget about everything he thought he wanted and instead join me. Become my expert. I laughed out loud. I was gonna get my own expert.

I picked a man who lived in Key West. Out of all the profiles of people with computer related jobs he was the closest and as far as I could tell the most qualified. I called him at home at 8 a.m.

"Dan?"

"Who's this?"

"Opportunity."

"I can't remember when the last time a B&B called offering me opportunity."

"Caller I.D."

"Don't pick up the phone without it."

"I want you to come here. Your flight leaves in an hour. A car will pick you up."

Dan laughed. "Are you crazy?" he asked.

"I've been getting that question a lot."

"Look, I'm sure that an operation your size does not need the kind of protection I provide."

"I'm not the B&B, Dan. I'm Joy Humbolt. A car will be at your place in 30 minutes. See you in a couple of hours."

Years later, while Dan and I were getting drunk together in this shit hole in Peru, he told me that he hung up the phone and was about to go to work and forget about the phone call. But as he was walking out the door wearing his suit, he thought about how fucking hot it was out and that he was wearing a tie. Dan said that he threw his briefcase on the ground, pulled his tie off and was kicking off his shoes when the car pulled up. He arrived in St. Thomas wearing shorts, flip flops and an old cotton T-shirt.

Growing up in New Jersey and bored out of his mother-fucking mind, Dan started hacking when his grandmother gave him a computer for his 11th birthday and his parents gave him his own phone line. When he was a teenager his mother worried about him spending too much time online, but Dan figured it was better than going to the mall to drop acid, jump in the fountain, and get kicked out.

One of those kids who could have gotten straight A's if he'd just cared a little more, he floated along in a sea of B's, the occasional C and, of course, he failed gym. But it wasn't because Dan was some pencil-necked geek who couldn't climb to the top of the rope. It was just hard to get up in the mornings after spending all night chatting with kids in Japan to go play dodgeball.

Dan went to college in California where he fell in love with warm weather and learned that his computer skills could be used to make a living by stopping other hackers. He went to work for a company in Key West because he liked the color of the water there and the idea that gators floated just under the surface of the swamp. But after six years of helping protect the networks of large corporations, he was sick of his bosses, his peers and his life.

When he found the site about me, or at least the site for people who liked me, he found something new. It was a different type of person who networked through my site. Beyond the normal complaints of their lives, the people on the site wanted to do something. They wanted more than what they had, and not in a material sense, but they wanted to be more important to the world.

The night before I called Dan he was sitting in front of his computer scanning through the latest postings on a blog about algorithms and he started to wonder what would happen to the world if he was eaten by an alligator. First he imagined his own death, the struggle to escape the prehistoric beast's grip, the spin underwater, the last desperate gasp for breath. His body eventually giving up and sinking into the depth, leaving a red sheen to the swamp's surface.

His boss would be the first to notice. He'd leave some messages on the machine, the last one probably firing him. Dan's mother would eventually get worried enough to come down and file a police report. She would cry, pack up his house and go back to New Jersey. And though he knew his disappearance would break his mother's heart, it would do little else. His friends online would miss him but not enough to find him. His stuff would end up at the Salvation Army. There was nothing that Dan would leave behind.

So my phone call came at just the right time. Dan was looking for a challenge; he was looking for actual human contact, friendships that involved looking at each other's face. He was looking for something to do. Do.

Easy brought Dan to the hotel. I was by the pool sunbathing and thinking. Izel had just called and let me know about her new hires. My bank in the Caymans was more than happy to oblige setting up the necessary wire transfers. I was trying to think about the next step when Dan blocked the sun pouring through my closed eyelids. I blinked looking up at his silhouette. He was a medium-sized guy in a dirty t-shirt.

"This is Dan," Easy told me. I sat up and put out a hand. Dan shook it.

"You know who I am?" I asked Dan. His hair was brown. It needed a cut; his shaggy bangs tickled his eyelashes. He pushed it aside and looked at my face. I pushed my shades up.

Dan smiled. His teeth were straight and white, they looked like they'd grown up in Jersey. "Oh, shit," he said. "I didn't really believe it was you on the phone but..." he trailed off into a grin.

"Sit down." I motioned to the chair next to me. Dan sat, resting his hands on his knees and leaned towards me. "Dan, I need you to do something for me. I don't know if you'll be able to, hell, I don't know if it's possible. I basically don't know anything about computers." To be honest, I thought the internet was basically a bunch of pneumatic tubes that shot information around the world using the power of our imaginations. I still kinda think that, but whatever.

"What do you need?" Dan asked.

"I want into an email account."

"That's possible."

"What about into a computer? I mean, can I see what's on the hard drive? Stuff like that."

Dan pursed his lips. "Depends on the security system."

"I imagine it's a good one. It's a private investigation firm."

Dan sucked air through his teeth. "That could be tricky."

"Also, I want into a Mexican Senator's email."

Dan laughed. "Sounds like fun."

"Would you like a drink?"

"Sure."

I wrapped my towel around me and led Dan back up to the room. I went into the bathroom to change. Removing a tag from a recently purchased blue sundress, I pulled it on. Dan was standing out on the balcony, leaning on the railing enjoying the view. I picked two sparkling water bottles out of the mini fridge and joined him. Passing Dan one bottle, I opened the other. It foamed over the cap, bubbling and cold, down my hand and wrist, dripping onto the floor. I jumped back with a laugh.

Dan ran inside and grabbed me a towel. He wiped down my wrist and then taking the bottle from me, cleaned my hand. "You have beautiful hands," he said. I smiled and laughed, wondering what he would think of my hands if he knew the things they'd done. He looked up at me, making eye contact. "You're beautiful." I blushed and turned away, he held my wrist lightly. "Seriously, I've seen pictures of you, but they can't capture your eyes."

"Thank you," I said. He handed the bottle of seltzer back, releasing me.

I sipped the water, it was cool and bitter. "You don't seem to worship me," I said.

Dan laughed and turned away. "I respect you, I like you. I think you're drop-dead gorgeous, but I don't worship anyone."

"That's good to know." I sat down in one of the white plastic chairs and Dan sat in the other. I looked out at the island across the way. It was as deserted as ever. "Don't you want to know why I'm asking you to hack into a private investigation company and a senator's email?"

"I kinda figured you'd tell me when you were ready." Dan held his bottle of soda over the edge and unscrewed the top. It opened with a soft fizz. Dan took a long sip and then turned to me. "Do you want to tell me?"

I smiled. It was nice seeing someone my own age from my part of the world. I'd felt so strange for so long it was nice talking to another East Coast kid. "Yeah, I do."

Dan leaned back in his chair, put his feet up on the railing, placed his soda bottle on his stomach and waited.

"Well," I leaned back, putting my bare feet up on the ledge. I explained to him about the last three years of my life. The normal cases I'd been on hunting down missing people, solving murders in a controlled manner for the wealthy who preferred these things be handled quietly. Returning of stolen property, solving and hushing up of unpleasant matters of all types.

I went into detail about meeting Blane, the first couple days of our investigation, my intuition that he was hiding something. When I got to the part about Alejandro inviting me out on the boat, he asked, "Romantic?" I shook my head with a resounding no. He was shocked by Alejandro's brutal death.

"I don't get why," Dan said.

"I know. I mean, I guess it makes sense that they don't want him working with Juanita's opponent to unseat her but murder seems like an overreaction. Blane said that he was trying to take down the government but I don't believe that."

"Maybe he was," Dan said.

"You didn't meet this guy. He wasn't one for conflict. I really couldn't see him starting a blood bath. Some sort of international conference on the rights of indigenous people, that I could see, but a bloody revolution, it just doesn't fit."

Dan put his feet back on the ground. "Then why?"

"That's one of the things I'm hoping you'll find out. I want you to hack into Juanita's emails and Pedro's. I want you to get into Mulberry's computer. I want to know if he's in on this thing."

"That's a lot of work."

"I'll pay you well."

"It's not that." He looked a little hurt. "It's just time. You're talking about seriously secure systems here."

"SSS."

"What?"

"Seriously Secure Systems." He smiled. I cleared my throat and brought my feet down to the floor. "Can you get help? Do you have friends who would be interested?"

He nodded, his eyes narrowing in thought. "Yeah, there's a couple guys I could ask."

"Can you trust them?"

He shrugged. "I think so."

"How long will it take?"

"I don't know, I'll have to do some research."

"All right. There's one other thing." He nodded. I leaned forward and, resting my forearms on the balcony railing, scooted to the edge of my seat. Laying my left ear on my hands I looked over at Dan. He was smiling and I thought how very sweet and sloppy he looked with his shaggy hair and soft green eyes. "I need a secure form of communication," I said. "I want to talk to my people from anywhere in the world without it being traced."

He smiled. "You have people?"

"You're not my only lieutenant," I told him with a smile.

"Yes, Captain." He laughed. I stood up to head inside and he rose too, blocking the entrance to the hotel room. I looked up at him and felt a rush of warmth run over me when he smiled. Dan placed his left hand on my hip and with just the slightest pressure moved me toward him. His other hand caressed my neck as he brought his face slowly toward mine. I closed my eyes and holding the base of my skull, Dan pulled me into a gentle kiss. His lips were smooth and warm.

The hand on my hip slid to my back and hugged me closer to him. I felt the shape of his chest. The muscles that moved under his ratty old T-shirt were strong and hard. Dan's lips became more insistent as I leaned against him, bending back as he pressed into me. A quick gasp for breath and we melted back into each other.

It felt like one of those dreams where at one second you're in one place and then the next you're in an entirely new one. We bounced against the balcony door and then knocked into a dresser before he had me firmly pressed against a wall. A knock at the door broke through the haze and when I heard Ana Maria's voice, I pushed Dan back. He looked down at me, his eyes bright. "Just a minute," I called out.

Dan went for me again, but I pushed him away. He let go easily. "Not now," I said, breathing deeply. "We have work to do."

"Yes, Captain," he said with a smile.

I laughed.

14

Spending Time with Cinderella

DAN WAS ON THE COMPUTER SETTING UP SECURE EMAILS FOR everyone on the team when Izel called. "I saw Blane," she said, breathless and excited.

"How'd he look?"

"His arm is bandaged."

"Where was he?"

"He was going into Pedro's office."

"Anything else?"

"I am waiting outside now."

"All right, good work. Stay with him."

Dan looked over at me after I replaced the handset on the receiver. "Izel, the lawyer right?"

"Yeah. She saw Blane, he's still around."

"What does that mean?"

"I don't know yet."

Malina called later that day. Ana Maria took the call and reported back to me as we walked toward a giant cruise ship. "Her girl met Pedro last night and stayed with him." We passed small shacks with their hurricane shutters flung open. The sounds of families talking, cooking and watching TV spilled out onto the street. "She said that he thinks the girl speaks no English so was not afraid to talk on the phone."

"That's great." I turned to look at her, she was smiling.

"Yes, he was on the phone with Blane."

I stopped walking and looked over at her. "And?"

"She didn't understand it all except that they are looking for us. Actually she only heard your name mentioned, Sydney Rye that is." Ana Maria started toward the ship again. "They know you were in the Caymans."

"So they've traced us that far. It's only a matter of time before they connect us to Easy."

"She didn't hear Easy's name."

"That's good."

We approached the ship through an abandoned mall. Its wide halls and glass storefronts were all empty. People didn't want to shop right off the cruise ship. They all wanted to get bussed into the historic district to buy their duty free liquor and perfumes. Our steps echoed in the dusty space.

It opened up onto a huge dock where the behemoth was parked. It was a Disney cruise with Mickey's ears painted all over the damn thing. Ana Maria and I joined a group climbing out of the van and followed them toward the gangplank. "I just wish we got to spend more time with the characters," one of the fathers said to the other.

"Yeah, I know what you mean. We might as well have stayed in Disneyland. At least there you get to spend some real time with Cinderella," another man answered him. A small girl wearing all pink started crying and the man who'd been lamenting about his lack of time with Cinderella hefted her onto his shoulders. We passed those guys and moved ourselves more to the center of the group as we started up the gangplank.

The guards nodded to us as we passed. Once aboard, we separated from the tourists and headed toward the staterooms. Dan suggested that we steal passenger's cell phones. He said we could use them until they're docked. They'd have no idea until they got home.

We checked every door until we found an open one. I knocked, no one answered. We went inside and locked the door behind us. It only took about 30 seconds to find the couple's passports, cash and cell phones buried in the wife's underwear drawer. We just took the phone's smart chips and then returned it all to its super-secret location.

I poked my head out the door and was about to step into the hall when a giant mouse walked around the corner. I ducked back inside and closed the door but not before he had a chance to yell out, "Hi there!"

"Who's that?" Ana Maria whispered.

"Mickey-fucking-Mouse."

"Don't be shy," he called through the door.

"Are you fucking kidding me?" I whispered to Ana Maria.

"Come on, now," he said in a high-pitched voice. "I don't bite."

"No thanks," I called. "I'm not feeling well."

"I bet a hug might cheer you up." I looked over at Ana Maria who wore a horrified expression.

She mouthed, "What the fuck!"

He knocked on the door. "Really, I just want to be alone," I called. He pushed on the handle and it gave. I stepped against the door and slammed it shut again. "Hey, back off!" I felt him put his weight against the door. I planted my feet but he still managed to move me about an inch. Sweat pricked on my forehead and I turned to Ana Maria. She stepped up next to me and helped to get the door shut. I turned the lock using all my strength to keep the bolt in line with the jam.

"Hey," I heard out in the hall. "You're not supposed to take your helmet off." Blood was thumping through my skull. "And what are you doing outside my door?" I heard a whomp, a low groan, and the thud of a body hitting carpeting.

The door securely locked, I ran to the window hoping for an escape but it opened up onto a thirty foot drop into the harbor. I turned back to the room. Ana Maria was peering through the peephole. I went to her side and she moved out of my way. The hall looked empty. Then again it was pretty easy to hide from a peephole. He could be right up against the door. Or just a little down the hall.

I went into the bathroom looking for a weapon. Whoever it was out there faced a large disadvantage. He was covered in a stuffed suit. The thing had to hinder his movement. Then again, if I was going up against him with a, I pulled a Lady Schick out of a toiletry bag, and he had a gun, I might be the underdog. If I hit him anywhere besides the face he wouldn't feel it.

I looked over at a pile of dirty towels on the floor. Maybe if I could cover his face and knock him down, he'd be like a turtle, stuck on his back. I picked up the towels and then pulled down the shower curtain rod. If nothing else, it had good reach.

Ana Maria was still looking out the peephole. I heard a soft groan from the hall. Quickly explaining my plan to Ana Maria, I opened the door. We stayed behind it inviting the giant mouse in. But nothing happened. Was he just patient? Was he waiting for us to come out? Who was he? Did he leave after hitting the tourist?

I peeked around the door and saw a pair of pale hairy legs. I stepped out from behind the door, my towel and shower rod ready. But nothing happened. Turning left and then right I just saw a long, ugly carpeted hall. The man right in front of the door was holding his face and rolling back and forth, occasionally moaning. He didn't appear to know I was there.

Ana Maria followed me into the hall. She looked at the man on the floor and asked, "What do we do now?"

"Run." I dropped the towels and rod next to the semi-conscious man and hurried back the way we'd come. The hair at the back of my neck was at full attention and every nerve in my body vibrated.

At the gangplank I stopped for a moment, shielding my eyes against the bright sun. I looked out over the abandoned mall to Frenchtown. I couldn't see our hotel but it wasn't far. Obviously it was time to move on. I just hoped that everyone back there was

OK. And then I saw him. That Mickey Mouse motherfucker was just exiting the dead halls of the mall.

"There he is," I said, pointing him out to Ana Maria. His head was gone and so were his gloves but there was no mistaking that body. His hair was a light brown and that's about all I could see before he disappeared into the small streets of Frenchtown.

"Do you think he knows where we're staying?"

"He followed us onto this boat; unless that was just coincidence I think he knows where we're sleeping." I didn't have a phone so couldn't call my friends and warn them. Easy was in the room with Blue. Dan was in town buying equipment. I figured Easy and Blue were the targets but only an idiot would go after that girl and dog without at least a gun.

I ran down the gangplank. Ana Maria's feet pounded right behind my own. The dead mall seemed full of life. Everywhere I turned a shadow was moving, a Disney character was lurking. I picked up my pace, sprinting through the decaying center of commerce. One guy was selling T-shirts and as I flew by him he offered, "Ganja?"

It felt good to be running. Passing houses with their storm shutters open and the smell of frying foods floating out of them, I took a deep breath. This guy, whoever he was, held some answers. Maybe he could tell me why I was in this mess. Tell me why Alejandro had to die. Why Ana Maria was so willing to take down her own parents.

She was right behind me. Keeping up with my fast pace. I admired her as I listened to her heavy breathing. She was a tough girl. I thought her love and admiration for her cousin unique and not unlike the relationship that my brother and I had shared. But would I ruin my parents over it? Maybe, I thought, as air burned in my lungs. I was willing to kill a man.

We reached the hotel out of breath. I stopped in front of it and grabbed onto an electric pole to help support me while I recovered. We didn't pass Mickey so either he wasn't at the hotel or was related to Speedy Gonzales. I looked up to my balcony and saw Easy sitting there. I waved to her and she waved back.

"She's safe," I said to Ana Maria.

"Yeah, I see that. Where do you think that guy was going?"

I shrugged. "Maybe he didn't know where we were staying. Or he's decided to change before another attack."

"Who is he?"

"Don't know. But I want to find out." I watched Easy stand up and go inside.

We climbed the steps to the lobby. There was no one behind the front desk. We ducked into the cool stairwell. It was a relief to be out of the sun. My run from the ship left sweat on my forehead and pooling on my back. Ana Maria's face was red with exertion and we climbed the steps slowly, enjoying the shaded path.

Our door stood slightly ajar. I leaned against it to open it more, but it stopped six inches in. My heart started racing. Where was Blue? Why hadn't he greeted me yet? I jumped back, knocking into Ana Maria as a piece of wood smashed into where my head had been. "Ana, run!" I heard her feet racing back down the steps as a man stepped through the door. He looked like a boxer. His nose was so mashed that it looked abstract. His forehead was small, a patch of white between his brown hair and his dark eyebrows. His eyes were sunken and black. They looked like the eyes of a rodent, a mouse.

I held my fists in front of my face preparing for a fight. He swung his board of wood at me, I ducked under it. The furry costume was slowing him down. On the balls of my toes, I stepped to the left and struck at the side of his face. I hit his ear. He turned to look at me, but I was already back in front of him. I struck at his lip this time and stepped around again.

Blood pooled on his split lip and mixing with saliva, journeyed down his chin. I went in low with a right hook and put all my weight into his stomach. It was like punching a stuffed animal. He grunted, recovered quickly and I felt the breeze the wood made as it missed my face by less than a millimeter. This guy was slow-moving. He wasn't as good as me.

Blane knew my training; Ana Maria's parents wouldn't be so stupid to send an amateur after me. He swung again and this time I caught the wood, twisted it against his thumb and wrenched it from his hands. He looked surprised as hell when I went to bash him in the face but stopped a half an inch short. "Who are you and what are you doing here?"

His eyes rolled in their sockets away from the wood to my face. "I was gonna bring you in."

"How about you answer some questions instead?" He nodded his head. "Firstly, where is my dog?"

15

Mickey Mouse Interrogation

HE DIDN'T KNOW WHERE BLUE WAS. "EASY?" I ASKED. HE looked as confused. "The woman occupying this room?"

"Oh, she's in there," he said, smiling, happy to help.

"Easy!" I called.

Mickey's face fell into a frown. "I had to wallop her one."

"Wallop?"

"Just knock her out so she wouldn't warn you or nothin'."

I motioned with the piece of wood for him to step inside. He moved backwards into the room. "Sit on the bed," I told him. A groan came from behind the door. I took my gaze off Mickey for just a second to check on the sound. Easy was behind the door, on her side, holding her head. "Your trademark?" I asked.

Mickey shrugged. I looked around the room searching for something to tie him up with. The strings from the curtains caught my attention. "Hey," I said to him. "Pull down those cords." I motioned to them with the wood.

Mickey got off the bed and ripped the whole window treatment off the wall. He smiled at me sheepishly and I saw that he was missing a few teeth. Blood was drying on his chin and he looked almost like a kid. A kid who'd spent his time in the womb boxing. "All right, lie down on the bed with your hands behind your back."

Ana Maria came in as I was tying his hands with my knee in his spine. "You're OK," she said, a big smile on her face.

"Yeah," I looked over at Easy. "Help her, would you?" Ana Maria turned and saw Easy on the ground. Her face whitened.

Once I finished wrapping the curtain cord around Mickey's wrists, I moved onto his ankles. Ana Maria crouched by Easy's side. "Her eyes look clear," Ana Maria said.

I rolled Mickey over and told him, "I should fucking wallop you for what you did to her." He didn't answer. "Who are you?"

"Jimmy Toll."

"What are you doing here?"

"I'm a bounty hunter."

"Not a very good one."

"I done better before."

"Yeah, who's got a bounty on me?"

"I don't know their name. I just know it's a lotta money."

"How much?"

"Hundred thousand."

"What about the girl? Anything for her?"

He turned to look at Ana Maria. "I never seen her before."

That was good at least. That meant that if we separated no one would be going after Ana, they just wanted me.

"What's my name?"

"What?"

"Say my name."

"Sydney Rye."

"How did you hear about me?"

"It's just going around."

"My picture?"

"Online."

"How'd you find me?"

"I got lucky. I saw you buying dresses and I followed you."

I looked over and saw that Easy was sitting up. She was rubbing her temples. I helped Ana Maria lift her onto the other bed. I propped her up on a couple of pillows. Ana filled a glass with water and brought it to Easy.

"There was a man," she said.

"That one." I pointed at our hogtied guest. He was still wearing the fuzzy body of Mickey Mouse.

Easy looked at him blankly. She raised a hand to her swollen cheek then brought it down quickly. "Ana, do we have any aspirin or anything?" I asked.

She went into the bathroom and I heard her rummaging through our bags. "You all right?" I asked Easy.

She smiled. "Takes more than a punch in the face to stop me."

I smiled. "Good. Easy? Where's Blue?"

"Dan took him for a walk right before that guy showed up."

I let out a breath of air I didn't even know I'd been holding. "Good, good."

"Who is he?" Easy asked.

Ana Maria came back into the room with two white pills. "Here you go."

Easy took the pills and then looking over at me asked again, "Who is he?"

I shook my head trying to clear it. "He's a bounty hunter."

"Wow, really?"

"Yeah, but there's good news. He's just after me which means that either whoever hired him does not know or care about the rest of you guys."

"I guess that's good," Easy said.

"Either way we've got to move." I stood up. Easy went to follow but I stopped her. "You rest for awhile. Ana and I will pack."

She went to protest but then I think her swollen face got the better of her and she laid back down. Ana and I packed quickly and by the time Dan got back we were ready to go. He came into the room all smiles. "Did you get the smart chips?" he asked before noticing the man tied up on the bed. "What the-"

"We've had an incident," I explained. Blue went over and

114

sniffed the bound man. Mickey or Jimmy, whatever his name was, looked scared as hell while Blue gave him the once over.

"Who is he?"

"A bounty hunter. We've got to get out of here."

"Hey, Jimmy?" His eyes left Blue and landed on my face. "You tell anyone about me?" He shook his head no. "You didn't tell anyone I was staying here?"

"No. Why would I do that? Then maybe they get you instead of me."

"Does anyone else know I'm on this island?"

"I didn't tell them. Everyone knows you're in the Caribbean but they don't know where." In that case, I thought, we've got to get the fuck out of the Caribbean.

The phone rang and everyone turned to look at it. Ana Maria went for it but I was there first. It was Malina. "My girl just left Pedro," she said. "He was very upset."

"About what?" Ana Maria was looking at me and chewing on the inside of her left cheek.

"He says that his daughter is missing. He says that he is very worried."

"Did he say where his daughter went?"

"He would not tell her. But she thinks she has been kidnapped."

"Really?" I cupped the phone closer to my ear, trying to keep the conversation private in a room full of people.

"He was on the phone and he was very angry. He was yelling at a man. He said…" Malina stopped to clear her throat, "he said 'she killed my nephew, she kidnapped my daughter.' What is he talking about?"

"I don't know." I looked down at the bedside table. It was marked with cigarette burns that turned the honey-colored wood black. "You are doing great," I said to Malina.

"He is so sad," she said. "He misses his daughter very much. He says he loves her and he wants her back very badly. Do you know where she is?"

"I've got to go. I'll get back to you soon." I hung up the phone and turned to the man on the bed. I was going to ask him again who sent him but I honestly didn't think he knew. The guy didn't look like he knew much.

"What was that about?" Ana Maria asked.

"It was Malina checking in." Ana Maria almost said something but instead she turned away from me.

I chewed on my bottom lip and looked around the room. Easy on one bed holding a cool compress to her face, Jimmy on the other watching Blue with a wary eye. Ana Maria was standing looking out onto the balcony. Dan moved close to me and his nearness felt calming.

"All right, folks, it's time to move."

Having a private plane and pilot makes escaping easier. Her ex working in customs and willing to lie about your flight plan helps, too. The bound man dressed up like a mouse who just screams ex-convict hinders things but not so much that it makes them impossible.

Maude did not like it when I dragged him into her office. "What are you doing?" she asked, her eyes huge, taking in the full picture of Jimmy.

"I don't want anyone to see him," I said.

"I don't want to see him."

"Yeah, sorry about that."

Maude pushed herself into the opposite corner of her office.

"Nice poster," Jimmy said, using his chin to point to the kitten encouraging us to hang in there.

"You need to get out of here," Maude said.

"I was thinking the same thing."

Easy opened the door and stepped into the already cramped office. The baggage between the two women did not clear up any space. When Maude saw the bruise swelling on Easy's face, she stepped forward and asked just above a whisper, "What happened?"

"That shithead," Easy told her.

Maude turned angry eyes onto Jimmy who didn't look back. "Why?"

"He is a bounty hunter who attempted to hunt me," I answered.

"Kill you?"

I looked at her, "Good question!" I couldn't believe I hadn't asked him that before. "What were you supposed to do with me Jimmy? Where did you plan to bring me?"

"I was just gonna take you to my house and then contact a guy."

"Which guy, Jimmy?" I walked toward him till he was pressed in a corner. Blue growled and showed Jimmy how big his teeth were.

"I just have an email address. I was just gonna email him."

"You use the internet, Jimmy."

"What?" He looked up at me with his eyebrows raised. "I'm not a plebeian."

"Coulda fooled me," Easy said.

"What's the email?" I asked.

"It's in my pants," he said.

I unzipped Jimmy's costume. He'd been sweating like a man in a Disney costume and his smell filled the tiny office quickly. He smiled as the relatively cool air touch his skin. Jimmy's pants were tight and his pocket was right next to his manhood. I did not want to go in there to get anything out.

"If you untie me I'll get it," he said with just the ghost of a smile on his lips.

"Yeah, I'm sure." Instead I reached in. His leg was warm and his pocket moist from sweat. "Nasty," I muttered as I felt around. There was a small scrap of paper that I pulled out. In pencil, in what looked like little boys handwriting it said: bgk26053@gmail.-com. "I'll be right back." I motioned for Blue to watch Jimmy and left the small office. As I walked away, I heard raised voices start. All right, one raised voice. Easy was yelling at Maude. Whatever, let them sort it out, I thought as I crossed the dock toward Dan.

He was standing next to the plane with Ana Maria. The luggage was loaded, they just needed me, Easy, and our new flight plan to get going. "Can you break into an email real fast?" I asked, handing him the slip of paper.

"I haven't even had a chance to work on the other two." He looked down at the slip and smiled. "This actually shouldn't be that hard." He pulled his laptop out, connected a cell phone with a borrowed smart chip, and went to work.

"I'm going to give them a little time," I said, motioning toward the exes having it out in the office. "I think Jimmy might be able to mediate." Ana laughed. "Hey, take a walk with me?" I said to her.

"Sure," she shrugged.

We left Dan hunched over his laptop and moved down the dock. "Are you sure you want to do this?" I asked her.

"Do what?"

"Ruin your family."

"My parents ruined our family when they killed Alejandro."

Long-necked white birds skimmed along the surface of the harbor. "I know, but you're very young and you might come to regret this."

"My parents are bad people. I told you my mom is full of shit. She says she wants to help women but she doesn't really. And my dad is such a fucking hypocrite."

"You know, a lot of kids think their parents are full of it until they get a little older and realize everyone is full of it."

Ana Maria stopped walking and turned to me. "Most parents don't kill their nephews." I watched a bird dive into the water, disappear completely below the surface and then burst out again, water dripping off its wings as they spread. A small fish struggled in the bird's beak. The bird threw its head back and the fish fell down its gullet.

"Right," I said, not looking at her. "But, Ana, if they are behind Alejandro's murder, why are they trying to bring me in, alive no less?"

"I don't know," she said. "I can't understand why anyone would want to hurt Alejandro." She sniffled. "I'm sorry," she said, swiping at tears. "I just can't think about him. The only thing that keeps me going is knowing that we will revenge his death." She looked up at me, her eyes searching my face.

I nodded. "OK," I said.

I left Ana Maria looking out at the boats buzzing around the harbor and headed back to the customs office. Easy stormed out of the little room, slamming the door behind her. She strode toward me and said as she passed, "What a fucking coward."

Maude stepped out of the room, leaving the door open a crack. She looked at Easy's retreating back and then to me. I gave her a smile which she returned with a grimace. She was playing with the hem of her shirt when I stepped up to her.

"How you doing?" I asked. She laughed the way you laugh when you're nervous and have to speak in front of a large audience of not-naked people. "I'm going to talk to our prisoner for awhile." She nodded but didn't move. "Would you mind giving me some alone time?"

She nodded and walked away in the direction of Easy. I stepped into the little room closing the door behind me. Jimmy was pushed into the corner with the potted plants. His body pressed several of them against the window. Blue sat right in front of him, his eyes trained on Jimmy's bound body. "OK," I said, to Blue. He looked over at me and took a couple of steps back but didn't really relax.

"Jimmy, do you mind if I call you Mickey?" Jimmy eased off the plants and nodded his head. "Have a seat." I motioned to the chair I sat in a couple of days earlier when I asked Maude for her help. Jimmy sat.

"Mickey, I've been thinking and there is a bunch of stuff I just can't figure out. I'm hoping you can help me."

"I don't know anything," he said. "I just found out about your bounty. I'm just trying to make some money, just like everybody else."

"Not everybody is just trying to make money, Mickey." He

started to laugh but looking at my face stopped him. "You said my bounty did not mention a girl I was traveling with."

"No."

"Did it say anything about me being a kidnapper?" He shook his head again. "Killer?"

"No."

"So what did it say?"

"That you were dangerous but needed to be taken alive and not to hurt you."

"Didn't think that wood was gonna sting, did you?"

He shrugged. I paced the floor, walking the short distance from the front of the room to the back, then I went over to the small jungle by the window. "Have you ever killed anyone Mickey?" I looked out the window and watched Dan smiling over his computer. Jimmy didn't answer me, but I heard his chair scrape on the floor. Blue growled and I turned in time to see Jimmy standing up. Blue rose to his feet and barked. Jimmy sat again.

"I just had an itch is all," Jimmy protested.

"Mickey, are you a killer?"

"No," his skin looked soft and loose. I could see a bruise the color of a fresh plum forming where I'd hit him.

"Even by accident in the ring?" I asked

"Maybe."

"I wish you would be more helpful. I really do. See, I'm in this shitty situation where I don't know who to trust. The only thing I do know is not to trust you but that doesn't do me much good." I looked back out the window again hoping that Jimmy would say something useful. He cleared his throat once but other than that, he was silent.

When I turned around he was staring at the cat poster. I left the room. Blue stayed behind to watch Mickey the Mouse.

16

Flight Times

I WALKED DOWN THE DOCK TO WHERE MY SMALL GROUP OF cohorts waited.

"Ready?" Dan asked.

"We should get going," Easy said.

I looked out at the harbor, busy with traffic; the birds swooping in over the fishing boats, the tourist on jet skis making figure eights. I watched the crystal blue water rising and falling and I said:

"We're staying here."

"What?" Maude said. "They know you're here you need to go."

I turned to look at her. Maude's eyes were big, her hands were shaking. "You know what? Let them come. I didn't do anything wrong and I don't want to hide. I don't want to run." A smile spread across my face. "I want to set a trap."

I looked at each one of them in turn. Easy was smiling and nodding her head. Dan pressed his lips together and nodded. Maude shook her head silently. Ana Maria shrugged. "Whatever you say, boss."

"I'm with the kid," Easy agreed.

"Don't leave me out," Dan said.

"What about you, Maude?" We all turned to look at her and she looked back at us.

"I can't, I-"

Easy turned away with a snort of disgust. "You don't have to do anything you don't want to," I told her. I held my hand out for her to shake it. "We'll leave you in peace." She just stared at my outstretched palm. "But you could be a great help. If you could just let us know if anyone arrives through this port with blonde hair and a bandaged arm. Maybe if you could mention to your friends that you'd like to know when that guy gets here. That would make a world of difference to us."

Maude looked at my hand, suddenly unsure of what she was shaking on. If she took my hand did she agree to help or was I letting her out of it, free to go back to her life with her doilies and her plants. She looked up at my face and I smiled at her.

"I want to help," she said, her chin wobbled and her voice broke, "but I am so scared." I stepped closer to her and put one of my arms around her small shoulders.

"Life can be very scary," I told her. She started crying over much more than my offer. Her shoulders shook and her body heaved. I patted her back. Ana Maria held out a napkin, it fluttered in the breeze until Maude took it with an unsteady hand. She brought it to her face and pressed it into her eyes. Easy looked over at us, then turned down the dock and walked away.

"I want to help," Maude said through her tears. "I really do."

"You can Maude. You can and you will." I stepped in front of her, Maude sniffled and looked up at me. Her big brown eyes were blood shot and the skin around them swollen. "Maude. This is your life and you can live it however you want."

She nodded slightly then wiped the tissues across her nose.

I found Easy in Maude's office. Jimmy was back in the corner with the plants. Maude followed me in the room sheepishly. "All right, ladies," I started. "I need both your help. I know you guys have been through some shit and I'm sympathetic, but you've got to get over it for the larger good here." That sounded stupid to me but Easy seemed to like it.

"OK," she said. I turned to Maude and she nodded. Jimmy smiled like a goofball.

"I'm glad to see you two getting along now," he decided to say. Easy got up with her fist clenched and was heading toward Jimmy in a way that made him push further into the corner and squeeze his eyes shut.

"Hey!" I yelled. "What are you doing?"

Easy looked over at me, un-balled her fist and muttered, "Nothing."

"All right, first things first. We need a place to stay." Neither of them said anything. I looked from one to the other. "Come on, guys, you live here."

"I don't, she does," Easy said.

"You can stay at my place," Maude offered.

"It is sooo not big enough," Easy said.

"What about you Jimmy? Where do you live?" I asked.

His eyebrows jumped up his forehead. "What? Me?"

"Yeah, you said you saw me shopping, you must live on the island."

Basically he was too dumb to lie. I could see the thoughts run across his eyes, the attempted lies came to the surface and then dove back down again until he finally said, "Yeah."

"All right, we'll go to Jimmy's place. Easy, why don't you go rent us a car and Maude, you start making phone calls letting your buddies know we're looking for a blonde-"

"I know, with a bandaged arm." I smiled at her and nodded my head. This was gonna turn out just fine.

Easy came back with a 4-door Jeep Wrangler and the four of us plus Blue piled in. "All right Jimmy, where to?"

Jimmy directed us up into the hills behind the old town center. The roads were narrow, winding, and a steep drop replaced the shoulder. In St. Thomas, they drive on the left side of the road. The cars are all American so the steering wheel is also on the left. I kept getting confused and would think for a fatal second that we were on the wrong side! Good thing Easy was driving. Though with Blue panting hot breath onto her left ear, she might have felt otherwise.

We passed over a hill that blocked the town and Caribbean from view. The center of the island didn't look like the coast. Poverty and reality both lived there. We drove by a Home Depot where cows crossed the parking lot. Men in dirty clothing and no shoes walked along the side of the road. In the jungle that lined the streets, I could see broken-down shacks with clean laundry hanging outside. We had to swerve to avoid hitting a chicken.

Cresting another hill, the Atlantic was suddenly in front of us. Dark blue and stretching as far as the eye could see. Rocky islands dotted the shimmering expanse of ocean but other than that it was clear sailing straight to the horizon. We wound along the coast, high up on a cliff until Jimmy pointed for us to go down a very steep hill.

Jimmy's road was once concrete but the ocean air, many rains, and island life was turning it back into dirt. His driveway was the third in and when he pointed to it, Easy turned to look at me first. I nodded. Trees hung over the path blocking our view of the house until we were almost upon it.

Jimmy's house was not what I expected. His storm shutters were thrown open to reveal screened windows. We climbed out of the Jeep and Jimmy asked to have his hands untied. I refused. His door was unlocked and I walked into a breezy open room. The front wall was all screen doors that lead out to a balcony with a stunning view of the ocean.

A small, galley style kitchen to my right was tidy and clean. It was separated from the living room by a counter with enough room for two to eat. To my left a hallway led to two bedrooms. One with a queen bed unmade, but the room was clean besides that. The next room was an office. Jimmy had a computer, two guitars, and a pull-out couch. Posters of boxers covered the walls.

"Jimmy, this place is nice," I said.

"Yeah," Dan said. "I like it."

"Nice view," Easy said from the porch.

"Thanks," Jimmy said, trying to hide a smile.

"All right," I said, turning to my people. "Dan, I want you to send an email to whoever hired Jimmy saying that he caught me and wants to arrange a meet. Also, if you can break into the account so we can see what we will see."

Dan nodded. "I'll set up in the office," he said.

"Great, Ana Maria, I need you to call Izel and give her the number here. Find out what Blane is doing."

Ana Maria went to a phone hanging on Jimmy's wall and started dialing.

"What can I do?" Easy asked.

"Go lie down," I said. She started to protest but I shook my head. "Easy, you got knocked out today. Take it easy, please, for me."

She smiled. "Fine."

"Thank you. Take Jimmy's bedroom."

Ana Maria motioned for me to come to the phone. "Izel wants to talk to you."

I crossed the room and took the receiver. "Yes?"

"I followed Blane to the airport. He boarded a flight for Miami."

I bit my lip thinking, he must be on his way to the Caribbean. "What kind of luggage did he have?" I asked.

There was a pause on the other end of the line. "I think just a briefcase. I do not think he checked any luggage."

"OK, thanks. Good work. Take the rest of the night off. I'll call you tomorrow."

I hung up and then turning back to the room saw that the sun was setting. A gorgeous orange glow filled the room. Jimmy was looking at it with a peaceful smile on his face. Strange guy, I thought.

17

Disrupt, Corrupt, or Interrupt

THAT NIGHT I COULDN'T SLEEP. AND IT WASN'T JUST BECAUSE I was sleeping on the couch in Jimmy's living room. I couldn't slow down my mind. It felt like a live electric wire ran along my spine. I got up, threw my blanket to the floor, and scrounged around in the kitchen until I found a bottle of whiskey. I filled a glass and headed out to the balcony.

A huge moon lit up the water with a bright, white stripe. I sipped at the whiskey, enjoying the sting with the sweet. The door creaked behind me and Dan stepped to my side. "Couldn't sleep?" he asked.

"Restless, I guess. You?"

He shrugged. "I'm a night owl."

"Whiskey?" I asked, offering my glass.

He took it and sipped then handed the drink back. A breeze blew rustling the palm trees and raising goosebumps on my flesh. "You cold?" Dan asked. He moved closer to me so that our hips touched. Placing his arm around me, he squeezed. Dan leaned over and kissed the top of my head. I rested against his chest and listened to his heartbeat. It picked up pace when I slipped my arm around his waist.

"What is it about you and balconies?" he asked. I looked up at him. Dan's eyes glowed in the harsh moonlight. "That makes you so damn irresistible."

He ran his thumb against my cheek, smiling down at me. I blushed and felt his touch like a burning coal against my skin, rough and hot. Dan leaned down and kissed me on the lips, gently, almost chastely. He moved down to my neck, opening his mouth and kissing me deeply. I looked out at the ocean's vastness and felt grounded by the kisses Dan was laying on me.

His hands ran up and down my back, using their strength to pull me closer to him. My dress strap slipped off my shoulder exposing my breast. Dan took the whiskey glass out of my hand and finished it looking at me in the moonlight. I felt my nipples hardening under his gaze. Dan placed the empty glass on the balcony railing then leaned over and kissed my breast, softly, slowly. I shuddered with pleasure. Dropping to his knees, Dan took my dress with him. It fell to the balcony floor without protest.

I ran my fingers through his hair and then pulled him back to his feet. I fumbled at his T-shirt and pulled it over his head. Dan's skin felt soft and silky against mine. His chest was lean and sculpted.

Dan unbuttoned his jeans and they dropped to the balcony floor next to my dress. Urgent now, Dan kissed me like if we stopped something disastrous would happen. I wrapped a leg around him and he followed my cue picking me up off the ground. Both my legs wrapped around him, Dan turned and leaned me against the building.

He caught my eyes as he breathed heavily, our noses almost touching, his fingers hooked into the waistband of my panties. He tried to say something but I stopped him, pressing my lips against his. Dan didn't try to ask for permission again.

I woke in the morning feeling rested for the first time in a long time. I blinked and looked around Jimmy's office, light filtered through dark curtains casting a slate grey onto the room. The posters of the boxers in their ring-day finery, gloves up, eyes mean, seemed to be watching me.

Rolling over I found my dress laid over a chair. Dan must have brought it in, I thought, a smile pulling at my lips. I heard the clinking of cups and then the scent of coffee reached me. Slipping the dress on, I headed out to the living room.

Easy looked up from a cup of coffee she was pouring and smiled at me. "Want one?" she asked.

"Thanks," I said.

Dan was at the stove and he looked over his shoulder at me. His eyes searched my face and when I smiled at him, he grinned back. "Eggs?" he asked.

"Sounds great." I took the cup Easy offered me and sat on one of the stools at the bar. Moments later, Dan spooned scrambled eggs onto a plate for me and Easy dropped a piece of toast next to it. "You guys are awesome," I said, before digging in.

Ana Maria emerged from the room she'd shared with Easy while we were doing dishes. Dan offered to recreate our breakfast for her and she happily agreed. "Make enough for Jimmy, too," I told him.

"Have you checked on him yet?" Ana Maria asked.

"No," I said. "I'll go get him now. I'm sure Blue needs a break."

I headed to Jimmy's garage, which he kept as neat as his house. Shelves lined with labeled boxes covered two walls. Against the third was an old couch, which Jimmy slept on, snoring up a storm. Blue looked over at me from where he lay on a jumble of towels.

"Good boy," I said. Blue's tail wagged as he came over to me, his head low and ears flat. I knelt down and pet his face, rubbing his ears. "What a very good boy."

Jimmy stirred and blinked his eyes open. "Good morning," I said. "Would you like some breakfast?"

He looked up at me with puffy, sleep filled eyes and nodded. After he'd eaten and enjoyed some coffee I sat down on one of the couches in the living room and sat Jimmy in a chair across from me.

"Jimmy, I need a gun."

He looked up at me. "I don't have a gun," he said.

"I figured as much, hence the piece of wood."

"That's right."

"But Jimmy, I'm guessing you know where I could get a gun."

"I don't know," he said, shaking his head.

"I've read the paper. This island's got quite a gun violence problem I can't believe a guy who does bounty work wouldn't know where to get a gun."

"I don't do so much bounty work. I just needed to make a little extra because my niece is getting married and I wanted to do something nice for her."

"Jimmy, do you know how crazy that sounds?"

He pouted his lips and sat back in the chair. "I don't care how it sounds. I don't know nothin' about guns."

"All right." I stood up. "Blue," at the mention of Blue's name, Jimmy sat up straighter. "Take his toes off." Then I whistled one short burst.

"What!" Jimmy yelled. Blue does not have a command for taking people's toes however, a single whistle tells him to act aggressively toward the person I'm talking with. Which he did. Jimmy started sweating and stood up. Easy came in off the porch and Dan looked at the scene from where he stood in the kitchen drinking a glass of water.

"Now Jimmy, if you just find me a gun or two I can stop him, but once he starts it becomes difficult." Blue barked. Jimmy backed away from us. He knocked over a standing lamp, and turning back to look at it, he tripped. While he fell, he screamed. From the floor he started yelling, "I'll do it, I'll do it."

"Great. Where's your phone?" Blue stopped growling and went back to sniffing the house. Checking every crevice for evil, or a snack.

Jimmy was shaking as I helped him up. "That dog is scary."

"I know, Jimmy, I know. Now listen," he was still looking over at Blue so I held his chin and moved his face so he was looking at me.

"I'm going to untie you so that you can make phone calls. Don't do anything stupid."

"OK." Dan brought me a knife from the kitchen and I cut Jimmy loose. He rubbed at his wrists. They were red and for a second I felt bad about tying him so tight for so long. It only took one look at Easy to remember that this guy was not my friend. He might be stupid, he might have a nice house, but he was my enemy.

I watched as he dialed a number from a little black book he kept next to his phone. He put the book down and in the silence of the room I could hear the ringing on the other end of the line. It sounded like it was traveling through a tin can. I had a funny image of Jimmy in a tree house as a boy, but still with the mashed face, talking in a tin can with a string attached to it.

A voice broke into the middle of the fourth ring and Jimmy reacted. He sat up straight and went through the pleasantries that any phone conversation begins with. Then he asked about guns. Not in some special code or anything he just said. "Do you have any guns... yeah, I'll need a couple."

For some reason I was surprised. I'd thought that the illegal gun trade would be more along the lines of buying marijuana where you tell the dealer you're looking for trees or a green dress or something totally stupid like that but Jimmy was just asking for guns.

"It's for a friend," he told the guy at the other end. "Yeah, I'll bring her." Then Jimmy laughed and said, "Not like that." He hung up the phone and told me, "We're all set."

"You drive," I said. He shrugged.

Jimmy pulled out of his drive way and headed back up the hill to the top of the island. We passed by the Home Depot again, the cows were gone. He didn't take the turn off to town and soon we were in a neighborhood that made me glad I was carrying a straight razor and was riding with Blue.

Small houses lined the roads. Their wood sides chipped gray paint. Some of the roofs were blue tarps. "From the Hurricane," Jimmy said. "It's been ten years but the damage is still around. You see it all over the island." Children pointed at Blue from the side of the road. He rode with his head poking out the side of the jeep, his ears flapping in the wind and his nose sniffing at the air.

We pulled off the road, through a ditch, and onto the muddy lawn of a shack that didn't look much different than any of the others. A woman hung laundry on a line that ran from the porch to a nearby coconut tree. She looked over us, not bothering to stop her eyes on anything in particular. Her hair and her skin were the color of pure cocoa powder. Her dress was clean but worn. She could have been anywhere from 35 to 55.

Jimmy led the way inside. It was cool in the shade of the house. A small TV sat in the corner muted. Maury Povich spoke to a woman who was very young and crying very hard. He said something that made her scream and then a man came out on stage waving his hands in the air as the crowd yelled and clapped.

Maury's show cast a blue light in the otherwise dark room. To my left a small kitchen filled an alcove. Sunlight peeked through the closed slats of the storm shutters. A man wearing shorts and an old grey T-shirt smoked at a table that breached the line of the kitchen into the sitting room. He was watching Maury.

He nodded at Jimmy and as Maury went to commercial (that cute teddy bear who bounces on clean towels), he turned his eyes to me. A smile pulled his cheeks up toward his ears revealing a gold tooth a couple from the center. "You didn't say she was so pretty, man," he said to Jimmy.

"She's not," Jimmy said. He pulled out one of the empty chairs at the table and sat down. Then the man saw Blue silently seated next to me. He pushed himself up and out of the chair, his eyes glued to Blue's form.

"What the fuck is that?" he asked.

"A dog," I answered, moving toward the only remaining chair at the table. Blue stayed on my heel.

The man put up his hands and knocked his chair over trying to back up. "I don't like dogs, and I don't like that."

I took my seat and Blue sat next to me. "He won't hurt you." The man reached behind him, opened a drawer and pulled out a hand gun, swinging it around to aim at Blue. His hand was shaking. I smiled at him. "It still surprises me that so many people are so afraid of dogs."

"I'll fucking shoot it."

"That seems unnecessary," I said. He didn't look like he was going to shoot Blue but with the tremor in his finger and the fear in his eyes, there was little I could be sure of. "How about I have him wait outside?"

"How about you just get the fuck out of my house?"

I stood up and reached into my purse. "Hey," he turned the gun on me.

"I'm just getting money," I said. I moved very slowly ignoring the muzzle of the gun trained on my face. I pulled out a bundle of cash and slowly placed it on the table. "You give me that gun, another that looks like it, and some bullets, I'll leave the money and your house," I said.

He looked down at the money and then at Blue, then his eyes reached my face. "I don't like doing business this way."

"Me either, man, but then again, I'm not the one who pulled out a gun and started threatening people's pets." I smiled at him and I could see him relax. "He won't bite you," I said.

"Unless she tells him to," Jimmy added.

The man's eyes jumped to Jimmy. "How you gonna bring this into my home, mon?"

"Hey, I'm just bringing you business."

"Yeah right, mon. You bringing crazy in here."

"Look, Oscar," Jimmy's brow furrowed and his mouth turned into a frown that radiated into his eyes, "she's trying to give you money, mon. Her dog ain't going to do nothin' so why don't you just sit down. We'll buy some merchandise and then we'll leave."

"Thanks, Jimmy," I said, surprised by his impassioned defense of me.

Oscar looked back at me and Blue. His lips pursed and he brought the gun down to his side. I was happy to have the barrel with its black center and deadly intent off my face. Oscar put the gun on the table next to the money and then opening the fridge pulled out two more that looked almost like it. "Here," he said. "How many you want?"

I picked up the gun on the table. It was older and heavier than what I was used to but it looked well taken care of. On the handle where the serial number should have been was a file mark. "Do you know where it came from?" I asked Oscar. I aimed it at the back wall and looked down the barrel. It looked straight enough but I couldn't tell without shooting the thing.

Oscar sat back down. "What does it matter where it came from if it's here now?"

I smiled. "Well, Oscar, I just want to know what it's been used for before in case I get caught with it. I want to know what I'll be charged with."

Oscar laughed. "Lady, it don't matter what it done before, you get caught with that it's not like they going to care what it done, they just care you got it. Besides, I don't know where it been and I don't want to know where it's going." Oscar laughed again and Jimmy joined him.

"Fair enough," I said, recognizing Oscar's logic.

18

Driving

Turned out I bought those guns just in the nick of time because when Jimmy and I turned onto his street my window exploded about a millisecond after the bang of gunfire rang out. "Shit!" Jimmy yelled.

I slid down in my seat, Jimmy did the same while pushing the gear shift into reverse. Another shot was fired, this one tinged off the metal roll bar above our heads as Jimmy hit the gas. Our tires spun in the gravel for a second before catching and propelling us back up the hill.

We hit the paved road and nearly ran right into the mountain on the other side of it before Jimmy pushed it back into drive and swung the wheel around so that we were racing down the road. I turned in my seat, making sure to keep my head low, and peeked out trying to see if there was anybody after us.

Blue was in the foot wells in the back seat with his ears flat against his head. We were on a very curvy road so I could only see about ten feet behind us. At first I thought there was no one there but when we hit a straightaway, right as we were going into the next curve, I saw a black Jeep.

Jimmy was hunkered down in his seat with just his eyes high

enough to see where he was going. I hadn't seen the driver because of the glare off their windshield, but I had a pretty good guess who was driving the other Wrangler. While I hadn't heard from Maude about a sandy-haired man arriving on the island, that didn't mean he wasn't here. I turned back around and faced forward trying to think. We were headed back toward town and I thought that was OK. Blane couldn't shoot at us in town, right?

Around the next bend a chicken was in the road. Jimmy saw it and swerved into a rut to avoid it. It was a wild, out-of-control move and I grabbed at the door trying to steady myself. The Jeep jerked down and then up again as Jimmy powered us out of the ditch and back onto the road. "What the fuck!" I yelled.

"There was a chicken."

"Next time fucking hit the chicken!"

That's exactly what the guy in the black Jeep did. I turned around to see the feathers exploding with a mix of blood and guts against the guy's grill. He drove through the chicken into the shade of a tree and I saw him. I saw Blane. He was wearing wrap-around sunglasses - the kind douche bags think look cool. His mouth was a straight line, his face made of stone.

I rested my new gun on the shoulder of my seat and tried to steady my aim as we raced back past the Home Depot. Jimmy swerved around other cars, at times facing oncoming traffic, to further our escape. It was impossible to get a clear shot. I turned back around as we crested a hill and we could see the harbour below us.

Traffic became congested as we got closer to town. I turned around and saw that Blane was stuck several cars behind us. There was no way he could fire off any rounds with all these people around. We stopped at a red light and I waved to Blane. He raised a gun and I dropped down in my seat as I heard a window shatter. It wasn't our car but the one right behind us.

People started screaming and the light turned green. Jimmy and I were off. Blane was stuck in the traffic jam he had caused. I laughed as we pulled further away; I couldn't see his face but I was sure he was pissed.

I thought we would pull onto the street that runs along the water but the road was blocked. "Cruise ship just came in," Jimmy said.

"What?"

"Five thousand people all flowing into town at once causes traffic." He turned and looked at me.

I looked around to check for Blane. I heard Jimmy's door open and turned to see him running away from the Jeep into the heart of the town. Blane came around the bend, his hands empty. He saw Jimmy racing along the side walk and took off after him.

Sirens filled the air and I saw flashing lights headed toward Blane's traffic jam. Cops were running toward me. I decided it was time to go. People behind me were leaning on their horns. Grabbing my bag, I picked up Blue's leash and we left the car, walking toward Main Street. A cop bumped into me as he ran toward the "shots fired" site.

When they were around the bend, I took off in the direction Blane and Jimmy had been heading. For a moment, as my flip flops smacked the pavement and I reached into my bag for my gun, I wondered why I didn't just turn around and walk away. Let Jimmy and Blane do to each other whatever they wanted. This was my chance to escape.

But then I spotted Jimmy running up a staircase on the side of a building still missing its roof. Blane was only twenty feet behind him. Did Blane know that I wasn't with Jimmy? That I was behind them? I watched Jimmy disappear into the building. And then Blane, with his gun raised, went in after him.

I stood at a distance looking at the old brick building with its blue tarp, catching my breath. I checked that my gun was full of bullets, it was. I looked down at my flip flops and wondered at my stupidity. Not only was I not wearing the right shoes for this I was also wearing a dress. And who fucking cares about those two anyway? Was it my fault if Blane killed Jimmy? I mean the guy tried to take me in. He hit Easy!

The sun was high and hot. Sweat beaded on my forehead as I looked at the door my two enemies had gone into. But what if Blane didn't hire Jimmy? I needed to know because if Jimmy didn't tell Blane where I was, who did?

I started after them. The steps were old, metal and rusted. They creaked under my and Blue's weight. I just hoped the two men inside were too busy fighting to hear me coming. I stopped just outside the door and listened. I didn't hear anything. I looked back at Blue. I wished I could hear what he was hearing.

The door was open a crack and I peered into the gloom beyond but I didn't see anything. Fuck it. I kicked the door open, ducked and rolled into a dark corner. Resting on my haunches I looked around. Blane laughed and my eyes zeroed in on him. He had his bandaged arm around Jimmy's neck, holding his body close. His free hand pushed a gun against Jimmy's temple. The light from the door cut through the dark of the room illuminating Jimmy's petrified eyes.

I thought about shooting Jimmy and then Blane but figured that firstly, Blane would get me before I got him and besides I really didn't want to kill Jimmy. I'm not afraid of burning in hell, I just don't like to think of myself as a killer. I prefer avenger.

Blane spoke first. "You can stand up."

"You seem to be confused."

"Oh yeah," he smiled.

"The man you are holding so tenderly is not my friend so I don't give a shit if you kill him." A shadow flickered across Blane's face. "He's your bounty hunter dipshit." He looked surprise. I didn't think he had a bounty hunter. It also might have been the first time since grade school he'd been called a dipshit. He didn't know about Jimmy. How the fuck did he find me?

I stood up slowly and began to circle Blane. He continued to use Jimmy as a shield, shifting his position so Jimmy was always between us. "If you don't care about him why don't you just kill him? And then me?"

I laughed. "Blane, I feel bad for you-"

"If you don't kill him you're stupid."

"If I do I'm no better than you, and Blane, I really enjoy being better than you." I kept walking till Blane's back was to the door. He realized it only a second after me. Blue was already in the air when Blane threw Jimmy at him and fired off a shot. I took aim but Blane dove out of the way, I followed him with my barrel and started squeezing off shots feeling the reverberation in my wrist. It kicked as hard as a pissed off horse.

Blane ran through a shaft of light to an open door filled with darkness. I heard his feet pounding on the wood floor. Blue started after him but I called him back. I wasn't about to go crashing through a dilapidated building hunting Blane. I needed to call my friends and tell them to get out of Jimmy's house.

Blue came and sat next to me. My heart stopped for a second when I saw a red stain on his neck but looking closer I saw that it wasn't his blood. Looking back toward the door to the outside world, I saw Jimmy on the floor holding his shoulder and moaning. I stepped over him to get out into the sunlight. I planned on just leaving him there but he struggled to his feet and followed me down to the street.

Jimmy's face was pale. He was using his left hand to apply pressure to his right shoulder. His shirt was stained red and it leaked out of the sleeve and down his arms, dripping off the tips of his fingers. There weren't many people around because we were on a side street, but there was no way I could walk out into a public area with this bleeding man.

At the top of the alley a woman was selling sarongs and straw hats. I told Jimmy to wait for me; he leaned against the building and squeezed his eyes shut. I ran to the top of the block just hoping that Blane wouldn't come out and start shooting at me. The woman with the sarongs smiled as I approached.

"I'll take a hat and that red one," I said, pointing to a burgundy piece of cloth with fringes hanging off it.

"Very good choice," she said as she pulled it off the rack. "Very high quality. And only fifty dollar."

She handed it to me and I looked down at the cheap piece of cotton. I knew that it was worth about five bucks but glancing down the alley at Jimmy slumped against the wall I also knew I didn't have time to bargain. I handed her three twenties, grabbed a hat and started back toward Jimmy.

I scanned the block as I walked keeping all of my senses ready for another fight. The building was a large one and I was sure it had other exits. I hoped Blane had used one of them. I hoped he was out of my hair for just a couple of minutes.

I wrapped the sarong around Jimmy's shoulders covering up the blooming stain. Luckily the stain on the front had a matching one on the back so I guessed the bullet wasn't still in his shoulder.

I held his good arm, supporting him as we moved toward Main Street. I wanted to be around people where Blane wouldn't have the guts to start shooting. I pulled my cell phone with its stolen chip out of my purse as we hurried toward the crowds.

I called Easy. She picked up on the second ring. "Get out of there now," I said. "Meet me in town."

"What?"

"Do it now." We turned onto Main and the mass of people was almost suffocating. I held Blue's leash and Jimmy's arm and pushed through the throng. Jewelry stores lined the block along with T-shirt shops and liquor distributors. Every door was open and manned by someone yelling about the products inside. Air conditioning poured out of the stores onto the sweltering streets. Fat tourists sweated and held their fanny packs tight.

I stepped into a store selling china and crystal just to get out of the heat but inside was so full of bodies that I felt like I was going to scream. It was a feeding frenzy. People were pulling everything off the shelves, I heard them bargaining with the sales people demanding better prices. "You can't bring a dog in here," a woman wearing a name tag told me.

We walked back out to the street and stumbled on. My eyes darted through the crowd narrowing on every blonde head, every tall man. I didn't see Blane. Jimmy pulled on my arm leading me down an alley shaded by the buildings on either side. There were still people here but not as many. And in the middle of the alley was a bar. A round marble bar with a bartender standing in the middle of it, smiling.

"How you doing, Jimmy?" he said, holding his hand out.

"All right, mon." Jimmy wiped his hand on his pants before shaking. "Get me a drink, I'm going to use the bathroom." I sat down on a stool and watched him walk into a restaurant clearly affiliated with the bar.

Stores lined the alley. A Talbots stood next to a hand-painted T-shirt store. Looking down at my dress, I decided it was time to go buy some pants. The bartender put a rum and coke in front of me as I stood to go.

"I'll be right back," I told him. The Talbots was in a building that had been standing since the 1600s. Its exterior was a mottled yellow stone that had seen hurricanes, earthquakes and many a drunken tourist. Inside was some ugly ass clothing. I bought a pair of gray slacks that fit, although they did have pleats in the front which made me look like I was carrying either a child or several years of over eating. I also bought a long lavender (ewww) shirt so that when I tucked my gun into the waistband of the pants, you couldn't see it.

Jimmy was sitting at the bar when I came out in my new outfit. He smiled. "Nice duds." He looked pale and was leaning on the bar for support. Before I could respond my phone rang. It was Easy; she, Dan and Ana Maria were in town. I told them where to meet us and then sipped at my drink. It was mostly rum, as are most drinks in the islands. The stuff is cheaper than water so the bartenders don't bother to hold back.

Jimmy and I sat in silence while we waited for the rest of our crew to show up. I felt that he was on my side now. I think by not blowing out his brains I'd managed to make a friend. That's a nice story, I thought, as I finished off my drink.

The bartender offered me another but I turned him down. "Come on," he said. "It's the islands, you have to drink."

"Sorry buddy, I've got work to do."

"Nonsense, no one works here."

"Really, I'm OK."

"I insist." He started making me another drink and I figured I could just let it sit there. I didn't have to drink it. My head was already getting soft and my belly was warm. The mix of adrenaline and rum in my blood could turn on me at any moment.

Easy was the first down the alley, Ana Maria was right behind her. Dan brought up the rear carrying a laptop case and a worried expression. They sat down and the bartender forced them all to take a drink. Dan leaned close to me and said, "I got into Mulberry's email."

"And?"

Dan bit his lip. "You're the first person I've told."

"OK?" I didn't know what he was getting at.

"Blane is saying that you kidnapped Ana Maria."

"Right."

"And that you are asking for a ransom."

"What?"

"A big ransom."

"But that doesn't make any sense."

"Shhh," Dan warned. He looked around. The bartender was flirting with Ana Maria who looked annoyed; Jimmy was telling Easy what happened. "I think we may have a mole."

I almost laughed. "A mole?"

"Look," he leaned closer and I could feel the warmth of his breath on my neck. "Mulberry is convinced of your innocence but he is the only one. The whole agency is out to get you. They think you kidnapped her. The ransom note was sent from here."

"St. Thomas?"

"Yeah."

"Why would anyone be stupid enough to post a ransom note from where they were holding the prisoner? That's insane."

"That's what Mulberry said, but do you get what that means?" I stared at him blankly, my brain refusing to make the connection. "The ransom was posted the day you got here, Sydney. It was sent before anyone who wasn't with you could have known about it."

"What are you-"

"Hey, so what's going on?" Ana Maria asked, leaning across the bar. I looked back at her, the hair on the back of my neck rising toward the sky.

"Blane's here," I said. She didn't look nearly surprised enough.

19

Change My Friends to Enemies

INSIDE ME A NUMBNESS WAS SPREADING LIKE FROST ON A WINDOW pane. I knew someone had betrayed me, I was just wrong about who. As I looked at Ana Maria, at her long lashes and the roundness of her still so young face, I felt my brain clicking in place. That little bitch used me. She played on my weakness; knowing how I lost my brother, she killed off her cousin. This whole thing was a set up and it wasn't Bobby Maxim or Mulberry or even Blane behind it. It was all Ana Maria.

"What are we going to do?" she asked. I just stared at her. Dan cleared his throat and turned to his drink. He knocked it over and Coke bubbled across the marble surface of the bar. I stood up and gently took Ana Maria's arm. She looked down at my hand as I guided her away from the others toward a small opening in the walls. It was a dark and foul-smelling passage between the alley I was standing in and the next one over.

I pushed her into it rougher than was necessary. "Hey," she said. "What are you doing?"

"Kidnapping you."

"What?" I pushed her forward making her walk through a stinking puddle in her flip flops. "Joy-"

I grabbed her arm and pulled her face close to mine. "Don't fucking call me that. My name is Sydney."

She nodded, her eyes big and growing wet. "What are you doing?"

"Cut the crap."

She did, much more than I expected. She turned back at me and her eyes were dry and hard. "You're already cooked."

"Cooked?" I smiled, happy to have my adversary out in the open.

"You're done. My parents think you took me, Bobby thinks you took me. You're a common criminal and now everyone knows it."

I laughed. "Honey, there is nothing common about the crime I'm about to commit." I pushed her forward but she didn't move.

"Blane will come for me."

"This isn't the Princess Bride."

"He loves me," she said. "He's here to take me back." She pushed passed me heading back toward the bar. I grabbed her arm and swung her around. I was about to say something really clever when Blue let out a bark, Ana Maria's eyes focused on something behind me and she smiled.

I pulled out my gun and put it in her face at the same time turning my head to look down the passage. A figure who looked a lot like Blane was walking toward me, a pistol raised at my face. His arm was no longer bandaged and he looked ready for a fight. "What does she have a tracking device in her pussy or something?" I called down to him.

Ana Maria went for my gun. It was a clumsy attempt. She just grabbed my hand with both of hers and pushed the muzzle toward the patch of bright blue sky above our heads. I turned and punched her hard in the face. Ana Maria stumbled back with both her hands raised to her nose. I turned back to Blane while Blue covered Ana Maria.

"Drop the gun," he said.

"You drop the gun."

"I'll shoot the dog."

"I'll shoot you."

He was close enough now that I could see his face. There was a small red scratch on his right cheek that was beaded with blood. He smiled at me.

"Come on Sydney, it's time to put the gun down."

"I don't know what makes you think you have the advantage. Just because you have a child on your side doesn't make you the winner of this contest. I've got a dog. He's smarter than her and a better fighter. So why don't you go ahead and put the gun down." I smiled at him. My arm tense, my finger caressing the trigger. I thought about just pulling it. Killing him was quickly becoming my only option. Then I wondered why he didn't just kill me. Why not take me out and save Ana Maria? He could get rid of my body, tell Ana Maria's parents that I got the money and disappeared. Instead he was standing there asking me to surrender. Why?

Blane's lips tightened into a white line. He looked behind me to Ana Maria. I didn't take my eyes off him. He was close enough to shoot but too far away to touch. That was an OK distance. If he came any closer I wasn't going to have a choice. I was going to have to shoot him.

"How about you take Ana Maria and walk away, and I'll walk away and we'll all pretend like we never even knew each other?" I suggested.

"OK. That sounds like a plan."

He started to walk towards me. "Stop where you are."

He smiled. "What? I'm just gonna grab my girl and go."

I waved for Ana Maria to walk past me with my free hand. "You guys can go out the other way. My friends are waiting for me in that alley. I've got a nice cold drink out there too." My arm was getting sore holding up the gun and I crooked my elbow a little to alleviate the weight. I stepped to the side of the alley, pressing Blue against the wall as Ana Maria walked past me. She was so close I could see the sweat on her neck. Blane put his hand out to her and she grabbed it.

"I can't let you go," Blane said.

I smiled. "You don't have a choice."

I started backing down the hot, still alley toward my friends, toward the bar and the crowds. Blane walked forward toward me. I steadied my gun and prepared myself to shoot when a voice behind me said. "Sydney?" It was Dan and I fucking turned to look. Such a stupid move. Blane was on top of me in a second. He jammed the butt of his gun into my face knocking me to the ground. I heard Dan yell and saw through spotted vision Blane train his gun on Blue.

Blue has faced the open end of a gun before and he knows not to fuck with it. You don't jump straight at that darkness. I reached up to touch my face and felt wetness. I pulled my hand back and saw that it was wet with puddle water. The stink filled my nostrils and I gagged. Blane grabbed me by the arm and hauled me to my feet wrenching my shoulder in its socket. He pushed me forward at a run, I stumbled but he carried me along.

"Now!" Blane yelled to Ana Maria as he forced me forward. An explosion ripped loose rock and dust and all hell behind us. I turned to see just a cloud. We left the small passage for a slightly bigger one. My mind was starting to clear as we hit the promenade that ran along the water. I wrenched my arm free from Blane and stepped back, almost losing my balance. He reached out and grabbed me again. I tried to pull away but he was stronger than me. He pulled me close and pushed something into my hand.

"Put in on Blue." I felt a gun in my stomach and looking down I realized I was holding a muzzle. "Put it on," Blane said through clenched teeth.

"Or what? You'll shoot me. Obviously you need me alive for something or I'd be dead along with anyone close enough to that blast."

"Put it on or I'll shoot him." Blane pulled the gun out of my stomach and aimed at Blue's head. I weighed my options quickly. I could try to disarm him but it's not like he didn't know all my moves. I could try and run away from him but his hand was like a vice on my bicep. I could trying screaming for help but as I watched the terrified tourists running around us I knew it wouldn't do any good. The bomb was taking up everybody's attention. My problems were my own.

I muzzled Blue. Ana Maria came up to Blane. He pulled a small leather pouch out of his jacket pocket and handed it to her. She unzipped the thing and passed Blane a syringe. Blane jabbed me in the arm with it. "OW!" I yelled. We started down the street. I walked next to Blane until my feet became too heavy to lift and the world became so colorful it was too hard to look at. I closed my eyes and went to sleep.

20

Waking Up

I WOKE UP IN FIRST CLASS SITTING NEXT TO BLANE WITH BLUE at my feet. I looked out the window and saw a city filling a valley below. I was wearing a silk shirt and my head hurt. "Good morning, sleepy head," Blane said. I looked over at him and tried to remember how I got there. What was going on? Wasn't I on St. Thomas?

Ana Maria leaned across the aisle. She had a black eye. I looked down at Blue again, he was wearing a muzzle. Why would Blue be wearing a muzzle? "What day is it?" I asked.

"What day do you think it is?" Blane asked.

"What?"

The intercom crackled and a female voice told us to prepare for our descent into Mexico City. I leaned my head back on the seat and closed my eyes. Everything was so blurry but slowly my adrenaline started pumping. I remembered fighting with Blane in the abandoned building. Had he taken both Ana and I captive, but when? My veins were filling me with energy and my hands twitched on the arm rests as I remembered Ana Maria's betrayal. What a fucking cunt, I thought, as the plane dipped toward the earth.

That little bitch sold me out and for what? That was the question wasn't it. Why was I sitting here in Melanie Franks's clothing descending into Mexico City? What were Blane and Ana Maria up to? With a tightening in my chest I remember the explosion in the alley, the suffocating dust, the flying bricks. I hoped that Easy and Dan were OK. I wondered if I'd live to tell them how sorry I was. How sorry I was that I failed them.

A tear ran down my cheek and I brushed it away quickly. I opened my eyes and looked out the window as the plane touched the tarmac with a reassuring jolt. We were on the ground. I didn't join the enthusiastic crowd this time.

We passed through customs like it was nothing. Like I was Melanie Franks and Blane was Peter Franks and Blue was Fluffy and Ana Maria didn't even know us. I thought for a second, just a millisecond really, of pleading for help. Of dropping to the ground and begging for the authorities to take care of me. But I didn't have the right. When you break your contract with society you can't go running back for help once trouble finds you. I was on my own.

A limo was waiting and the three of us climbed into it. "Welcome back to Mexico City," the driver said as we pulled away from the curb. I sat by the door staring through the tinted windows wondering if at the next red light I could jump out. As we merged onto the highway I turned into the interior of the car. Ana Maria and Blane were sitting very close to each other on the long bench running along the side.

Blane reached across the car to the bar. He poured a vodka and soda for Ana Maria then a Scotch for himself. Blue sat next to me and I had to lean across him to reach for a drink. I ended up having to stand up and hunch awkwardly as I poured a long shot of tequila. I added ice and cranberry juice. As I sat back down, I laid my arm across Blue's neck. I lifted my glass toward the happy couple and said, "mazel tov." Ana Maria looked at me like I was a useless piece of shit and Blane ignored me.

I sipped my drink and returned my stare to the outside world. But I wasn't looking at the buildings passing under the highway or the bright blue sky or the other cars on the road. I was wondering why I was sitting there; why Blane and Ana Maria were taking me back to Mexico City.

If they wanted the ransom money for themselves then fine, kill me and keep it. It just didn't make sense bringing me and Blue back. Unless they were trying to set me up for more than just the murder of Alejandro and the kidnapping of Ana Maria. But what else did they want? What else could they need? Why were they dragging me along?

Before long we were pulling up in front of the same hotel Blane and I stayed at on our first trip to Mexico City. "Welcome to Casa Vieja," the doorman said. I looked up at him and smiled. He offered me his hand and I took it. The day was sunny and crisp. The hotel was as beautiful as ever. Blane kept his hand in the small of my back as we walked into the lobby.

I started to laugh when the woman asked about our reservations. She looked at me with a furrowed brow. "Deja vu is all," I said. Blane threw me a look that just made me laugh harder. He had to move his hand to fill out the paperwork and I decided it was time to leave. I backed away from him. He looked up at me, his eyes fierce and his lips pursed.

"I'm just going out for some fresh air, dear," I said.

"I think you should stay with me."

I kept backing away. Ana Maria put her hand on my arm. "Come on now, you're not well enough to go outside."

I laughed again, the doorman and the woman checking us in both stared at me. "I'm going outside now." Ana Maria tightened her grip on my arm and tried to pull me back toward her but I wrenched my arm free. She looked at Blane and he looked at me. I turned around and sprinted out the door. I heard Ana Maria right behind me.

Blue was by my side and I thought that if I made it to the main street I'd be OK. No one was going to shoot me or Blue in front of Dolce and Gabbana. Besides, clearly they needed me alive. The block was short and I reached the corner with Ana Maria still close. I could have kept running but the combination of high heels and a still-drugged brain tripped me up over a cobblestone and sent me flying onto the ground in a classic splayed position.

Ana Maria grabbed my arm and started to haul me up. I turned and sunk my teeth into her wrist. She dropped me back on the ground, holding the wrist to her chest. Blane ran up and stopped next to her, panting. I looked up at them from the ground and smiled.

"Come on, Melanie, let's get you back inside."

"If you touch me, I'll scream bloody murder." I looked around and saw women wearing clothing worth the down payment on a small home talking on their cell phones and watching us. If they hadn't been wearing sunglasses that made them look like giant bugs, I bet I could have seen the glee in their eyes.

"Come on, Melanie, you're not well, let's get you inside."

I sat up and rested my hands on my knees. "What exactly is wrong with me?" I asked.

Blane saw the crowd of women watching and started to reach for me again. Blue growled through his muzzle. I slapped Blane's hand away.

"Unless you plan on shooting me right here in front of all these ladies, I suggest you answer some questions."

Blane's fingers were fidgeting at his sides and his eyebrows were holding quite the little conference above his nose. Ana Maria was looking at him to do something. I smiled. "So, what is wrong with me?"

"Your nerves, Melanie," Ana Maria answered. "Your anxiety," she raised her eyebrows. "Why you fly with the dog. I hope it hasn't become paranoia."

"Like, for example, if I thought that you two were actually lovers and you'd kidnapped me for some unknown reason." I said 'lovers' and 'kidnap' really loud. A murmur ran through the crowd and I could sense them all leaning forward, desperate for the next line.

"Don't be silly, honey," Blane said. "We both love you."

A small dog in a fat woman's arms started barking at Blue. I turned to look at her and mouthed the words 'help me.' I couldn't tell if she understood me or not. I started to stand up. I heard Blane let out a breath of air. I thought about continuing to run, to just taking off again but was feeling a little light-headed. I'm not going to blame the tequila but it might have been a factor.

"Do something," Ana Maria said to Blane quietly so the crowd would not hear.

Ana Maria reached into her bag and pulled out a syringe, cupping it in her hand so the crowd couldn't see. She started toward me slowly. Blue growled but she didn't stop. Blue raised his hackles and braced himself to leap on her. "If he attacks me in front of all these people he will be put down." Ana Maria said. "We'll call the cops and have him taken away. So how about you just call him off and we'll all go back inside."

Blane launched himself at me and Blue blocked him. Even without teeth the dog is still a giant. Ana Maria jumped on me, I pushed her off but she was on me again. I punched her hard in the stomach. She stumbled away gasping for breath. I felt woozy and looking down saw the syringe hanging out of my leg. "Blue, come." He was instantly by my side. Blane pulled me toward the open hotel door. Blue followed, keeping his eyes on me. I was asleep before we got to the room.

21

Drugs, Booze, and Rock and Roll

I WOKE IN A DARK ROOM. THE ONLY LIGHT WAS A SHAFT OF yellow that came from a door standing slightly ajar. I heard voices in the other room. My brain fought through a thick fog trying to catch up to my surroundings.

"It will all be over soon," a man said.

"Can you believe she was in Juarez, campaigning for a friend? It wasn't even about her. She was helping a friend. That's how much she cares about me," a female voice responded. Ana Maria crossed in front of the door and blocked the light for a second. I closed my eyes and pretended to be asleep.

"Don't worry," the man said, and I recognized it as Blane. "They will both be there."

"Shouldn't she be waking up soon?" Ana Maria asked.

"I'll check," Blane answered. I heard footsteps approaching and laid still. His breathing even, Blane unzipped a case near me. A sharp prick made me wince and I felt myself floating away again.

A fire burned in the corner of the room sending black smoke up the wall and billowing at the ceiling. A lanky figure rocked gently in a chair to my left. "Joy," said the figure without turning to look at me. In the flickering light of the fire I could see that it was a man with a large beard and wild hair. He tapped his fingers against the arm of the rocking chair and soon his foot joined. Gentle humming followed, a song he used to sing to me when I was a child.

The fire sparked and shot out an ember that landed at my feet. It glowed deep orange and bright yellow. "We've all got a switch. It goes on when we need to survive." He hummed a moment more and then the fire spat again, the flames leaping towards the ceiling suddenly angry. They engulfed the wall filling the room with light but also deep black smoke. "Some people's switches get stuck."

Despite the raging fire I felt cold. "Watch out," he said. "Don't get stuck." I heard whining and turned to see Blue standing in the doorway. I could hardly see him through the smoke. He whined again, his high pitch whine that means he wants my attention, that he wants me to wake up. I felt his nails against my forearm and his wet nose press at my neck. I blinked and the smoke was so thick now that all I could see was the matte black of it.

"That dog is in there again!" I blinked again seeing the outline of Blue's head inches from me. His fur shone in the moonlight. I felt a bed of leaves beneath me and smelled the mossy scent of fall and decay. Then the smoke came back and filled my brain, blocked my vision, and put me down.

"She has to have some strength." I smelled bacon and blinked my eyes open. Sunlight poured in the windows and I closed them again quickly. Behind my lids I watched a green and yellow display of color. "Sydney!" I blinked again and Ana Maria was standing over me. "Sit up."

I tried to swallow but my throat was dry and painful. Rolling onto my side I pushed into a sitting position. I saw that my wrists were duct-taped together. Ana Maria handed me a glass of water and I took it with shaking hands. The water sloshed in the glass as I brought it to my parched lips. It was cold and I could only take a little in, feeling it travel down my throat into my empty stomach.

"You need to eat something," Ana Maria said.

"What are you giving me?" I asked.

"Eat it," she said, pointing to a table by the window set for breakfast.

"Where is Blue?"

"He's safe."

"Bring him to me and I'll eat. Don't bring him to me and I'll kill you."

She laughed. I had neither strength, depth perception, or precision but raw emotion powered me off the bed on to her. She squirmed under me but I leaned my forearm against her throat, using the dead weight of my atrophied body to crush the life out of her. She stared up at me, her eyes huge and wild with rage. Ana Maria scratched at my arm then turned her nails on my face.

A kick to my stomach rolled me off of her. I laid still, staring at the ceiling above me. A crack in the white plaster snaked from the corner toward the light fixture in the center. Another kick rolled me onto my side and I brought my bound wrists up to protect my face. That old familiar prick brought the smoke rushing over me.

"In about a half hour."

"Good. I want her to be a little drowsy when it happens. I don't want her trying to save anyone."

"I think you're right," Blane said. "She's still out." Footsteps approached and I felt a person standing right above me. Blue growled.

"We should just kill that dog now," Ana Maria said.

"No," Blane answered. "He's muzzled and safe. If we kill him now it won't make sense. Why would she kill her dog?"

"I guess you're right." Blane walked away. I heard his foot falls on the thick carpeting.

"I love you," he said and then I heard kissing followed by a low groan. The door clicked shut. I heard the TV turn on. Blue hopped onto the bed with me and I unclasped his muzzle. He pushed his face against my ribcage and curled up into a ball. I softly rubbed behind his ears and breathed in his musky dog smell.

As I lay with my face pressed into Blue's fur, my eyelids closed and the world dark, I tried to wrangle my floating thoughts into some kind of order. The TV in the other room roamed from channel to channel. It was loud and kept interrupting my brain. There was something pulling at the back of my mind. Some detail I knew I'd missed. How could I have let this happen? When did it turn around and I became the prisoner, the kidnap victim? Exactly how stupid was I?

They landed on a TV show that sounded like it was some sort of contest with very excited contestants. The high-pitched scream of a winner brought my head up off the pillow. It felt as though its gravitational pull increased. I let my head fall back down again. I've had a lot of hangovers. This was one of the ones where you feel like there has been an explosion in your brain and some of the tunnels that allow information to pass from one part to another have caved in. At least I knew I hadn't embarrassed myself by dancing on the bar or telling somebody, at the top of my lungs, I thought they were totally gay.

Blue pawed at his muzzle but I pulled it tight again. Even though it was unclasped we didn't want them to know he wasn't muzzled. I heard footsteps and propped myself up on my left elbow. The door opened letting in bright light from the living room. I squinted at the dark figure approaching me. Ana Maria clicked on the light next to my bed and looked down at me. A confident smile was on her face, despite the blossom of color around her nose and eye where I'd, as Jimmy would say, walloped her. I checked her neck but didn't see any bruising. Was it a dream?

"Morning," she said.

"I thought it was evening." I turned to double check and the windows were indeed dark.

"It's an expression."

I turned back and looked up at her. "Oh."

She threw a protein bar onto my lap. "Eat that," she said, and then left the room again closing the door. The lock turned.

I sat up all the way and if it weren't for the shooting pains in my head, I would have sworn my cranium was floating somewhere above my neck. With weak fingers I opened the Power Bar and devoured it. As I was about to pop the last bite into my mouth, Blue caught my eye. I wondered when he'd last eaten. Slipping the muzzle off him I gave him the last morsel. He chewed it quickly and I pushed the muzzle back over his snout.

I tried to move my legs but they refused to separate. I pulled off the blanket and seeing that my ankles were duct-taped together started to pull at it.

Blane came in and stopped me. He grabbed my hands and pushed me back onto the bed. "Geez," I said. "If this bed wasn't so soft that might have hurt." It actually did hurt and there were little white lights shooting across my vision. Blane moved over to the dresser and opened a drawer. I heard a bang in the other room and figured it was Ana Maria. Blue jumped down off the bed to investigate. "Your girlfriend's a real peach. Takes things in stride. I bet she's a real pleasure when she's on the rag."

He turned back to me. His eyes were slits and he strode across the room with two easy steps. He hit me hard with the back of his hand and I tasted the metallic tang of blood. "You don't talk about her that way."

"Wow," I said, exploring my split lip with the tip of my tongue. "Must be love." The sharp pain was bringing my brain back into focus.

"Put your hands together," he said.

I raised my hands over my chest. He wrapped them so tight that the skin around the tape bulged red. I was about to say something clever when he ripped off a piece of tape and put it over my mouth. Breathing through my nose I watched him pull a knife out of his pocket and cut the tape off my legs. It made me wonder what happened to the straight razor I stole from him. I bet he took it back.

Blue trotted back into the room. I smiled through my tape at him. Neither of us could open our mouths. Made you think they might be our most dangerous weapons. Ana Maria came back into the room dressed in jeans and a blue T-shirt the color of the deepest parts of the Caribbean. Blane left the room and Ana

Maria said, "We need to get you into some sensible shoes, some running shoes." She smiled at me like that was some kind of funny joke. I would have said something that wiped the smile right off her fat little face but I was gagged so I just raised my eyebrows and shrugged. She went to the closet and brought out my sneakers.

"Blane brought all of Melanie's stuff from Playa Del Carmen. I think when all this is over I will spend about a month or two there convalescing." She smiled again with that I'm-so-funny smile and then dropped the shoes onto my stomach. "Put them on."

My wrists were bound but I still had use of my hands. I sat up, feeling that heaviness in my head again, and pushed the shoes onto the floor. My socks were more like stockings and I stood up to try and find something more appropriate but Ana Maria shook her head. "Just stay seated." I looked up at her and thought about how easy it would be to kick her feet out from under her and bash her face with my bound hands. Pulling a gun from her waistband she shook her head. "Oh no, not again." The gun was small but its barrel lengthened by a silencer.

I pushed my feet into the shoes and tied them tight. Ana Maria nodded as she watched me. Blane came back into the room. He was now in jeans and a white, collared shirt that had a little croc-odile on the breast. Loser, I thought. When he turned around to check his reflection in the mirror over the dresser I saw a bulge in the back of his pants. A gun, I supposed.

Blane pulled me up by the arm and pushed me toward the door. Blue followed not even bothering to growl. Ana Maria clipped a leash onto him and said, "Ready?"

Blane nodded and opened the front door. The stairs were dark and the lobby empty. Out front under the dim yellow light of the street lamp, a black, non-descript car waited silently at the curb. The air was moist from a recent rain and fog hung in the night. The scent of fresh flowers and wet cement filled my nostrils.

Blane pushed me into the back seat and Ana Maria climbed in next to me, Blue followed her. Ana Maria had her gun out and put it right up against my neck as Blane got into the driver's seat. Blane started the car with a rumble that disturbed the quiet night. We pulled out into the empty street, turned left and drove by the darkened stores of Gucci and Hermes. We passed a restaurant where the last of the wait staff were putting chairs up on tables. The low hum of a vacuum barely reached my ears. We turned off the main road and travelled down darkened residential streets. The glow of lamp lights filtered through the thick air giving the streets a look that made me think of old Sherlock Holmes movies. Who knew what would come out of this mist?

Blane pulled up in front of a large mansion that I recognized as belonging to Ana Maria's parents. I felt a chill work its way through my limbs as we climbed out of the car. I didn't know what was going to happen. There was a part of my mind that thought it was possible, but I wasn't willing to believe it.

Blane used a key to open the door. He didn't turn on his flashlight until the door was closed behind us. He ran the beam over the large staircase and crystal chandelier. Except for the sound of the four of us breathing, I didn't hear a thing. Without a word they started moving down the hall.

I followed the bright beam of light and with the help of a gun barrel in my back I made it into the sitting room where my initial visit with the bereaved parents had taken place. Blane brought me over to the bar and poured a drink. He ripped the tape off my mouth and it took every ounce of will I had not to scream. He pushed the glass of warm tequila into my hand and in a low whisper said, "Drink it."

I brought the glass to my lips and took a small sip. His eyebrows bunched together and he lifted his chin gesturing that I should finish it. I took another sip. It was warm and I like my tequila iced, but what can you do when a man is pointing a gun in your face and telling you to drink?

I went to raise the glass to my lips again, but instead of taking a sip I threw it hard into Blane's face. The bottom of the glass hit him right in the nose and then fell to the carpeted floor with a low thump. I used his momentary daze to bring my fist down onto his gun arm. The gun skittered across the ground into darkness. Before I could do anymore, something hit me hard in the back of the head and I fell forward, spots dancing in front of my eyes. Blane, his nose dripping blood, hauled me off the ground by the back of my shirt.

A noise that sounded like the footsteps in the hall made us all freeze. The air felt thick. The smell of blood filled my nostrils. The footsteps stopped and we all held our breath. Somewhere in the room a clock ticked. Ana Maria was standing close to my left arm. I could see blood glistening from a cut on the bridge of Blane's nose. The footsteps started up again. They were retreating.

Ana Maria pushed me into a chair. I landed hard. She grabbed my legs and pushed my feet together. Pulling duct tape out of the darkness, she bound my ankles. Blane paced the floor; I could see his dark form occasionally reaching up to touch his nose. Blue sat by my side, his muzzle was a little tilted but neither of them seemed to notice. Ana ripped off one last piece of tape and put it over my mouth.

I concentrated on calming my breathing. It's easy to get freaked out when your mouth is covered. Think about if you were watching a scary movie. You could be sitting there on your couch, breathing happily through your nose, but when the boogie man jumps out of the closest or grabs the girl's ankle from under the bed, you scream. You intake air fast. If you don't have your mouth to do it, you're likely to pass out. My nose was clear but my heart beat was up and I could feel that it was going to be hard to maintain enough breath if anything exciting happened.

22

Something Exciting Happens

Blane whispered something to Ana Maria who nodded back. He crossed the room and climbed on the couch. I squinted my eyes trying to make out what he was doing. I saw a large dark rectangle swing out from the wall and then the beam of his flashlight illuminated the paint. It passed over whiteness until landing on a metal door, in the middle of which was a dial.

He turned to Ana Maria, the beam of light gliding across the room in her direction. For a second it lit her face. I was struck again by how young she was. Her features still soft with the collagen of youth. She scowled into the light and waved her hand through it. Blane immediately dropped it to the floor.

Then she screamed. It was loud and unexpected. I jumped in my seat, bucking against the tape binding me. Her voice vibrated off the stone walls around us and you could sense a whole household waking up. Blane jumped down from the couch, knocking over a table stacked with large volumes. They spilled onto the floor, the pages squished by the weight of their binding.

Blue looked up at me and I looked back down at him. Blane positioned himself in front of the door. Ana Maria, without breaking her cry, squared off, raising her gun at the entrance. I watched them, not understanding what the hell was going on. Did they expect Pedro to come running and then at gunpoint force him to open the safe? But then why did they need me? Why have me bound in a chair?

All I could hear was Ana Maria screaming. It was making it hard to think and I had to concentrate on my breathing. In and out but not too hard. The pressure of air racing through my nose was starting to give me a headache when Anna shut up. Footsteps echoed throughout the large house. I heard shouts from indistinguishable voices saying unintelligible things.

The steps became more focused, the yells closer. I saw Blane's hand begin to tremble from the weight of his gun. Why were they both aiming at the door? What were they doing? Then there were steps running down the hall right for the door. They came so quickly that I was surprised when the door was flung open. A shaft of warm yellow light fell on Ana Maria right before she opened fire.

The silencer muffled the shot making it sound like little more than quick intake of breath. The darkened silhouette in the doorway crumpled to the ground without so much as a cry. "Ana Maria! Ana Maria!" A woman was yelling from close by. Blane ran forward and dragged the dark lump into the room. He stepped back and joined Ana Maria in the shadows, just out of reach of the hall's light. I was in a corner, invisible. Blue leaned against me, his body warm and heavy on my leg.

The woman kept yelling Ana Maria's name until she was in the doorway. I couldn't see her face but from the thin frame and perfectly coiffed hair, I was pretty sure that it was her mother. I steadied my breathing and closed my eyes. "Ana Maria!" she called one more time, her voice more of a sob than a name. The intake of breath filled my ears. I heard her body hit the stone floor and struggled to fight back the tears.

If you cry, you will die, I told myself. If you get stuffed up you won't be able to breathe. A tear slid down my cheek and I sniffled, my mouth pulling against the tape that covered it. I opened my eyes and saw Ana Maria grab under her mother's arms and pull her into the darkness with us. There were still more footsteps in the house. I thought about the size of the staff that kept a place like this going and wondered who would die next.

"How many left?" Blane asked my question out loud.

"The chef and the maid." She didn't use their names.

"Do you think they're coming?" The footsteps did not sound like they were getting closer.

"Probably not," Ana said. "They'll just call the cops."

I saw Blane nod in the semi-darkness. He closed the door, locked it, and turned on the light. I blinked against the sudden whiteness. Blue stood up and his hackles raised. I blinked again and using my shoulder got some of the tears off my face. Ana Maria saw the red around my eyes and smiled.

"Are you crying for them?" she asked, using her gun to point at the slumped bodies piled by the door. My eyes riveted to them. Her mother was in a bathrobe, untied it hung open to a short night-gown made of worn cotton. She was on her back, her arms splayed out to the side. Her body twisted at the waist, both her legs leaning left. Her face was turned away from me but I could see the dark red matting in her hair where part of her skull was missing. At least she died quickly, I thought. Next to Juanita, Ana Maria's father lay on his side. He was also in his pajamas. He had on one slipper. Blood leaked slowly out of the hole in the middle of his forehead.

I swung my eyes to Ana Maria. She was staring at me. "You feel an awful lot, don't you?" she asked. Blane crossed the room and poured himself a drink. I could see his hand shaking from the corner of my eye, and I didn't think it was from the weight of the whiskey.

"See, I wondered," Ana Maria continued, "if you felt or not." Blane downed the drink in one go. "When I read about you, about you killing Kurt Jessup, I thought it was amazing. It really inspired me, you know?" Blane's hand was steady as he poured himself another drink. "That a girl with no experience could kill. That you could go from not killing to killing. I wondered if you did it because you felt a lot, or nothing."

Blane turned to look at Ana Maria. He didn't say anything but he watched her closely as she crossed the room toward me. "You think I'm a monster don't you? For killing my own parents. But what if they were monsters, Joy, what if they made me this way?"

Her eyes were bright and she pointed the gun at the bodies again. "They forced me to do this. They gave me no choice."

"That's right, dear," Blane said. He intercepted her before she stood directly over me. "Now let's get everything done that we need to. I'm sure the police will be here soon." Ana took her eyes off me and turned to look at him. She nodded. "When this is over, everything is going to be just perfect," he told her.

"I think it already is," she said.

The smell of blood was heavy in the room and I was sucking the taste of adhesive with every breath. Blane kissed Ana Maria lightly on the forehead and then moved back to the bar. He dumped the clip out of his gun and emptied the chamber before coming back to me. He forced the gun into my hand, curling my finger around the trigger. I sort of tried to resist but what with the not breathing really, the being all bound up and the general confusion, he got my fingerprint on the trigger with little difficulty.

"You think you're some kind of a hero, don't you?" Ana Maria asked me. Blane turned to look at her and I thought I saw a flash of fear cross his face. "You think you can be some kind of avenging angel or something. You'll build your little army and help the less fortunate."

I looked up at her and filled my eyes with ice. She smiled. "You do think you're a hero." She leaned in very close to me. Her cheek almost touched mine as she whispered into my ear, "We don't need another hero." Sweat trickled down from my hair and slid around my eye. Her breath was even and calm. It was clear to me that Ana Maria was not a victim. She wasn't caught up in some older man's scheme. She was a sociopath. And I was her inspiration.

The tape ripping off my face made me shout in pain and

shock. I took some big breaths, the skin around my mouth tingling. She pulled out a knife, it glinted in the overhead light. I squeezed myself back into the chair and raised my bound arms. She laughed.

"I'm not going to cut you. I'm letting you go." I darted my eyes to catch a glimpse of Blane. He was putting the bullets back in the gun. Ana Maria crouched in front of me and gnawed at the tape around my ankles with the knife. Once she'd cut through it she peeled it off my pants and laid it on a nearby table.

She stood up, took aim at the safe in the wall and opened fire. I threw my hands over my head and curled into a ball. I heard the ping of bullet against metal and just hoped it wouldn't ricochet into my head. The firing stopped and I peeked out from behind my hands. Ana Maria was smiling down at me. "Here," she said, and threw me the gun. It was headed right for my face. I blocked it with my wrist. It hit that little bone on the pinky side.

"Ow, fuck," I said. The gun landed at the side of my chair.

"Pick it up," Ana Maria said.

"You pick it up, you dumb cunt," I said.

Her lips quivered. "Pick it up."

"Go fuck yourself."

"Sydney, be reasonable," Blane interrupted.

I looked over at him. "Are you as bat shit crazy as her? Did you catch it while you were fucking her or is it something your mom gave you?" His face turned red and I smiled. "Why don't you pick it up, bitch boy? That will make your little tyrant here happy."

"We're going to let you go."

"Let me go? Let me go? Really? You're going to let me go." I stood up and Blue came to my side. I took off his muzzle. Blane raised his gun.

"If you shoot me, won't there be questions as to why I'm bound? Why there was duct tape residue all over my wrists and ankles? Why my mouth is red and raw? These are the kinds of questions cops ask. Especially when a fucking senator has been killed."

Blane kept his gun trained on me. "Look," Ana said. "How about I cut the tape off your wrists and you just leave through that window?" A siren wailed in the distance and we all stopped to listen.

"I guess we're running out of time here," I said. I looked from one of them to the other. Ana Maria's expression was blank, but Blane's eyebrows were forming a nice little furrow above his nose. The fact was I needed to get out of there for all our sakes. I was, after all, already a criminal on the run. It wouldn't take them long to figure out who I really was. I glanced down at my bound hands.

Ana Maria held up the knife. "Let me cut you out of that." I held my wrists toward her and she sliced right down the center. I unwrapped myself and let the used tape fall to the carpeting. The sirens were getting closer. I backed toward the open window. Ana Maria smiled and Blane kept his gun focused on me.

I climbed onto the ledge and looked out into the darkness. The jump was only about three feet into some bushes. Blue went first and landed on the lawn. Beyond him was the empty street with the wail of the police getting closer. I followed him into the darkness.

23

Speaking of Heroes

I LANDED IN THE BUSHES. THEY WERE A DARK, HARD EDGED LEAF that scratched at my bare arms. I heard a bullet fly through the air over my head. I stayed low as I pushed my way out onto the lawn. Blue was lying down, his face pressed into the dew soaked grass. I belly crawled over to him. The thwap of the gun stopped.

The street was empty except for several dark cars. The dew covered them too. In the street light the cars looked like they'd been bedazzled. The moisture was soaking through my shirt and pants. I stood up and so did Blue. I started toward the street figuring that at least I could get into a neighbor's yard and from there onto another street. The other houses on the block were dark. I looked back at the mansion I'd just jumped out of. It was ablaze in electric comfort.

The sirens were very close now. My body was taut. It felt like a spring ready to bounce. "Hello," a voice whispered into the night. I froze. I could feel my wet clothes sticking to my skin. A light came on in a house at the head of the street.

"Joy?" I looked down at Blue. He was focused on a nearby parked car. I strained my eyes and saw that the driver's window was down. I looked past it and saw the tell-tale red, white and blue lights bouncing off buildings. A window in the house directly in front of me filled with light.

The sirens were so loud that I didn't hear the sound of my feet hitting the pavement as I raced across the street. I yanked open the back door of the car and jumped in. Blue followed. The driver did not wait for directions. The car pulled out into the street and sped away. I looked back. Ana Maria was standing in the window watching me drive away.

"Are you alright?" the driver asked me as we merged into city traffic. A buggy cab in front of us blew its horn. I could see the silhouette of the cabdriver's fist pumping in the air.

"Who are you?" I asked, sitting up for the first time since getting in the car. The woman turned to face me.

"It is me, Izel," she said.

I leaned forward and recognized her face. "You look better in person," I said.

She laughed. "You are referring to my picture on the web." I nodded and leaned back into the seat. My clothing was wet and it stuck to my skin in that obnoxious way that wet clothes do. "I am a different woman since that picture. You have given me new purpose. New life."

I closed my eyes and didn't respond. What could I say to that?

"You are a hero," Izel said.

I laughed. "No honey, you're the hero. You just seriously saved my life." I could see her beaming in the rear view. "What were you doing there?"

"I have been watching the house like you told me. When I could not reach you I figured I just keep doing what you say and you would contact me again. And now you have."

"Have you heard from Easy or anyone?"

She shook her head. Izel had shoulder length dark hair. It was the kind of thick, straight stuff that I dreamed about when I was kid. Growing up blonde left a soft spot in me for luscious, long, dark locks.

"Where do you want to go?" she asked.

"Somewhere safe. You know of anywhere like that?"

"How about my house?"

"Sounds lovely."

Izel's neighborhood was a twenty minute drive on quiet streets. The buildings were about five or six stories. Their large windows and detailed facades told of a better time. Now, half the windows were boarded and the gargoyles were missing their wings. Izel parked on a wide street and turned the car off. "Here we are," she said. Izel turned in the seat and smiled at me. "May I pet him?" she asked.

"Sure," I smiled. Izel's eyes grew wide as she reached her hand out. Blue stretched to sniff her fingers. Then he shot out his tongue and licked her wrist. She giggled and pulled her hand back.

"I bet you guys will be good friends soon," I said. Climbing out of the car I reached toward the sky and stretched. My body felt bruised and tired. I needed to shower, sleep and then I would think. Then I would figure out what just happened and what came next.

Izel lead me up crumbling steps, past a door from behind which a baby screamed. The smell of clean laundry mixed with the scent of onions cooking. Izel opened a large door. She flipped a switch and a shaded lamp lit the room. The place had high ceilings, huge windows and a fireplace. Izel hurried around tidying up the living room, moving magazines into piles, putting pillows in the corners of the couch. It was a cozy place. It reminded me a little of my apartment in New York. The furniture was mostly found, but instead of looking used it appeared loved.

"It's wonderful," I said.

Izel beamed. "You want some food or something?" she asked.

"Yes. And something to sleep in." Izel left the room. I sat down on the couch feeling the weight of my limbs. Izel came back with a pair of sweat pants and a T-shirt three sizes too large. I took off my damp clothing and pulled on her dry ones. She brought me a pillow and a blanket. I laid down on the couch and put the blanket right up to my chin. Blue climbed onto my feet and tucked his face under his back leg.

Izel went to work in the small kitchen that covered the back wall of the living room. The sound of chopping and the clinking of bowls felt like a lullaby. I closed my eyes and listened to the crackle of chicken frying. Izel hummed a song I didn't know. The melody continued into my dreams.

Izel's voice drifted across an open field. I was standing in the center of it, the perimeter lined with palm trees. I heard a scream and turned around in circles but all I saw was the empty field. Then my mother was right in front of me. She was crying and the tears were carving tracks in her thick makeup. I turned away from her and looked down at my feet. I was suddenly sinking into the ground. I struggled, trying to pull my feet out and flailing my arms but it didn't do any good. I tasted dirt in my mouth and I breathed it in my nostrils. Izel's sweet humming was drowned out by the mud filling my ears.

24

Sometimes All You Need is a Good "To Do" List

THE BLUE LIGHT OF DAWN FLOWING THROUGH IZEL'S WINDOWS woke me. I didn't know they were Izel's windows at first. In fact, I was pretty sure they were mine. That I was in New York and my windows were just really big. But after a couple of blinks, turning onto my side and a yawn, I figured out where I was.

Blue was awake, too. He sat at the foot of the couch and whined at me. "Hungry?" I asked. "Me too." I sat up and rested for a minute with my elbows on my knees and my forehead in my hands. I looked down at my feet and thought that I needed a pedicure. Then I thought about what a stupid thought that was in a situation like this. I stood up and stepped right into the coffee table, smashing my shin so hard that I actually had to sit down, hold it, and squeeze my eyes shut. "Shit," I said in a pained whisper. Blue whined at me.

"All right, all right, I'm going." I rolled back into a sitting position and this time was careful to avoid the coffee table on my way toward the kitchen. The pale light coming through the windows made the place look like it was filled with mist. On the counter was a note. Izel's handwriting was small and tight. Each letter carefully drawn. I looked down at Blue who groaned impatiently. "It says here you already had your dinner, young man."

He stretched his front paws foreword, stuck his tail in the air and whao-whaoed at me. "It says there is chicken in the fridge for me, and she gave you yours." Blue sat and wagged his tail. "I'm not falling for it."

I opened the small fridge. It was clean, not like my old one with its sticky stains where juice spilled and was never cleaned. I pulled out a plate covered in tinfoil. It said in the note that I could put it in the oven at such a temperature for such and such an amount of time but I just took the cold plate back to the couch.

Under the tinfoil was a chicken breast, yellow rice and beans. I had to go back to the kitchen for a fork and when I looked back at the couch, Blue was sniffing awfully close to my food. "Hey," I hissed. He skulked away. The food was amazing. I love cold chicken and this was some of the best I'd ever had. I piled beans and rice onto my fork and took bites way too large for me. I swallowed and got that weird pain in my throat when you've taken in too much.

I breathed for a minute and the feeling passed. "What I need," I said to Blue, "is to make a list." He was lying on the floor looking at my food. "I need to figure out what I need to do." I took another heaping bite of chicken and went back to Izel's note. Next to it was the pen she'd used to write it.

I went back to the couch taking the note and pen with me. The paper was blank on the opposite side and I wrote at the top of it: Things To Do. I took a bite of chicken and sat back looking at it. A fine beginning. Then I wrote a 1 and put a circle around it. A bite of rice brought me to the conclusion that the most important thing was to find out what happened to Easy and Dan in that alley, were they OK? Did they need my help? I wrote down: Locate friends.

I looked at the word friends and wondered if that's what they were. I crossed it out and wrote soldiers. That seemed absolutely ridiculous so I crossed it out and wrote: Easy and Dan. I cleared my empty plate to the kitchen while I considered my next item. I found a beer in the fridge and returned to my spot with it.

Item number two: Find Out What Ana Maria Told Police. I wanted to know exactly how she was setting me up. Would she tell them I was Joy? Would she tell them about the website? Would they know about Easy and Dan? Izel?

I took a sip of the beer. It was cold and bubbly just the way it's supposed to be. It was possible, I thought, as I sat looking at my list, that she would tell them about Izel. It was quite possible we needed to get out of there. I stood and went to the window. The street below was quiet except for an old man walking his small white dog. I watched them progress slowly down the block until they turned the corner. The sun was rising above the houses across the street. The top of it cast a warm yellow light onto me. I took another sip of beer and squinted against the light.

Turning back into the room I approached my list. I wrote a 3 and circled it. I remember reading somewhere that you should only put three things on any to do list because it makes the list seem more accomplishable. If you put thirty things on it you won't ever get any of them done because it is so overwhelming.

I wrote: Come up with Brilliant Plan to get us out of this one. I sat back looking at my list. I took another sip of the beer. It was almost empty so I had to block my vision with the can as I sipped. Looking back down at the list, I smiled. Sure, real accomplishable.

25

Working on That List

I PICKED UP THE PHONE AND LOOKED AT THE KEYPAD. IT WAS one of those phones attached to the base by a curlicue cord that reminds me of pasta. I wrapped it around my finger. It was so tight it made my skin bulge and change color. The dial tone was consistent. I put my untied hand on the key pad but didn't dial. I looked over at my list. Then at Blue. He wagged his tail, sweeping it across the floor.

I stood up taking the phone with me and walked to the window. The sun was hovering a couple of inches above the buildings across the street and the low hum of early commuter traffic floated up. I put the handset back on the phone and then immediately picked it up again. I dialed the number. Closing my eyes, I listed to ringing on the other end.

Mulberry picked up quickly.

"It's me," I said. "Is this line safe?"

"Yeah. Where are you? Are you OK?"

"I'm fine." I looked down at my wrist where a nice rash formed an outline of the duct tape. "I learned I'm allergic to certain adhesives." I tried not to think about the itching on my face.

"This is no time for jokes."

"That wasn't a joke. I've spent the last couple days as a prisoner, bound by tape it turns out I'm allergic to." I turned away from the window and stared into the room. "What's going on Mulberry?" A lump caught in my throat as I realized how scared I really was, how incredibly well Ana Maria had fucked me. I swallowed.

"Who killed Juanita and Pedro?"

"It was Ana Maria."

"The girl?"

"Yeah, the girl." I walked over to the couch and sat down. "She's crazy." I put my feet up on the coffee table and looked at my toes.

"What happened?"

"You know, Mulberry, I don't even know anymore. This has gotten so out of hand."

"Where are you?"

I looked around the sweet little apartment. The bookshelves filled with paperbacks, the kitchen, small but neat. Izel's world was so pretty and taken care of. "I can't tell you that."

"Come on, Joy!"

"Don't fucking call me that!" I sat up, my feet hitting the floor.

"You need my help. I can help you."

"Really," I stood up, "how Mulberry? How are you going to help me?"

"Look, if she's guilty we can fix this." He lowered his tone and sighed at the end of his sentence.

"How can this be fixed?" I waved the phone base in the air. "She's the victim of a horrible kidnapping murder plot and I, Sydney Rye, don't even really exist. And if anyone figured out who I really was, they'd just ship me back to New York."

I turned around and saw Izel standing in the hall. Her eyes were heavy with sleep and she smiled at me. "Sorry," I whispered. She shook her head and waved a hand of dismissal at my apology. Then she turned and went into the bathroom.

"Who are you talking to?"

"No one."

"I know you've got contacts in Mexico City. Jimmy told me."

"Jimmy was working for you."

"I was trying to find you."

"He tried to beat the shit out of me."

"Well, that was stupid."

"Yeah it was." I paused for a moment and stared out the window. Rain was moving in and I could see the clouds headed towards me. "What about Easy and Dan? Are they OK?"

"Sure, sure they are."

"What do you mean sure?"

"Dan had some burns but he'll be fine and as far as I know Easy came out of it with barely a scratch."

"Where are they?" The sky darkened and suddenly rain arrived. Big droplets splattered onto the street below. I watched a mother run to her car carrying a kid tall enough to walk. She opened the door and the little boy climbed in. The mother ran around to the driver's side. Her hair was plastered to her forehead and her shirt clung to her body.

"I don't know. It's not like Jimmy hung around. He was shot."

"Right. How is he?" I watched the car drive away. Turning away from the window I paced the floor, being wary of the coffee table.

"He's OK. He'll be fine. But I don't think he will be taking any more jobs from me." Mulberry laughed into the phone.

"What should I do Mulberry?"

"We've got to find a way to prove she's guilty." He took a deep breath. "We can do this, Joy."

"Don't call me that. The whole reason I'm in this mess is because I was trying to kill her off. Have you talked to Bobby?"

I flopped down onto the couch and cradled the phone to my ear with my shoulder.

"He is as confused as us."

"Do me a favor and stop talking to that Jack Ass. Seriously, why are you still in contact with that guy?"

"You're not giving him enough credit. He's not all bad."

"You're nuts. This whole mess is his fault."

"I'm telling you he has no idea what is going on. You think he was a part of the plot to kill Pedro? That just doesn't make any sense."

"Who knows Mulberry? With that guy…"

"Sydney, you can't seriously think he could convince Ana Maria to murder her parents, do you?"

That did seem far-fetched but when it came to Bobby Maxim, I was not going to underestimate him. "Just tell me where you are," Mulberry said. "I can be in Mexico City by tomorrow night."

"All right. I'll call you back." I hung up the phone while he was trying to say something.

Izel came out of the bathroom as I was replacing the receiver on the base. She smiled at me. "How did you sleep?" she asked.

"Fine, thanks." She nodded and moved into the kitchen. I watched her put coffee into the coffee maker and turn it on. Then she pulled down two mugs. "Izel," I said. She turned to look at me. "I'm very grateful. You saved my life."

Her face turned crimson and she turned away. "De nada, you're welcome."

"Izel, I'm worried."

She turned back to me again.

"See, Ana Maria isn't who we thought she was. I mean, she wants to do me harm and I'm afraid she might want to hurt you, too." Izel cocked her head in confusion. Why am I talking to her like she's a child? "Izel, last night Ana Maria murdered her parents and she is trying to set me up for it."

Izel frowned and furrowed her brow. "I don't understand."

"Basically, Ana Maria is crazy. I don't know what her personal reasons were for killing her parents, she implied that they forced her into it. But I imagine the hundreds of millions she stands to inherit were a contributing factor. At least, that's why Blane is helping her."

"Blane?"

"Blane and Ana Maria are lovers, they plan on getting

married." I couldn't help but roll my eyes at that one. The coffee machine began to sputter and Izel turned to look at it. "The point is that you need to go somewhere safe. You need to hide until all this blows over. We need to tell Malina, too. Ana Maria knew you guys were helping me and it won't take her long to figure out where you live." A siren wailed outside and I hurried to the window. An ambulance raced by, spraying water in its wake.

I turned back to Izel who was looking past me out the windows. "You are probably right. She will find this place before long," Izel said.

"So you've got to get out of here." I took a step toward Izel, she turned to pour the coffee.

"I'll go with you."

I stopped walking. "No, no, Izel, I want you to go somewhere safe."

"Where would I be safer but with you?"

I thought about the last people to follow me. Easy and Dan ended up in an exploded alley. "Izel, you can't come with me."

She turned to me, a coffee cup in each hand. She smiled. "I want to. You'll see, I can be a great help to you."

"It's not that I don't think you'd be helpful-"

"So then we are decided."

"No, Izel, I don't want you to get hurt."

Her face darkened. "I don't think you can say that now. I am already in harm's way. If you will not let me help you, at least let me save myself." I started to speak but she cut me off. "The best way for me to survive is to help you stop her. That is what I will do."

She crossed the room and pushed one of the cups into my hands. Her eyes were glowing. What could I say? "Thanks."

Malina was as much of a pain in the ass. I called her as Izel started packing up her life. I sat on the couch. Malina picked up on the second ring. "Hola," she said. I could hear the TV in the background.

"Hola, Malina."

"Sydney?"

"Yes, it's me," I said.

"How are you?"

"I'm alive but in deep trouble."

"Si, the TV is full of speculation. What is happening?"

I sighed before repeating the horrible events of the night before. Izel stepped out of her bedroom and leaned against the wall listening. Tears glistened in her eyes by the time I was done. Malina was silent so long if it weren't for the murmur of the TV in the background, I'd have thought that I'd lost the connection.

"Malina?" I said.

"Si," she whispered.

"We know that Ana Maria knows about you. I'm afraid she will tell the police. I think you need to get some place safe."

"No."

I rolled my eyes and looked over at Izel. She was staring back at me. "You sound just like Izel," I said.

"I want to help. You helped me when no one else would and now I am getting the chance to repay the favor. Where are you?"

"Malina, think about the women working for you, what will happen to them?"

"Do not play with me, Sydney, I am not some little girl. I know what I am getting into. I am not afraid."

"Jesus," I muttered.

"What?"

"Nothing. Fine. I'm not going to fight with you."

"Good. Call me tomorrow. I will be ready to go."

"Where are we going?" Izel asked as I hung up.

I looked over at her and felt the weight of my responsibility to these women. I promised them that they could make a difference and now I was going to have to do it.

Izel and I checked into a hotel so cheap that they didn't even ask for Izel's ID. Leaving Blue in the room we went out to a bar to get a bite to eat. I wore a big brimmed hat and a baggy sweatshirt.

The night was cool after the day's rain and I pulled the fabric tight around me as we walked down the street.

Izel carried a small bag. She had her ID, a change of clothes, and her most precious belongings. As we'd left her apartment she'd looked back at it, and I could tell she didn't think she was ever coming back. "Izel," I said to her, "we will win this; you will be able to go home." She smiled at me and told me it was OK.

I looked over at her as we walked toward the warm glow of the local cantina. She was thin and had an intelligent face. Izel was a couple inches shorter than me. Her face was long and her nose tiny. She was ordinary looking. I thought that was good. Ordinary was good in this game.

The cantina was quiet. About five people leaned against the bar. A couple who stood very close and three single men. All of them were watching the small TV mounted in the corner of the room. Izel and I sat at a table. A waitress in her teens took our order.

She came back with two beers and then disappeared through swinging doors to the kitchen. The TV program switched from a game show to the news. The attention of our fellow patrons fell from the screen while Izel and I both leaned forward.

Footage of Ana Maria, her face red and tear streaked, being loaded into an ambulance filled the screen. Izel translated for me. The anchor was talking too fast for me to understand. "They are saying that she has suffered a great trauma. That her captor kept her for many days. That she was blindfolded and bound. They did not feed her." The footage of Ana Maria turned to footage of Alejandro's body being pulled from the ocean. "They are talking about how it began with the death of her beloved cousin in front of her eyes."

The other patrons returned their glassy stares to the TV. A dead body gets everyone's attention. The screen cut to a female anchor sitting at a desk, above her left shoulder a graphic of a person's head with a ? over the face floated. "She says that they do not have a suspect yet."

A picture of the outside of Ana Maria's mansion appeared. "They say that the kidnapper forced Ana Maria's father to open the safe and then killed him and his wife. The only reason that Ana Maria survived is that Blane arrived on the scene and scared the fugitive away. They say that he is a hero."

I sipped my beer and stared at the screen. The news went to commercials. When it came back they were talking about a different story. Something to do with a new project to help the city stop sinking.

Our food arrived. Rice and beans and some kind of meat. We dug in, eating in silence. I looked over to the crowd at the bar. On the TV was an image of the cathedral in Mexico City's central Zocalo. In the shot you could see how it was breaking apart because of its sinking foundation.

At the bar the man with a date stood up and headed toward the bathroom leaving the lady alone. I watched one of the single men at the bar eyeing the woman. The man took a step toward her. She noticed and averted her eyes. The man said something to the single woman but she did not respond. The man said something else, the woman looked up at him, her cheeks were red.

The woman's date came back from the bathroom. The single man stepped back but not before the guy saw what was happening. I looked over at the door. It was close to them but if we hurried we'd be able to get out of it. I stood up and grabbed Izel's arm. "What?" She cried right as the guy with the date punched at the guy without one. I reached into Izel's purse, pulled out some money, dropped it on the table and then moved along the wall.

The guy with the date had missed and now the guy without the date was aiming. The other men at the bar were all standing up, not sure which side they were on yet. The woman held her hands over her mouth in horror. I squeezed behind one of the unsure men and opened the door as the guy without a date hit the other guy right in the nose. He stumbled back into the woman and we were out the door.

26

My Favorite Mode of Transportation

I DID NOT SLEEP WELL. THERE WAS A STREET LAMP RIGHT outside our window and cats fucking right under it. I laid awake listening to the screaming felines below and thought about my life. It was one of those conversations you have in your head that you're trying not to have the whole time. One voice telling me I'm a fuck up, another telling me I have a chance at greatness, a third just begging me to go to sleep.

When the sun began to light the sky and the cats voices faded, I slipped into a restless sleep. Izel woke me. I jumped away from her. She backed up her palms toward me. "It's OK," she said. "It's me."

I nodded and looked around the room. It looked used up. I felt like I fit in. Blue was waiting by the door. "I think he wants to go out," Izel said.

"Yeah, I'll take him." I pulled back on my big sweatshirt and a pair of jeans I'd borrowed from Izel. They were tight and short but not painful. I opened the door to the dark hallway and looked both ways. Not a creature was stirring...

On the street Blue did his business and I looked around the dilapidated neighborhood. The houses appeared to be falling in on themselves. But the people who passed wore pressed clothing and carried themselves with dignity. Blue and I wandered around the block. He inspected the ground while I appreciated the crisp morning.

I stopped at a food stand and bought bread and coffee for Izel and me. I got a large sausage, uncooked, for Blue. Upstairs Izel was coming down the hall. Her hair was wet and she carried a damp towel. "If you want to shower it's down there," she said, pointing to the communal bathroom.

"Maybe after breakfast," I said. We ate our meal in silence. Blue finished first and curled into a ball in front of the door. His snoring was the only sound except for the chewing in my head. When we'd finished I turned to the phone. It was time to call Mulberry. It was time to start all this, whatever it was. This was its beginning.

Mulberry sounded sleepy. "I'm near the airport," he told me. I heard him sip something.

"I can meet you there," I said.

"I've got wheels, I'll pick you up."

I told him where I was and then hung up the phone. He was a good hour away and knowing his morning routine he wouldn't get going until his cup of coffee was empty.

I called Malina. "You know you don't have to do this." I could hear her bristle over the phone. "Never mind," I said, and then told her where we were.

I went to take a shower. It was worse than I expected. I thought there would be a shower, not a room with a spigot, a string and a rotted out door. I stepped into the dark space, the only light came from the hole in the bottom of the door. I kept my socks on but took everything else off. I flung my clothing over the top of the door. My towel was there too. The bar of soap went on the floor by my feet. I pulled the string and a gush of cold water hit my head. I immediately let go and gasped.

"Jesus Christ," I said out loud. I thought about just putting my clothes back on and foregoing the shower until we were somewhere more hospitable but knew that it could be days before that. Hell, I might be dead before that. For all I knew the cops were on their way to get me right now and this was my last chance to shower before prison.

I pulled the lever again and leaned my head back. Using my free hand I moved my hair around getting it all wet. I released the string and grabbed for my soap, it was slippery and I dropped it. I tried not to think about Mexican prison as I picked it up again. I ran the bar of soap in my hair and over my body. Then one last pull of the string and I rinsed it all off. I grabbed my towel and wrapped myself in it trying to stop my chattering teeth.

I dressed quickly. My skin was still wet so my clothing stuck to it. I hurried down the hall in my wet socks making squishy noises all the way. When I got back to the room Izel was not alone. Malina turned when I came in and lit the room with her smile.

She crossed the room and enveloped me in a hug. Her beauty had only improved with age. Malina was shorter than me with her compact body squeezed into a pair of jeans and sweater that just barely fit. She pulled away and held me by the shoulders. Looking up at me she said, "It is so good to see you."

I smiled, conscious of my wet socks. "Yes. Only I wish it was better circumstances."

She hugged me again, pressing her warm body against mine. I held my towel and soap in my hand, but I managed to hug back. I heard her sniffle on my shoulder and realized that she was crying softly. "It's OK," I said. "Shhh."

She stood back and wiped the back of her hand across her face. Malina had subtle lines around her eyes and on her forehead that were not there three years ago. However, her rich, hazel almond-shaped eyes were just as beautiful, maybe even more so since they now held a note of wisdom missing before. "Hey, it's going to be OK."

"Yes, yes. It is just so good to see you. I'm sorry."

A horn honked outside. Blue stood up and followed me to the window. I pushed the curtain aside. Parked in front of our dilapidated motel was an RV. A rental. I grinned as I watched Mulberry climb out of the cab, reaching for the sky in a stretch. "He's here," I said.

Quickly pulling off my wet socks, I put my feet into my sneakers and we all hurried downstairs. When Blue recognized the broad man, he took off at a run. He jumped around Mulberry, swinging his tail, his tongue hanging out. "Hey boy, good to see you," Mulberry said. He squatted down to Blue's level and rubbed his left flank. Blue stopped his jumping, twisted around and sat on Mulberry's foot. Then he looked up at him with his big mismatched color eyes.

"Has he gotten bigger?" Mulberry asked.

"Not as much as you," I said, motioning toward his ever-increasing waistline. When I met Mulberry he looked like he was made of stone. His arms and shoulders still shared that boulder-like appearance but the last couple of years behind a desk had turned his washboard stomach into a plump little gut. His brown hair had a dab more silver at the temples but his green eyes still sparkled with glints of yellow when he smiled at me.

Mulberry reached out, and grabbing me, pulled me into a bear hug. I put my arms around him and squeezed back. It felt so good to be enveloped in his arms. I almost started crying, but Blue's nose in my belly reminded me of my responsibilities. I reached down a hand and pet his head. We felt almost like a family.

"And who are these two lovely ladies?" Mulberry asked. I pulled away and looked at Izel and Malina. I smiled.

"This is Izel," she nodded her head.

"Nice to meet you," Mulberry said, he held out his hand and Izel shook it, a blush of color rising to her cheeks.

"And this is Malina." Mulberry let go of Izel's hand and offered it to Malina. She shook it with narrowed, suspicious eyes.

"Well, ladies," Mulberry said, "welcome to your chariot." He swung his arm at the RV. Izel and I smiled. Malina looked at the RV like it was an animal, one that might turn on her at any moment. Mulberry opened the side door. I climbed in.

It surprised me how many memories came back as I looked

around the small space. Mulberry and I used an RV during our escape from the States, a time I think back on with both fear and fondness. Directly in front of me was the kitchen - a sink in the corner, a small three-burner stove, and above that, a microwave. Right next to me was the fridge. I took a step and was in what would be called the living room. A small table sat between cushioned benches against one side. Across from them was another bench, this one longer. Beyond them was the windshield and the captain's chairs. A foam mattress filled the crawl space above the front seats.

I turned to look toward the back of the RV. The curtain was pulled across the bedroom. I went and pushed it aside. Mulberry's bag was sitting in the center of the plastic-wrapped mattress. To my left was the shower and to my right the small toilet stall. When I looked up, Izel was standing in the doorway. "Come on in," I said. She climbed the few steps and then stood staring at the kitchen. She reached out and ran her hand across the back of one of the benches. She pulled away from the scratchy material.

"Don't worry," I said. "You get used to it." Malina stepped into view. She smiled at the small living space. "Cute, right?" She nodded at me.

The side door slammed shut and a moment later Mulberry climbed into the driver's seat. "Buckle up," he called. "We're moving out."

Izel and Malina turned to me for direction. "Here," I motioned toward the bench on the side of the table closest to the front. "Sit down," I said to Izel. "Malina, you can sit here." I pointed to the bench across the aisle. Once seated, I showed them where the seat belts were. Then I climbed into the front. Blue laid down in the aisle between Izel and Malina. Mulberry turned to me with a big grin brightening his face.

The RV roared to life and we pulled out of the parking lot. "Here we go again," he said as we merged into traffic. "Are you holding wet socks?"

"Yes, yes I am."

27

The Plan

"ANY THOUGHTS?" MULBERRY ASKED.

"About?"

"A plan?"

I looked over at Mulberry, his eyes were glued to the traffic in front of us. "I was thinking you might have some ideas. I mean, you've got a recreational vehicle, you must have a plan."

Mulberry smiled. "I figured this way we're on the move. And there are lots of hiding places. I figure I'm just a tourist and if anyone asks you're not even here. And this baby is pretty easy to defend." He lowered his voice. "I've got a gun for each of us under the kitchen sink, just in case." He took his eyes off the road and made eye contact for a moment. Despite all the joking, we both acknowledged how dangerous this game was.

"Right," I said.

"So?" Mulberry asked, turning his attention back to the road.

I looked out the window and watched a man on a bike in my mirror as he expertly maneuvered through traffic. He pulled up alongside us and I looked down at him. He wasn't wearing a helmet. Looking both ways, he blew the red light we sat stopped at.

"Well, I was thinking about maybe heading south," I said. The light turned green and with a wheeze the RV moved forward.

"South?"

"Yeah, get out of Mexico, maybe head down to Costa Rica." We passed a collection of food stands set up in front of a church. The smell of cooking meat reached my nose and made my mouth water. "I would rent a place on the ocean." I could almost see Blue and I jogging on the beach as the sun rose. Me drinking tequila as it set. "I figure I'll just disappear."

"And what about Ana Maria?"

I turned to Mulberry and smiled. "What about her?"

"Well?"

Izel and Malina were leaning forward from the back, hanging on every word.

"I guess she'll get away with it. I guess I don't much care that she killed her parents or any of that shit. I should just let Bobby Maxim handle the whole damn mess. He's the one who got me into this."

"That's not true," Izel said. "You do care, you must."

I turned in my seat and looked at her. "I do?" I sat back and closed my eyes, the image of Blue and me on the beach replaced by one of Ana Maria's mother's dead eyes. "I guess I do."

"And you will do something about it," Malina said. I turned to my window and watched trees that some gardener had shaped into perfect little balls pass by. "You will."

"Yeah, I guess I will."

"And that brings us back to what?" Mulberry said.

I laughed. "I don't know."

A silence fell over all of us. Mulberry turned on the radio and we listened to a woman singing something upbeat. I didn't bother trying to understand the words. Mexico City passed around me. It felt like I was watching a movie screen.

"Another option, of course, is just killing her," I said. I didn't see anyone's reaction to this because I was watching two garbage men load up their truck. They wore jumpsuits. One of them turned and I saw his lined face frown as he looked past me at the giant advertisement for RV rentals that graced the side of our truck. "I mean that solves the whole 'her being a danger problem'. It doesn't clear my name but it's not like Joy Humbolt isn't already a fugitive."

"Shut up, Sydney," Mulberry said. "We're not killing anyone." I looked over at him. He was exasperated with me. "We need to come up with a way to expose her, not kill her."

I turned back to my window and listened to the music. Malina coughed and I thought she might say something but the radio continued to be the only sound louder than the traffic outside. Minutes passed and I thought about how I could expose such an incredible fake. Who would believe that the young girl who'd lost both her parents, who was crying in front of news cameras and sequestering herself in a hotel was really a killer with no conscience?

The music was interrupted for the news. The weather: good. The economy: bad. Then I heard Ana Maria's name. "What are they saying?" I asked, turning to Izel.

"It says that-" she stopped to listen again. "That Juanita was to be the keynote speaker at a benefit for the women of Juarez. Ana Maria is giving an undisclosed contribution-" she listened again. Her eyes got wide. "And she will be giving her mother's talk in her place."

"Of course she is," I said.

"Full of shit, yes?" Malina asked.

Mulberry laughed. "Yes," I said. "She is totally full of shit."

"Can't we explain this to people?" Malina asked.

"I'm all ears," I said.

Malina bit her lip. "What about if she confessed?"

"That would be great," I said. "But I think impossible."

Malina chewed on her lip for another second and then said slowly, "Could we record her speaking, without her knowing?"

"What do you mean?" I asked.

"If you talk to her, she says things that she would never say in public and then you play it for the-" she waved her hand in a tight circle trying to think of the word.

"The audience?" I said.

"Si, the audience. What if you played a tape of her to the audience?"

No one spoke for a second. "That's a good idea," Izel said. "I think you could do it."

"I don't know," I said.

"Yes," Izel said. "You could talk to her, either at the benefit or before. Mulberry you could find a way to wire her."

"Wire her?" Mulberry said. "Where'd you learn that?"

Izel bristled. "I have a law degree."

Mulberry laughed deeply. "All right, Izel. I'll wire her up."

"But how am I going to get close to her? She's got tons of security, not to mention Blane. And it's not like she's some wilting flower. Hell, she might even kill me."

"No, no," Malina said. "I think she will talk to you. She will not kill you. She is not that good."

"Besides," Mulberry said, "we could sneak into her hotel room or something. We'd get the recording before the benefit and then just play it there. Hey, I like this plan. It's got balls."

"Balls? Don't you mean holes? Even if we do get this recording, how are we going to play it at the gala?" I asked.

"Through the sound system," Izel said.

"Yeah, but how are we going to get into the sound system? Any sound experts in this RV?" No one said anything. "Hell, I don't think any of us could even program a VCR."

"Yeah, but that's really hard," Mulberry said. I looked over at him giving him my best glare. "What? It is."

"Not to mention outdated. You're showing your age, Mulberry."

"You brought it up," he said.

"You think hacking into a sound system is going to be easier?" I asked him.

"I bet it would be for Dan."

The name made my stomach lurch. "Yes," Izel said. "He could help."

"I don't know how to reach him," I muttered.

"I do," Mulberry said.

"I doubt he will help me. I almost got him killed last time."

"Doesn't hurt to ask," Izel said. "Besides, you didn't think that Malina or I would want to help but we do."

I chewed on the inside of my cheek thinking about the explosion in the alley. The dust, the confusion, the heat. "I don't know."

Mulberry was grinning. "I like this plan," he said. "I like it a lot."

"Me, too," Izel said.

"Me, too," Malina said.

I turned to look at their smiling faces and grimaced back. "OK. We'll call Dan." They grinned.

"My cell's in my bag," Mulberry said. Izel jumped up and headed to the back to retrieve it.

"Right now?" I said.

"No time like the present."

"Please, don't start with clichés, it will kill me. This whole plan belongs in a fucking 80's movie. Except it should be my cheating boyfriend I expose, not a child who killed her parents."

"What?" Malina asked.

I shook my head. "Nothing, nothing. It will be fine."

She smiled. "Yes, very good."

Izel came back with the cell phone and handed it to me. It was a Blackberry. I imagined Mulberry bent over the thing getting frustrated by trying to hit the little buttons with his big thumbs. "Nice phone," I said.

"I'm a businessman. I need to email on the go sometimes." I laughed. "What?"

"Nothing."

"What?"

"It's just funny, you being a businessman."

"Yeah, whatever, just call him would you?"

"Where's the number?"

Mulberry sighed and took the phone out of my hand. He scrolled through the address book, flicking his eyes between the phone and the road. "It's dangerous to text and drive you know?"

"Shut up," he said, but he was smiling. "Here." He handed me the phone. It was ringing. Dan picked up on the third ring, sounding sleepy and curious. Hearing Dan's voice made me smile and my heartbeat quicken.

"How you doing?" I asked.

"Sydney? Is that you?"

"I heard you survived St. Thomas with only a couple of scratches."

"Yeah, yeah. What about you?"

"I'm OK."

"I saw that Ana Maria's parents were murdered. What is going on?"

I explained to him what happened as succinctly as possible. It sounded like the story of a crazy person, I realized, as I retold the tale of my capture and release.

"Jesus Christ," was his first response, followed quickly by "how can I help?"

I smiled. "Let me tell you what I want and then maybe you can tell me if you can help."

"Sure."

I explained our convoluted plan. About how I wanted to record a confession without Ana Maria knowing it and then patch said confession into the sound system of an auditorium crawling with security. When I was done I took a deep breath closed my eyes and said, "Exactly how crazy does that sound?"

Dan laughed. "It sounds completely insane."

I let out my breath. "Impossible."

"Nothing is impossible. Difficult, arduous, tricky, but not impossible."

"How?"

Dan laughed again. "You want me to explain it to you or do it for you?"

"When can you get here?"

"I'm already booking my ticket." I could hear the tapping of keys on the other end of the phone. "All right, I'll be on the-" more tapping. "I get in at 5am. You wanna pick me up at the airport?"

I smiled. "We are full service. See you at dawn."

28

Old-Fashioned Detective Work

THE HOTEL WHERE ANA MARIA HAD TAKEN UP RESIDENCE WAS modern. The sun reflected off its glass walls and made me squint. I was in the back, sitting on the bench behind the driver's seat, leaning over Mulberry's shoulder. I reached into the bowl of popcorn that sat on the table without turning to look at it. "What do you think?" I asked, before pushing a handful of popcorn into my mouth.

Mulberry shrugged. I struggled to chew, my mouth was so full it needed my undivided attention to figure out how not to choke. "Her security is insane," Mulberry said. I nodded. "Not only is she guarded by the hotel's security which is some of the best in the city, but the president has loaned her some of his presidential guard. Those are some serious motherfuckers."

"And what's that mean?" I asked with my mouth still half full. Blue leaned up and plucked an escaped popcorn from my lap.

"Basically we'll never get near her," Mulberry said.

"Really?"

Mulberry laughed. "Oh, I'm sure you'll come up with something. Maybe there's a secret tunnel that leads straight into her toilet."

Malina looked over at him from the passenger side, her brow wrinkled in a question. "He's joking," I explained. She looked back at me. "Because of the tunnels I found before." That didn't clear it up for her. "In New York I discovered tunnels left over from the American Revolution that led from a nearby park into the Mayor's office. It by-passed his security. I don't think we will have that opportunity here."

"You can't even get a room," Malina said. Ana Maria had basically shut down one of her father's, excuse me, her hotels. It was filled with her security (headed by Blane, of course), and the specific media she wanted around her. Any reservation made in advance of the sudden tragedy had been honored but no new ones were being offered. Malina turned back to face the hotel, I let my eyes go there, too.

I was looking at the door. I was looking at it so hard, just willing Ana Maria to walk out of it. But it remained closed. A small crowd of paparazzi, their cameras slung around their necks and cigarettes drooping from their lips waited for her, too. I wondered if when I exposed her they would want her more or less. Or maybe their passion would be unwavering for the girl.

As I worked on another giant handful of popcorn, the door opened. I leaned forward, my face almost even with Mulberry's. The paparazzi all crowded against the metal gate that separated them from their subject. It was a woman, but she was blonde. The photographers recoiled into resting position.

The woman exited the hotel and made her way down the street. She was short and plump. One of the tourists booked into the hotel before the national uproar. Her face was pinched. Her lips a tight line just above her small chin. She wore round glasses and as she hailed a cab, I imagined her peering through them at the wonders that the National Museum held.

I reached back for another handful of popcorn and found only kernels. I turned to look into the bowl and my hand's initial findings were confirmed. Izel was in the kitchen, doing something that looked domestic. I licked the salt on my lips and contemplated asking her for another bowl of popcorn. I looked at the clock on the dashboard and calculated that there were a hell of a lot of hours between now and when we'd pick Dan up at the airport. Blue abandoned me now that I was no longer littering food and went to sit in front of Izel.

Izel looked over at me and said, "Do you think we should change your hair?"

I heard Malina sit up, "That's a good idea," she said.

I heard Mulberry laughing under his breath. "You could shave it all off and dye it pink," he said before letting out a belly laugh that Mrs. Claus might have recognized.

"I think that makes sense," I said over Mulberry's hysterics, "but perhaps something simpler. Just change it a bit so that I don't look quite so much like me."

Malina stood up and walked into the living area of the recreational vehicle. "What about," she said "if we dye it dark brown and put in red..." she struggled to find the word, "tints?"

"Highlights?" I said.

"Yes! Highlights, and cut it a little shorter, maybe? And maybe some makeup to make the scars go away?"

"You girls better get to work," Mulberry said, turning back to the hotel.

Malina went out to buy the hair dye and makeup while Izel made me another bag of microwave popcorn. Mulberry leaned into his seat, his chin close to his chest, and snored. When Malina came back, Izel and I both put our fingers to our lips and shushed her. She crept into the RV as we pointed at the slumbering Mulberry. Malina smiled then sat down across from me and rustling through her bags, pulled out an eyeliner.

Izel had to clamp a hand over her mouth to stifle the laughter. I took the pencil from Malina and pulled off the top. It was a liquid liner which meant that I wouldn't have to use any pressure at all to write on Mulberry's forehead. "What should I write?" I asked.

Izel giggled and then clamped her hand back over her mouth. Malina was smiling so hard her cheeks had to hurt. "I don't know, my English not so good," Malina said. That sent another wave of laughter through all of us. Blue was infected by our excitement, his tail hit against the leg of the table and my shin.

"All right, all right, I'll think of something," I said. I climbed into the front seat, my weapon at the ready. I was about to write Place Balls Here on Mulberry's brow when a cry went up from the paparazzi. Mulberry snapped to attention. I jumped into the passenger seat.

"What's going on?" Mulberry asked. I peered through the windows, squinting against the sun's reflection and there she was, posing for the camera, wearing all black. Blane was at her side standing up tall in a dark suit, a severe expression on his face, the obligatory dark sunglasses resting on his nose. Still gripping the eyeliner I leaned toward them. I was trying to tell what she was thinking, trying to read her next move. Her eyes wandered to where I sat but she didn't see me. She was staring off into space. She looked so fucking sad.

"Hey," Mulberry said. "What are you doing up here?" Malina and Izel burst into laughter.

Blane took Ana Maria's arm and she followed him, like an obedient child, into the waiting limousine. "Follow her," I said over Malina and Izel's laughter. Mulberry was looking back at them so I said it again. "Follow her!" He looked at me only for a second and then started the vehicle.

Following the dark, sleek car flanked by motorcycles through city traffic proved to be impossible. It was only ten minutes later that they made it through a red light we missed, turned a corner and disappeared. The sky was dark and a soft drizzle turned the windshield misty as we headed back to the hotel to wait for her return.

They came back a little more than an hour later. Malina jumped out and joined the crowd of other interested citizens to listen to Ana Maria speak. "They went out to dinner," she told us when she came back, her coat covered in a fine layer of silver droplets. "She sounded really sad."

"I bet she did," I said. "She's real good at faking feelings." No one said anything to that.

"Wait," Mulberry turned to me. "What were you going to write on my forehead? You were going to write something, weren't you?" Izel and Malina's fit of giggles confirmed his suspicion.

"Doesn't matter now," I said, staring at the building across the street. "You know we should get out of here. I wouldn't consider this vehicle stealth."

Mulberry pulled away from the curb muttering under his breath. We parked in a motel parking lot in a neighborhood where trash blew down the streets until landing in a puddle sludgy enough to hold it. Malina and Izel worked together to turn my hair brown with red highlights. Then with nervous, though not unsteady hands, Izel shortened my hair to just below my chin.

Blue picked up a chunk of chopped hair and tossed it across the small room. He pounced on it and lowering his front half, warbled at Mulberry. Mulberry laughed, and reaching forward, pushed on Blue's left shoulder. Blue play growled and hopped to the right. Mulberry growled back and Blue turned in a very tight circle. "I think he needs a walk," Mulberry said. Looking at me, half my hair still reaching my shoulders, he picked up Blue's leash and smiled. "It would be my pleasure."

We went to bed early knowing that we had to pick Dan up at the airport at dawn. Mulberry got the master bedroom. Izel, being the shortest, ended up in the dining area. The table flipped down and the benches stretched to meet each other. Malina slept on the bench across from the table, and I was above the driver's seat.

It was dark up there, the ceiling less than six inches from my nose. It smelled musty and I buried my face into the pillow breathing in the comforting scent of detergent. Of course I couldn't sleep and judging from the rapid breathing coming from below, neither could the two other girls. I leaned toward the small window running across the front of the RV and looked out into the dreary parking lot.

A rat ran from a dumpster into the yellow pool of a street light and then under a parked car. I waited for the sun to come. When I woke up, the sky outside was slate gray and I heard movement down below. Rolling over I saw Mulberry struggling with the small coffee maker. He had the grinds out of the cabinet but couldn't seem to figure out how to put the filter into the machine.

Izel climbed off her bed and went to help him. He smiled at her, his eyes still puffy with sleep. "Good morning," I said. They both looked up at me and smiled. "What time is it?"

"4:30," Mulberry answered me.

"We better get going."

"Yeah, we're not far from the airport so I'm not worried. He's got to get through security, gather his baggage and stuff so we've got a while."

The smell of coffee began to fill the small space. Malina rolled over and said, "Good morning." We all returned the greeting.

I climbed down from my bunk. Blue, who'd slept in the driver's chair, nosed my hand. I crouched down and gave him a nice petting. Then maneuvering past my bunk mates, I made it into the bathroom.

My face looked different framed so tightly by dark brown hair. The girls had done a good job. It didn't exactly look real but it also didn't look so fake as to draw attention. Malina insisted that when she did my makeup and thinned out my eyebrows my own mother would do a double take. I washed my face and thought that if I ran into my mother I'd do more than a double take.

As I scrubbed my teeth I tried to think of a way to get to Ana Maria. She was so protected. Surrounded by not only trained security but trained paparazzi as well. I stood in that tiny little bathroom with the sounds of domestic RV life right outside the door wondering not how, but if, I would I reach her.

Dan's plane was late. I was pretty sure one of the airport traffic cops was looking at us funny. "Of course he is, we're in a freaking RV," Mulberry answered my fears. "Everybody is looking at us funny. We're fucking funny."

"Too much coffee," Malina said from the passenger seat. Izel nodded. She was sitting right behind her on the bench. I was behind Mulberry and Blue was under the table. We figured people wouldn't notice a dark-haired woman but a giant wolf dog with mismatched eyes was bound to draw attention.

"I think we should get out of here," I said.

"Fine," Mulberry said. "Fine!" He swerved the oversized vehicle into a moving lane of traffic and revved the engine. One of the orange-vested traffic cops blew a whistle at us, but Mulberry just zoomed right toward the exit.

"We can just call his phone and tell him to catch a cab," I said.

"Fine. Whatever," Mulberry said as we merged into traffic. It was 6:30 and the morning commute was beginning.

"Just get off at the next exit and we'll tell him to take a cab to us."

Mulberry nodded his head and Malina started to say something about coffee but Mulberry shot her a look that clamped her mouth shut. We inched toward the exit in silence. I called Dan's cell phone and left him a message about getting a cab. I told him to just give us a call when he landed and we'd let him know our location.

We pulled into a gas station and Mulberry climbed out to fill the tank. His cell phone rang. It was Dan. I picked up.

"I just left you a message."

"Oh, I didn't listen to it. I just got off the plane." I explained where we were and he agreed to meet us there.

Two badly advised cups of coffee for Mulberry, a short walk for Blue, and a drunk man falling against the side of the RV happened before Dan's cab pulled up. I watched him climb out of the taxi from inside the RV. He looked up at our vehicle squinting against the sun. My heart fluttered in my chest. His grape-green eyes caught me in the window and I waved. Dan grinned, showing off his straight white teeth.

The cab pulled away and I watched him standing there with his luggage looking at me and it was like we were stopped in a moment of time. I thought that it was possible nothing would ever change, that we'd spend eternity in that moment but I heard the squeak of the door and saw Mulberry approaching Dan. He didn't take his eyes off me until Mulberry put out his hand and they shook.

Blue raced after Mulberry and leapt around Dan showing him how excited he was to see him again. I broke away from the window. When I stepped out of the RV, Dan didn't hesitate. He crossed to me with two, or maybe it was three steps and embraced me in a tight hug. Pulling away he brought a hand up and held my face, caressing my cheek. I turned away from him blushing.

"It's good to see you," he said. Malina cleared her throat behind me and I untangled from Dan. "Sorry," he whispered as he let his fingers trail along my hip before dropping them to his side.

"Malina, this is Dan," I said. "And Izel," I gestured to Izel who stood next to Malina.

They both were grinning. "Hello," Malina said, and reached out to shake his hand. Izel offered hers as well.

"Lovely to meet you ladies," Dan said. "I've heard great things."

"And us about you," Malina said, raising her eyebrows at me.

"Come on," Mulberry said. "We've got to get going." He walked passed us and around to the driver's side. Mulberry climbed behind the wheel without looking at me.

Dan picked up his bag and followed us into the RV. Malina climbed into the front and the three of us settled into the back. "How was your flight?" Izel asked Dan as we pulled out into the road.

"God, I hate flying," Dan said.

"Me, too," I agreed. "Turbulence scares the shit out of me," I said, feeling relief that we'd passed the awkward first moments.

"It's not really the whole crash and burn thing that freaks me out," Dan said. "It's the not being able to get out of there thing. The I'm stuck in this cylinder with all these people and there is no escape."

Something clicked in my brain. "Yeah," I said. "All that security, no way to be alone. Being watched all the time."

Dan cocked his head. "Yeah."

"I couldn't take it. Everyone always knowing where I was, what I was doing. She'll try and get away." I was smiling. "That's it. She'll sneak out. We won't have to get to her. She'll come to us."

"What are you talking about?"

"Ana Maria. Dan, she won't be able to stay under lock and key." Malina, Izel and Dan were all staring at me. "She'll sneak out. And we'll be there waiting for her."

"Sounds like a plan," Mulberry said. I looked up to see his eyes smiling at me in the rearview mirror.

29

Night Falls

MY EYES GREW ACCUSTOMED TO THE DARK AND MY SNEAKERS soaked the water off the wet grass. A car drove slowly down the street, its headlights cutting through the blackness. It stopped a couple houses down. The lights shut off. A man carrying a brief-case climbed out and closed the door with a sigh. His car beeped and the taillights flashed as he walked away from it. The sound of his front door opening was loud in the quiet neighborhood. Yellow glowed from the entrance before the door shut behind him.

I watched as he moved through his house turning lights on. His was the only one lit on the short block. I shifted my weight onto my other foot, my arm brushed against a branch knocking resting droplets to the soft earth. Waiting, never one of my favorite things to do, was satisfying this evening. I felt that I had all the time in the world. The evening was mild, the storm that had haunted the valley for days having blown away. The puddles glimmered in the moonlight and the smattering of fallen leaves plastered to the side-walks shone wet and slick against the dark pavement.

The air was still moist and I breathed it in feeling that for the first time since coming back to Mexico I knew what I was doing.

There was no confusion about why I was hunkered down in these bushes. I knew that the house I sat next to, shrouded in the darkness not only of night but also of tragedy, would pull Ana Maria to it as surely as it drew me. Here is where I would hear her confession.

This was my fifth night of waiting. It was easier for me than for the others. For some reason I had an incredible faith that she would come. Mulberry, on the other hand, was becoming impatient. That night, before I'd left he'd tried to stop me saying that I was exposing myself too much, that there had to be another way. But I knew this was it.

So Dan and Mulberry sat in the RV back at the motel watching a monitor that connected to a camera hidden in the folds of my sweatshirt. They could see and hear everything that happened around me. I imagined that Blue was also watching the monitor. I decided not to bring him; it is easier to hide one body in the bushes than two. Besides, I needed to do this alone.

I missed him, though. I was so used to him being at my side it almost felt like he was there. I could sense his breathing but when I turned to look, nothing. I imagined that this must be what it felt like to lose a limb and still feel it.

I heard her before I saw her. My ears followed soft footfalls across the yard. I saw her silhouette walk right up to the front door. She was only a couple of yards away. I heard the lock turn then she ducked under the crime scene tape and disappeared inside. My heart raced. Ana Maria closed the door behind her. I waited a moment catching my breath and calming the adrenaline coursing through me. Now was a time for calm, not for action, I reminded myself looking at the closed door.

I saw the beam of a flashlight run over a window and then disappear. She was heading to the study. I followed along the outside of the house, staying low and out of sight not only to anyone inside but also nosy neighbors. I found the window I'd jumped out of. Pulling a small mirror on a handle out of my pocket, I raised it to the window's ledge. The door opened and a round light entered. It raked across the floor until it fell on the dark red stain. There it stopped, steady as any spotlight.

I lowered the mirror and stood to my full height. The beam didn't move till I'd grabbed hold of the window frame and raised myself to my waist. As I put my foot on the ledge, the light flicked to my face. I squinted against it but continued to climb into the room.

"You should drop that light unless you want the neighbors to see," I said. Ana Maria lowered the beam and I leaned against the window sill, my feet out in front of me. Relaxed. I couldn't see her, but her light told me where she was. "How you doing?"

I heard the cocking of a gun. "I'm fine, and you?"

"I'm not here to kill you," I said.

A hushed laugh crossed the room. "You couldn't kill me."

I smiled into the darkness. "Sure. Want a drink?" I started toward the bar. Her light caught me.

"Stop."

I paused. "What?" I asked, squinting against the brightness.

"What are you doing here?"

"Waiting for you." I shrugged as if that was obvious. "I knew you'd come." Her light stayed steady on me and she didn't respond. "We are so alike you and me. I knew you couldn't stay trapped in that hotel with all those people around you all the time."

"We are not alike."

"No?"

"You're naive and easily tricked."

"We are different in that respect," I said. "But we are both unafraid. You're the most fearless creature I've ever met. I admire that."

"No, you're here for some other reason. Take off your shirt, do you have a weapon, what are you hiding under that sweatshirt?"

I smiled. "OK, then will you have a drink with me?"

"Take it off."

I unzipped my sweatshirt and let it fall to the ground. Underneath I wore a T-shirt which I pulled up so she could see I wasn't hiding anything.

"Turn around."

"So you can shoot me in the back?"

"I could shoot you right now." She took a step toward me and I heard an edge in her voice. "Turn around now."

"OK, OK, keep your pants on." I spun slowly letting her see that there was nothing on my body.

"Fine."

I picked up my sweatshirt and shrugged back into it. "You must need someone to talk to, Ana."

"What do you know about me?" she said.

"I think I know you pretty well. I knew you'd be here, didn't I?"

The flashlight roamed to the bar. "Close those," she said, gesturing to the curtain behind me. I closed them, blocking out the street and crossed to the bar. A small lamp sat next to the bottles. I clicked the switch and the room glowed. Ana Maria turned off her flashlight and crossed the room to close more curtains. "You better not get caught here," she said. "They're ready to kill you."

I poured us each a glass of her father's finest tequila. "I know. Don't worry, Ana, they won't ever catch me."

She came up right next to me and took the glass out of my hand. Ana Maria looked up at me for a moment and then immediately away. She left my side, a cool breeze took her place. I concentrated for a moment on the memory of her father's dead eyes. Then turned to her.

I sipped the tequila, felt it burn down my throat and warm my belly. "How's Blane?" I asked.

She laughed, the gun held loosely in her hand. "He's driving me crazy." Ana Maria clicked her flashlight back on. She was looking down at the place her parents gurgled their last breath. "I tried to have it cleaned up- hire someone- but the police said no." She turned to me. "How long did you have to wait before they let you clean up your brother's blood?"

"I never went back there," I said, maintaining eye contact. I took a sip of the tequila trying to warm myself against the coldness in her eyes.

She returned her gaze to the stains. "History is a funny thing," she said.

"Depends on which part."

She turned to me and a smile pulled at the corner of her mouth but did not spread to her eyes. "I mean the way events are remembered, recorded. Who's to say that we won't be seen as the same type of woman? Me and Joy."

"And what kind of woman is that?"

"Strong," she raised her chin, "fearless." She licked her lips. "Avengers."

I couldn't help but smile. "Yes, that's possible. Remind me again, who were you avenging when you killed your parents?" I leaned against the bar. "And what about all that stuff with Alejandro, making the world a better place?"

She laughed and approached the bar to refill her glass. "He was so sweet, wasn't he?"

"I think he was." The image of Alejandro slumped and moaning on his sailboat came to mind. "Did it hurt to watch him die?"

She poured more tequila into her glass and then looked over at me. "Surprisingly little. It's as if I feel less and less every time. And it's the only way I feel anymore. Are you the same?"

I took the last sip of my tequila and put the empty glass down on the bar. I knew what she meant about the feeling, the rush, the justification that comes to you when taking a life. Ana Maria walked slowly back over to the stain on the floor.

"History is a funny thing," she said again. "The world will never know I killed my parents or my cousin." She raised her gun at me again. "All the world will ever know is that I killed you, revenging my parent's death and bringing to justice the famous Joy Humbolt."

"You gonna kill me?" I asked.

"Why wouldn't I?"

"It's not that you wouldn't, it's that you can't." Picking up my glass I threw it at her and ducked. She fired blindly and I heard a bottle on the bar explode. I pulled the light cord out of the socket and dashed for the open window. I dove through the curtains, rolling as I hit the wet grass. I landed with my feet under me in a low crouch. Standing up I sprinted away from the house, away from Ana Maria.

At the end of the block Izel and Malina sat in the car. They saw me coming and I heard the engine rumble to life. I got in the backseat, laid down and covered myself with a blanket and a bunch of clothing. Izel pulled away from the curb. She turned the radio on, pumped the volume and drove. A police car raced by us a block away and we just kept going. Soon we were on the highway, speeding toward victory.

I sat up and put a hand on each of their shoulders. "Did you get it?" Malina asked.

"I got it."

Izel slammed a hand onto the steering wheel and Malina let out a whoop. The music filled me and I wanted to sing and dance. We pulled off the highway and wound through deserted streets past poorly made, decrepit buildings until we got to where our RV was parked. Dan and Mulberry tripped over each other coming out the door to greet us.

"You did it!" Mulberry yelled. Blue's tail wagged and his tongue lolled out of his head as he joined in our excitement. "I can't wait to see her face."

"I want to see it," Izel said.

"Yes, yes," Malina said.

We all went inside, a group far too large for the small living quarters. We crowded around Dan's computer. Mulberry passed out beers. Dan hit play and I watched Ana Maria tell the camera that the world would never know she killed her parents. Mulberry clicked his bottle against mine. "You fucking did it."

"Yeah," I said, leaning against him. "I got her."

Dan looked over at me and smiled. "Congratulations," he said. I raised my bottle in a toast to him.

30

No Thoughts

I WOKE UP THE NEXT MORNING JUST HUNG OVER ENOUGH TO know I drank the night before. I was the first awake and turning to look down at my motley crew, I couldn't help but smile. Mulberry was squeezed into the dining area bed this time. Dan on the couch. The two ladies shared the room in the back.

Blue poked his head out of the driver's seat sensing me. I lowered myself down as quietly as possible. Slipping into a pair of sneakers and jogging shorts, I opened the door and stepped out into the cool morning.

Blue and I headed down the block. It'd been too long and my legs felt tired. My lungs struggled to keep up with my ambitions. I started slow letting my body remember what it felt like to run, not in the heat of a moment but as an exercise in endurance.

We were the only ones out at that hour. As my muscles warmed, my head emptied. All my little plottings, all my worries about the next couple of days, the nausea of my hangover, I left it behind as my legs stretched into longer and longer strides.

I'd lost my headphones so the only soundtrack to my run was the pounding of my feet and the in and out of my breath. I started sprinting and felt exhilarated. There was nothing in my head except the thought that I was flying. I was flying.

I came back to the RV with sweat coating my body and a clear head. Dan stepped out and I felt my heart thump again. As long as there were other people around I felt safe, but being alone with him...

"Can I talk to you for a second?" he asked.

"Sure," I smiled. "What's on your mind?"

"You," he said, maintaining eye contact. Dan was several feet away and it felt like there was suddenly a wall of fire between us. He raised his left hand and rubbed at the back of his neck, smiling. "I get the feeling you're avoiding me."

"I can't, Dan," I said.

"Can't what?"

"I don't know, I just-" Struggling to put into words how now what I needed was space and room to think, I stood in front of Dan with my mouth open but nothing coming out.

"Is it because of Mulberry?" Dan gestured with his head at the RV.

"No," I shook my head. "But with all these people around, I just need to concentrate."

He stepped toward me and I didn't back away. "But you could in St. Thomas."

"I don't know."

"Maybe it has to be a balcony." He smiled and looked down at the ground. "I-"

I rushed at him and placed my hand over his mouth. "Don't, Dan. Don't say anything. Can't we just finish this?" He looked at me and I felt desperate for him to agree. For him to just be there for me until this was over. I couldn't bear to be responsible for this gentle, sweet man's feelings. He needed to be OK without me and I needed to be OK without him.

Dan nodded and I lifted my hand from his mouth. "Yes, Captain," he said.

I felt my body against his and stepped back. "Thank you," I said. "I'm sorry-"

He reached out and touched my hand lightly. "You don't ever have to be sorry with me, Sydney," he said, looking down at our hands. "I'm stronger than you think." He smiled up at me then and I felt an easing in my chest.

Mulberry stuck his head out the door and called to us. "You better come in and hear this."

When I opened the door of the RV, Malina, Izel, and Mulberry all turned and looked at us but no one said anything. The radio was on. "What's going on?" I asked

Izel answered, "They are saying that Ana Maria was attacked again by her kidnapper and that fingerprint evidence now confirms that it was Joy Humbolt, the fugitive."

"But it is strange," Malina interjected, "she says that you still have long blonde hair and they do not mention your scars."

Then I heard her voice. Ana Maria was speaking in Spanish and Izel translated for me: "Although this is hard, I will still be at the Juarez benefit on Friday. My tragedy is just one of many in this country. I, unlike the women of Juarez, had a chance to fight back; I want to give them the same."

"She's good," Mulberry said.

"Yeah, Jesus. If I didn't know better, I'd think she was amazing," Dan said.

"In her own way she is," I said. They all turned to look at me. "I mean it's amazing how full of shit she is." Everyone nodded. "It's amazing how well she is manipulating this whole thing. She doesn't really want me caught or else she'd give them a real description. She knows that the whole thing could fall apart if they get me."

No one said anything and the news changed over to the weather. Mulberry leaned forward and turned it off. "But for how much they love her now," I said. "They will hate her more when they find out they've been lied to. They will want their revenge."

I looked up and noticed that everyone was staring at me. Dan cleared his throat. "Well, I better get to work then." He reached into his bag and pulled out his laptop.

"I'll make some breakfast," Izel said. Malina stood up to help her. Mulberry climbed into the driver's seat and got ready for what looked like a nap.

It was three days until the benefit and while Dan was busy the rest of us didn't have much to do. Dan sat at the table in front of his computer. The rest of us just tried to stay out of his way. I worked out a lot, but it wasn't enough to exhaust me. I think we all had an incurable nervous energy. None of us would be able to sleep until it was over: when Ana Maria was up on that stage and behind her played the tape of her standing over her parent's death site, saying that the world would never know it was her.

History is a funny thing, I thought, as I laid awake in my bunk staring at the ceiling only inches away. I'd never really thought about my place in it before. But now my mind, with nothing else to do, kept wandering there. The idea that I would even have a place in something as big as history never crossed my thoughts before, but now I realized that, of course, I would be in text books. And not just criminology but high school. Any history of New York class, any history of politics, assassinations, millions upon millions of people would learn about me. But what would they learn? What would they know?

I rolled over and looked out the little window. It was dark out. Not even a rat was stirring. I felt like I had to get up. I couldn't just lie there. Blue jumped up when he saw me climbing down. I grabbed a beer out of the fridge and stepped into my sneakers. Without tying the laces I went outside. There was no moon, no street lights. It would feel like the country if not for the smells of so much humanity.

I popped the can of beer open and took a long sip. Leaning against the side of the RV I tried to think of something useful to think about. Something I could do to make this plan happen. Mulberry said I already did my part but I hated sitting around waiting. I heard a sound and turning quickly saw a stray dog. Its ribs exposed and its hip bones jutting through its skin. A shudder ran through me. It watched us cautiously then jogged away, large loose udders swinging from its belly. I didn't want to think about the fate of her.

I reached out a hand and rested it on Blue's head. He leaned his body against me. It was nice to feel his warmth. Looking down at him I felt a smile cross my face. "You're a good boy," I said.

He looked up at me. His eyes, full of emotion but empty of thought, brought a lump to my throat. Blue did not shy away from eye contact. He did not understand embarrassment. I turned away before he did, my eyes wet. I sipped from my beer again. James popped into my head as he so often did.

We were young and in the yard. Our father was still alive. James and I were working together to make a fort. One that would hold against the invading army. We'd brought all the kitchen chairs outside. Then James carried out the Transformers blanket from his bed. I helped drape it over the chairs. Inside the light was blue. We sat on the grass. James put his arm around me and told me that when the enemy came we'd be ready. With a big smile on his face, he showed me the slingshots he'd made for us. We gathered rocks and waited. James saw them first. Giant, hairy beasts coming across the yard. We fired through the chair legs.

"I've been hit," James cried, and fell back onto the grass holding his arm. I fired at the imaginary beasts. James pulled himself back up and using only one arm launched stones at them, too.

"I've been hit," I yelled, grabbing my leg.

"Oh no, lava," James yelled.

"Sydney?" Mulberry was in the doorway looking down at me. "You OK?"

I turned away from him and swiped at my eyes. I took a sip of beer and tasted it mixing with the salt of tears. "Hey, you OK?"

"Yeah, yeah. I'm fine." I smiled for him.

He rested his back against the RV next to me. Taking the beer from my hand he took a sip. We stood there for a while not speaking. A breeze came and blew some of the clouds away. The moon, barely a sliver, became exposed. Mulberry handed me back the beer. "Bobby's been calling," he said.

"Have you been answering?"

"I did, after it was confirmed that the police were looking for Joy Humbolt. I thought he should hear our side of the story."

"What's that?"

"I told him about Ana Maria and what she did. He knows we are together but I didn't mention them," he motioned with his head toward our sleeping friends.

"Do you think he believed you?"

"Unlikely, Blane is his apprentice. He's trained him for years. Bobby has total trust in Blane."

"Jesus." I pushed off the RV. "What else are you keeping from me?"

Mulberry grabbed my arm and pulled me toward him. I bumped against his chest dropping my beer to the ground. "Let go of me," I said, pushing against him.

"Listen-"

"No, you lie to me, you are just so full-"

"Sydney, stop." His voice was soft but persistent. "Everything I don't tell you, everything I hide from you, is me trying to protect you."

"You don't need to protect me," I said.

His green eyes glinted yellow and he tightened his grip on my arm. "I don't know how to stop."

I stayed pressed against him. I felt suddenly exhausted and rested my head on his shoulder. He wrapped his arm around my waist and leaned his face against my hair.

"I think Bobby has people looking for us right now," he said quietly.

"Another thing to worry about," I said into his shoulder. "I guess we'll have to take what comes. I'm ready."

"Me, too."

31

Connections

THE NEXT MORNING DAN WOKE UP IN A HURRY. HE SAID HE knew what he had to do. He'd figured it out. Then he grabbed Mulberry, jumped in a cab, and headed into the center of the city. The bags they brought back filled the small space. When all the monitors were unpacked, they covered the table and spread across to the bench. The cords clogged every plug.

Malina, Izel and I stood in the kitchen watching Dan connect all the monitors to each other. His tongue peeked between his lips and his eyebrows met in conference over his nose. Mulberry was helping by passing cords when Dan told him to.

When he was finished connecting everything, Dan pushed the power button on his laptop. The generator chugged trying to keep up with the power drain. The lights flickered and the four new monitors glowed to life.

It filled the small space with a creepy blue glow. I felt like we were inside a TV. Mulberry grinned. "What's all this for Dan?" I asked.

He turned to me, a little boy's proud smile on his face. "This is where we are going to watch the show."

"We need this many screens to watch it?" Izel asked.

"Yes. Because we are going to watch it from the booth."

"Booth?"

"See, a show like this there are a bunch of cameras, right?" We nodded. "And since it is a live show there is a director who sits in a little booth and tells people which camera to put up on the screen, the TV that people see at home." The monitors blinked and then came back to life. Dan turned to look at them. He guided the mouse attached to his laptop and we all watched as the corresponding arrow jumped from one screen to the next.

Dan continued: "So this booth with the director also controls what goes up on the screen behind the performers, or speech makers, whoever is on the stage. So if all goes to plan we will be able to see what the director sees and if all really goes to plan than we will be able to change what goes up on the screen."

"So when Ana Maria is giving her talk we will be able to play her confession?" I said.

"That's right, it will go up right behind her head."

"There is a small catch," Mulberry said.

Dan bit his lip. "See we need to somehow get into the booth. I can't access it remotely. I tried but their security is too tight. The thing is about this event is that 'the booth' is actually a trailer outside of the theater. So we could sneak in-"

"I'll do it," I said, excited at the prospect of having something, anything to do. Dan and Mulberry both looked at me.

"I don't think so," Mulberry said.

"What? I'm the most qualified."

"And the most exposed," Dan said. "If you get caught, you're in jail forever."

"I'll do it," Malina said.

"I'll help," Izel said.

"No, wait. Look, I can do this."

Everyone looked at me and I knew I was beat. Dan put it into words. "No way, Sydney, you're sitting this one out."

"But-" there was nothing left to say. "Mutiny," I muttered. Which, of course, they all heard.

In addition to all the monitors Dan bought he also invested in some audio equipment. He held up the small ear piece. "This way I'll be able to direct you through it," he said to Izel. He handed one to Malina. "And if you need any help we'll be in your ear, too."

They both nodded. Dan typed away on his computer and within seconds, two of the monitors showed images of all of us. Malina and Izel looked down at the small cameras hidden in their clothes. I noticed that my hair looked really uneven in the back. I reached a hand up to touch it but Izel turned and all I could see was Mulberry's chest.

I was sitting on the bench next to one of the monitors, a hand gently resting on it to keep it steady. Izel and Malina were by the door, Mulberry stepped out of the RV and held it open for them. "Good luck, guys," I said.

They turned and smiled at me. Blue tried to follow them but he too was banished from the adventure. The door closed behind them and I watched in the monitor as they all climbed into Izel's car which they'd picked up from her place earlier in the day. Blue and I were banished from that ride as well. "You hear me OK?" Dan asked into a tabletop microphone.

"Loud and clear," Izel said.

"Roger that," Malina said, and then giggled.

The car started, a soft rumble over the computer's speakers and we watched the landscape move across the windows. They listened to the radio on their way toward the theater. It was a rock station and after two songs a woman's voice came on. "It's about the benefit," Izel said. "She says that the woman who sang the last song is performing there tonight. She sends her and the stations best wishes to Ana Maria."

"That won't last," I said to Dan.

"Let's hope they can plant this thing."

"Dan, even if it doesn't happen tonight we can use it another time. Worse comes to worse we'll just send it to the police."

Dan shrugged. "I guess, but I think this is really the way to go."

"It's dramatic."

"And if you don't have drama in life, what do you have?" Dan said with a smile.

"Boredom?"

"Exactly," Dan nodded his head.

"Yeah, I think after this I might be up for a little boredom."

"Yeah, right."

"What?"

But Dan didn't answer me, he was watching as the car slowed. "They're at the drop off." Mulberry was letting the girls off a couple of blocks away. They climbed out and we watched the people that they passed on the street. It was funny to watch all the men staring straight at the camera pinned to Malina's chest.

The theater came into view. It was surrounded by a crowd of fans even though the benefit did not start for hours. Malina and Izel bypassed the crowd in front of the entrance and began to circle the building. Metal gates separated the fans from a red carpet which a man was vacuuming. They followed the gate around the side of the building and there it was. A big white trailer with no windows. Miles of thick black cable led out of the trailer and snaked along the metal gate and out of sight.

"That's it," Dan said.

A guard, wearing a uniform, stood by it. Malina led with her camera. "Hola," she said. I could picture her leaning on the gate towards the man. He smiled and returned the greeting. Izel's camera showed her hanging back watching the scene. The man stepped toward Malina. And Izel slipped between two pieces of the gate.

She was hurrying along the side of the building and Malina was bringing the man ever closer to her. She began to walk away from the trailer and he followed. Malina was asking about his job and he was answering freely. "Unless my Spanish really sucks I think she just asked if he was the only one guarding the trailer and he said yes," I said.

Dan nodded, watching Izel's camera. She was right at the steps leading to the trailer. He pushed down on the mic and said, "Malina, ask if there is anyone inside."

I heard her ask him. He shook his head no and explained that they wouldn't be there for another hour or so. He had it all to himself. "I think he is implying that they could go have sex in the trailer," I said.

"Can't blame a guy for trying," Dan said to me with a wink. I shook my head at him and he shrugged then laughed. Turning back to the mic he said, "Izel, there is no one in there. Go for it."

We watched, holding our breaths, as she climbed up the three short steps and turned the handle. Inside was dark and it took the camera a moment to adjust for the sudden light change. Before it even had a chance, Izel closed the door and the screen went black. We heard her shuffling around; meanwhile, Malina's chest was getting grinned at.

Izel's monitor turned white and then the camera adjusted and we could see a cramped space. Along one wall was at least fifty monitors, at seat level was a control panel that stretched the length of the trailer. Three chairs marked where the technicians sat. Izel scanned her camera over the controls. Buttons and more buttons. And at each seat a joy stick.

"Alright, you're doing great Izel. What I need you to do is pull out the middle chair." Izel did as she was told. "OK. Now look under there. The camera lowered as Izel climbed onto her knees. It was dark under the table but I could just make out what looked like computer towers. "Turn your flashlight on." The sound of clothing rustling was followed by a spot of light roaming under the dark space. "Slow down, slow down," Dan said leaning toward the screen. "Stop. That's it. No go back a little. Right there."

On the screen Izel's light was centered on a row of slits in the side of the computer. I recognized them as USB ports. "Get a little closer," Dan said. Izel moved the camera closer. "Alright, let's see." Dan reached out and touched the screen, running his finger along the ports. "Izel, it's the second in from the left."

The melody of Malina's conversation faltered and I turned to her screen. The guard was no longer looking at Malina, something to his right had grabbed his attention. Malina turned and I saw another uniformed men heading toward her. "He is my replacement," the guard said. "Let me buy you lunch?" Malina's camera turned back to him, but she did not respond. "Are you alright?" he asked.

I felt the same fear gripping my chest that was paralyzing Malina's vocal cords. "Dan," I said.

"Hold on," he waved me away. "That's it, yup," he said into the mic. He banged his fist onto the table. "You got it. Izel I could kiss you." He looked up at me and the smile fell off his face. His eyes flicked to Malina's monitor. It showed two uniformed men staring into the camera.

Standing up I grabbed the mic off the table. Clicking down on the talk button I said, "Izel get up now. Get to the door. Malina don't say anything. OK. On the count of three Izel you are going to get out of that trailer. Malina when I say three you drop, faint, fall. If you understand move the camera." It moved. I looked back at Izel's monitor. She was by the door. "Izel turn the lights out." Her monitor went black. "OK." I tried to look at both monitors as I counted. "1, 2, 3!"

Malina's camera swung wildly. The two uniformed men were replaced by the sky, overexposed into a white blur. It curved passed the heavens and flew by the distant buildings before settling with half the screen pavement and the other half a view down the block.

Izel's monitor turned all white as the camera struggled to fix its exposure. Labored breathing and the swish of fabric against the microphone came through the speakers. The camera adjusted and we could see that she was hurrying toward the metal gate.

I was gripping the microphone, my eyes racing from one scene to the other.

A pair of black boots almost filled Malina's screen. One of the men was asking if she was OK. She mumbled something unintelligible. Izel's monitor showed her approaching the metal gate. I saw her swing over it in Malina's. She was a tiny distant figure behind the boots. Izel's camera stopped jerking as she slowed to a walk.

I dropped the microphone back onto the table. "That was too close," I said. "Way too close." My hands shook, I rubbed them together and felt a thin layer of sweat between my palms. "I should not have let them do that." I sat down on the couch, tipping the monitor on its side. I cupped my hands over my eyes and watched the darkness behind my lids explode with dots of light as I pressed into my eyeballs. "I should have just sent the tape to the police."

Laughter. I opened my eyes. Laughter was coming out of the speakers. I dropped my hands and turned to the flat screen lying next to me. Malina's monitor showed Izel's smiling face. "I did it," Izel told Malina. Malina's laughter echoed through both their microphones.

"We did it."

THE RV WAS STARTING TO SMELL LIKE A SOCK. A SOCK WORN BY a sweaty man with suspect hygiene. I noticed it when Blue and I came back from a walk. We'd been wandering for 45 minutes in fresh air. Stepping back into the RV after that kind of freedom made it clear not only that the thing stunk but that it was also filled to comedic proportions.

"I feel like I'm in a Marx Brothers' film," I said, as I pushed past Izel who was pouring a glass of water.

"What?" Malina asked, as I shimmied by her. She was perched on the edge of the table. Dan sat in one of the benches. Mulberry was in the other. I stepped over a cord to get to my bunk. Blue hopped up next to the monitor on the couch and it tilted over. Mulberry reached across and straightened it back up. I took off my shoes and put them up in my bunk then sat down in the passenger seat, twisting my body to face the group.

"How much longer?"

Dan looked at his watch. "Two hours."

"Everything all set to go?"

"As much as it was before you left."

I sighed and faced forward. There was nothing to look at,

nothing to do. I sighed again. "Jesus, Sydney," Mulberry said. "Stop it with the sighing."

"Sorry, sorry. I'm just bored."

"We're all bored, doesn't mean we go around sighing."

"You're right." I turned to look at him. He was playing a game of solitaire.

"You want to play a card game?"

He shrugged. "Gin?"

"Sounds good."

"Can I play?" Malina asked.

"We could play Hearts," Dan suggested. "That way we can all play."

"Great," Izel said.

An hour into the game I got up, climbed over the monitor cord, squeezed passed Izel's legs and got myself a beer. During the second beer I ended up with the queen of spades (a really bad thing in Hearts unless you're trying to shoot the moon) and decided to try and shoot the moon (get all the hearts and the queen of spades). And I would have got away with it too if that pesky Malina hadn't managed to get the last heart.

I opened a third beer in an attempt to console myself. As I stood in the kitchen taking my first sip I glanced at the microwave clock for the thousandth time that day. The show started in fifteen minutes. Dan turned on the computer, all the monitors glowed to life. A local TV station played on the monitor on the couch so we could all see it. The other three monitors were broken up into lots of small squares each showing a different camera in the theater.

"I need some fresh air," I said, stepping out of the RV. Blue followed. He took a piss and I stretched my hands over my head. Scanning the barren landscape of the motel's parking lot, I was surprised to see a parked SUV with two men hunched into their seats. I let my eyes rove past them. Then calling Blue, I got us both back into the RV.

Everyone was watching the TV as graphics for the benefit played across the screen. "We've got company," I said. Izel and

Malina turned to me with a curious glance. Dan was typing on his computer and hadn't listened. "Outside, black SUV, two men," I said to Mulberry. He turned his head slowly.

"Yup."

And as I looked straight through the windshield I saw two more men coming our way. "They're getting out." he said. One of the men in the front raised a big gun.

"Duck!" I yelled before dropping to the ground. Blue laid down next to me. Malina flopped off the bench onto the floor, Dan slid under the table and Mulberry flattened himself into the bench. Izel looked at us all dumbly.

"What?" she said before the first bullets started. They were coming through the windshield and from our right side, the windows exploded and the walls dimpled. I grabbed Izel's elbow and pulled her down, as she came toward me a bullet hit her in the shoulder. It splattered blood all over my face, it was in my eyes and then her body was on top of me, moaning. I couldn't see and the smell of blood was so strong in my nose and mouth that I thought I might puke.

Instead I pushed myself from under her. She was crying. Using my shirt I tried to rub the blood off my face. It helped. The RV was shaking, a monitor exploded in a flash of sparks. It was fascinating and for a moment I just watched it burnout, the screen a blackened hole.

Regaining myself I pulled a kitchen rag down off the counter and pushed it into Izel's wound. She screamed. "Hold it there," I said. Then I opened the cabinet under the sink. Reaching into the small space I pulled out the guns Mulberry had stashed there. I scooted till I was between the bathroom and the shower. I checked the clip of the first, found it full, pushed it back into place and then leaning across the floor, handed it to Izel. "Pass this down to Mulberry," I yelled over the deafening banging that rocked our little home.

With a grimace on her face and shards of glass in her hair Izel took the gun. She turned to the body next to her and passed it down the line. I checked the second clip, and then crawled into the back bedroom. The bullets stopped. The only sound in the RV was the TV. A commercial featuring a monkey eating a banana. Glass bit into my forearms. Blue followed me.

"We are the police," a voice announced from outside in English. I peeked out the destroyed window and saw a man wearing a leather jacket and jeans. A bang came from the other end of the RV and the man dropped to one knee. I dove back to the ground as the hail of bullets started again. The gunmen were circling the vehicle, I could tell by the way the dimples in the walls moved. A piece of wood exploded out of the closet door. He was moving around, he would be in front of my window in a minute.

When the wall right in front of me started to dent I raised my gun over my head and depressed the trigger. The sound of guns quieted to only me and someone near the front. I released the trigger and lowered my gun, careful not to touch the burning hot barrel. The other guns stopped, too. I could hear Izel crying and a man outside moaning.

The benefit was starting. I heard applause coming from the speakers. I looked into the other room and saw through the smoke that Ana Maria was mounting the stage wearing a long green gown. I watched the screen mesmerized by her big smile, her delicate throat, her sad eyes.

"Come out with your hands up!" A man yelled from outside. "We won't hurt you." Izel looked over at me, her face pale and her whole left arm drenched in blood. "We will give you two minutes."

Ana Maria started to speak: "Thank you all for coming," she said. I opened my clip and saw that I had two bullets left.

"Mulberry, how many bullets do you have?" I whisper/shouted.

"There are more under the sink," he whisper/shouted back.

"The situation in Juarez is unacceptable," Ana Maria told the crowd.

I found the box of extra bullets, poured out a bunch for me and then passed the rest down the line to Mulberry. "How many are out there?" I asked while pushing bullets into my clip. Blue came over to me and sniffed at my gun. I pushed him back. "Down, boy," I said. He laid down, protected between the shower and bathroom.

"One minute!" a voice warned.

"I saw four men before," Mulberry whispered. "Two with the big guns and then two with hand guns. I think you got one of the guys with the machine guns and I got the guy who was doing the talking. They still have guns though. They're not helpless."

I looked around at the destroyed RV. The air filled with an acrid smoke, the filling spilling out of the cushions, not an intact pane of glass anywhere. Izel was the only one shot, I couldn't see Dan because he was under the table. Malina was holding Izel's hand, her eyes squeezed shut. "Everyone alive?" I asked.

"Thirty seconds!"

Malina and Izel both nodded. "Yeah," Dan's voice came out from under the table.

"I would like to close with a poem," Ana Maria said. "One of my mother's favorites," I looked at the screen and saw that Ana Maria was crying.

"It will play, right, Dan?" I asked.

"It should."

"Good. Mulberry, I'll go out first, cover me." I heard him moving around, glass crushing under his weight, then I saw his gun prop up against the passenger seat.

"Ten seconds." Looking out a hole in the front door I saw that the men were hiding behind the doors of their SUVs. They were scared. They should be, I thought, as I cocked my gun.

I stood up and as I reached for the handle, I heard Ana Maria's voice: "History is a funny thing," she said as I kicked the door open and dove for the ground.

33

A Fire Fight

THE SOUND OF BULLETS WHIZZING BY BARELY FAZED ME AS I rolled under the RV. Mulberry was shooting at the men, taking most of their fire. From where I lay I had the perfect angle to shoot at their feet. The first one fell on his side, his head exposed. I shot out the other one's feet and he fell into the SUV. They were both screaming. I rolled until I could see the SUV in front of the RV. Mulberry had turned his fire onto it already. Its windshield exploded.

The engine started. Mulberry fired at the hood. I smelled gas, turning I saw that our tank was leaking. "Get out!" I yelled. "Move, move!"

The men who still had use of their feet were peeling out. I rolled out from under the RV. Aimed my gun but decided to save my bullets. Malina was helping Izel out of the RV. Blue ran to my side.

I approached the other SUV with the two injured men. They'd both managed to climb inside but neither of them could drive. It's hard without feet. I approached at a crouch. They didn't have toes but they had guns.

Blue was behind my left leg. I turned back for a second just to make sure everyone was out of the RV. I didn't know what happened, I just fell forward. I saw a man's face, peeking over the door, his grin showed off yellowed, crooked teeth. Blue didn't wait for a command. He launched himself at the gunman. His smile turned into a scream. Mulberry was right behind Blue. He pulled the other man out of the SUV, wrenched his gun out of his hand and then turned to the guy who shot me. I looked down at my leg. Blood oozed in a streak along my right thigh.

I swallowed. There was grit and dust lining my mouth. I looked up and saw Malina standing over me. Bits of sand clung to my eyelashes, they looked like huge boulders separating me from Malina. She looked down at my leg. Crouching down Malina reach a hand toward it but paused a foot away from the wound, her arm hung in the air for a moment and then reached over and picked up my gun. Standing, she headed toward the SUV, her legs wide and head low she looked like a tornado. I was glad she was on my side. Malina strode to where Blue had my shooter pinned to the ground and put the gun right against his forehead.

"Malina!" Mulberry yelled.

"You deserve to die," she told the man in Spanish. "I should gut you like the pig you are." I looked at her hand and saw that she was pressing on the trigger.

"Malina, No!" I yelled. The burst of sound was somehow louder than any of the others that day. I closed my eyes. When I opened them again the man was still alive. Malina was standing over him. Tears running down her face. She walked away, the gun held loosely in her hand.

"He's not worth it," she said as she passed me.

Mulberry picked up the men's guns and then stepped over the recently pardoned gunman. "Who do you work for?" he asked. The man shook his head. Mulberry dug the heel of his boot into the man's wounded foot. "Who do you work for!" The man screamed in pain. "Answer me and we'll leave," Mulberry said, leaning down into the man's face.

"Global," he said. "Global."

"That's what I thought." Mulberry left the man lying in the dirt and climbed into the driver's seat. "Come on," he yelled to us, "let's go." Dan bent down and wrapped his arm under my shoulders. He heaved me off the ground. I gripped him. Keeping my injured leg up, I used my good one to hobble to the SUV. Dan helped me into the passenger side. The other three piled into the back with Blue. Mulberry pulled out of the dusty parking lot.

My leg was aching but it didn't feel like there was anything inside me. Inspecting the blackened fabric around the wound I saw that it was a graze. The sun was setting. Mulberry turned on the headlights to navigate through the quickly darkening streets. "Izel, how are you?" I asked, twisting in my seat.

She smiled at me. The kitchen rag still pushed onto her shoulder. "OK."

"We need to get her to a doctor," I said to Mulberry.

"I have a friend," Malina said from the back seat. "He will take care of all of us for no charge. And he is not a talker."

"Sounds perfect," I said.

An explosion shook the air. We all turned to see a cloud of black smoke rising up from where the RV used to be. Mulberry stepped on the gas as the wail of sirens filled the air. I leaned back in my seat exhausted. My leg burned.

Malina gave Mulberry directions to her doctor friend. Then Mulberry turned on the radio and scanned until he found a woman talking. It was a call in show and they were discussing Ana Maria. Izel translated. "This woman says she thinks it is conspiracy against Ana Maria. The host of the show says maybe she is paranoid." We didn't need translation for the woman's yell of frustration and the sound of a phone slamming down. "OK," said the announcer, "let's see who's next. Jose, tell me what you think."

"She is guilty. She made the whole thing up, obviously."

"You really think she killed her own parents?"

"Yes. Yes, I do."

"All right, Jose knows what he thinks, what about you?"

"Guilty," Dan said. We all laughed a little.

"For those of you just tuning it we're talking about the surprise at the Women of Juarez benefit tonight. If you've been under a rock for the last half hour than you might not have heard that a video of Ana Maria Hernandez Vargas confessing to her parents' murder was played instead of a planned tribute to her family. The police are trying to verify the footage. Apparently, they have not arrested Ana Maria yet. But they are asking her not to leave the city. What do you think?"

The next caller was outraged. "How can they not just arrest her? If she was not rich, if she was like most Mexicans, like the ones her mother fought for, she would be in jail. Where she belongs."

"That's a good point..."

The gentle rhythm of the SUV combined with the whispers of Ana Maria's guilt lulled me to sleep. When I woke up we were in the driveway of a suburban home.

I opened my own door and went to step out but my leg screamed out in pain. It felt swollen and stiff. Malina came to my side and helped me up. We hobbled toward the front door. The light of a TV flickered in a window. Malina rang the bell and we heard it ring throughout the house.

The sound of cautious footsteps leading up to the door preceded it being swung open by a tall, good looking man in his late 50s with dark hair graying at the temples. "Malina?" he said looking at her. Then he switched his focus to my face then down to my leg. "My God, what is happening?"

Malina pushed past him into the house. "You have to help us," she said. Izel supported by Mulberry came in right after me followed by Dan and Blue. The owner of the house stood in his doorway with a slack jaw. "Please," Malina said. "Help us!"

He jumped into action. "Bring them to the garage. We don't want the blood in here." Malina and I did our best impression of three legged racers as we moved through the man's house, past his bright clean kitchen and into the garage.

There was a ping pong table and Malina helped me up onto it.

Izel sat next to me. The man came out with towels, a bowl of water and several sterilized packets of tools. "Something for the pain, doc?" I asked. He nodded, stepping over to a fridge in the corner and pulling out a vial of liquid goodness. "Her first," I said, gesturing to Izel. He gave her the medicine and within moments she was laying back on the pool table, her eyes closed and breath even. "What's your name?" I asked as the doctor approached with his needle.

"I don't want to know your name or you to know mine. Hopefully, you'll all forget you were ever here."

I smiled, then he stuck the needle in my arm. Moments later I was floating on a sea of comfortable foam. I heard Izel moan a little and turned to see him working on her arm, a bright light on his forehead, a pair of bloody tweezers in his hand. Later I felt the prick of a needle in my leg and looked down to see him at my wound. "A local anesthetic," he said. "You won't feel a thing." And he was right, besides a mildly uncomfortable pulling sensation I didn't feel a thing.

WHEN I WOKE UP I WAS ON A COUCH, A CLEAN BANDAGE wrapped around my leg. The doctor was asleep in a chair nearby. A thick white stubble covered his face. I looked around the pleasant sitting room and saw Blue snoring by the front door. It was still dark outside.

Sitting up I felt light headed but OK. My leg throbbed with pain but nothing unbearable. Swinging my legs around, I stood up gingerly, giving most of my weight to the good leg. My movements woke Blue and the doctor, both of whom hurried to my side. "Don't put weight on it for a couple of days," he said. "I have a crutch for you. Wait." He hurried out of the room and I rested a hand on Blue's head. He wagged his tail and smiled up at me.

Mulberry came down the steps and seeing me up, smiled. "How are you feeling?" he asked while crossing the room.

"I want to talk to Bobby Maxim right now."

"OK."

"He was the one who set those guys on us. That was not some police raid. That mother-fucker tried to kill us." I would have continued on my tirade but the doctor came back into the room with my crutch and I didn't want to freak the poor guy out anymore than he already was.

"Here you are," he said, handing me the crutch. I shifted it under my arm and rested on it.

"Thank you," I said. "Thank you so much."

"You're welcome." He smiled and nodded. There were dark circles under his brown eyes. "I'm going to go check on Izel."

I waited until the doctor was out of sight before turning to Mulberry. "He tracked your stupid phone," I said. "If he believed Ana Maria and not you then of course he would want to kill us both. Get him on the phone."

Mulberry pulled his phone out of his pocket and dialed the number. I took the device and sat back down on the couch, my leg pulsating.

"Mulberry," Bobby said.

"Nope, it's Sydney."

"Wonderful-"

"We had a deal," I said. "I get the girl back, you make Joy Humbolt a corpse."

"Calm down, Sydney."

"You just tried to kill me, Mulberry and our friends. I'm not going to calm down for awhile."

"Someone tried to kill you?"

"Don't play dumb with me. I know what you do with people you consider threats. Those 'cops' you sent - you think I'm stupid - that I wouldn't figure it out?"

"If the cops caught up with you-"

"They didn't and they won't. Don't waste your time trying to kill Sydney Rye, just take care of Joy Humbolt."

"Things are already in motion. I saw the broadcast last night. It was very illuminating. One thing you'll learn about me is that I keep my promises."

"You better." I hung up the phone.

Mulberry was staring at me. "Did he admit it? That he tried to kill us."

"No, but he's not an idiot. Why would he? I think he'll follow through now, though. He knows what Ana Maria is. He said he saw the broadcast and that it was very enlightening."

"Good."

Malina came down the steps and smiled at me. "You look better," she said. "You have color in your face."

"Thanks." I heard more movement on the stairs and turned to see Izel and the doctor making their way down. I stood, using the crutch for help. Izel looked drained but OK. She smiled at me as she reached the bottom of the steps.

The doctor cleared his throat and looked over at Malina. "We need to go," she said.

"I understand. Thank you so much for your help, Doctor."

"This never happened," he reminded me.

"Right. Malina, I think it's safe for you to go home. Ana Maria is not going to be going after any of us. The cops don't know about either of you and I'm sure you are looking forward to getting back to your lives."

Malina laughed. "Yes, but it will seem so boring now, no?"

Izel gave her a weak smile. "I'm OK with boring right now. But," she looked at me, "if you ever need me, please call."

"I will."

"I can drive them home," the doctor said. Turning to Mulberry he said, "You need to get yourselves and your bullet-ridden SUV off my property before I get back."

Mulberry nodded. "Thanks for your help."

"It never happened," was his response.

"Right."

"Where are you going?" Malina asked.

"I'm not sure," I said.

"You will call me?"

"Sure. I'll stay in touch."

She smiled but tears welled in her eyes. I felt mine shimmering. We hugged tightly. "Thank you for all your help," I said.

"De nada."

I pulled back and wiped tears from my eyes but they just reappeared when I looked at Izel. Another hug, this one gentler to avoid hurting her arm. "You saved my life," I told her.

"Thank you," she said.

Dan, Mulberry, Malina, and Izel all hugged goodbye. The only dry eyes left in the house belonged to the doctor who was trying to hurry us out of his home. After Izel and Malina left with the doctor, Mulberry went to get the SUV. He'd hidden it behind the back of the house so no one would notice it and wonder why the good doctor had an SUV full of holes in his driveway.

"Do you need to get back?" I asked Dan while we waited for the car to come around.

"Back to what?" he asked.

I shrugged. "Don't you have a life?"

"Not one that needs me."

"Do you maybe want to go some place with me?" I asked, not looking at him.

Dan stepped close to me and touched my face. I looked up at him and he smiled down at me. "I'd follow you anywhere, Captain."

I felt my eyes welling again and then he kissed me softly and sweetly the way only a boy from New Jersey can.

Dan helped me into the front seat of the car and then climbed in the back. Blue jumped up next to Dan. I turned on the radio as we headed for the highway. That Robert "Bobby" Maxim worked fast. The music was interrupted and news of a shootout followed by an explosion at Ana Maria's hotel was announced. Apparently, she was dead, along with an unidentified woman. Both bodies were badly burned but they expected DNA evidence to match that of Joy Humbolt who was named in the recording of Ana Maria's confession. Ana's head of security, Blane Nichols, survived with only minor injuries.

I closed my eyes and laid my head back against the seat.

"Where we going?" Mulberry asked.

"Not you, too," I said.

"How about into the sunset?" he suggested.
"It's dark out," Dan said.
"All right," I said. "Then find us a sunrise."

Turn the page to start Reading an excerpt from
Strings of Glass (A Sydney Rye Mystery,#4) now.

Strings of Glass

A SYDNEY RYE MYSTERY, #4

GOT TO BE STARTING SOMETHING

The road crumbled under my feet as I ran up it. There is no road surface strong enough to resist the pull back to dirt in this climate. In Goa, Mother Nature rules.

Blue touched my thigh with his nose, a gentle tap to remind me he was there. Thick jungle lined our path. This hill had the fewest homes on our route. No neighbors to wave a hello to or children to smile at as they raced by on bikes either too large or too small for them. There was just me, Blue, the burst of vegetation, and this road of rocks. I reached the top of the hill, my thighs and calves burned. Panting, I struggled to keep my pace.

A low growl narrowed my attention onto a black and white street dog in the brush. Ears flat to her head she curled her lips and showed us her teeth. Noting the swollen teats hanging low and exposed, I kept moving. "I'm not going to bother you, mama," I said in a steady voice. "We are just passing by."

Blue slowed and when I patted my thigh for him to catch up he stopped. I turned to look back at him, my senses on high alert. Blue was a mutt the height of a Great Dane with the coat of a wolf and the long snout of a Collie, with one blue eye and one brown. Blue has saved my life more than once so when he stopped, so did I.

I recognized a twitch on his lip and saw the hackles raise off his shoulders and back making him appear even larger. A deep and rumbling growl left his chest. It was answered behind me. There were suddenly three dogs in our path. None as big or strong as Blue but together they looked dangerous.

I'd been warned about this pack. Growing larger by the day, it was led by an aggressive alpha male the color of dirty water. This must be him, I thought, as the largest of the three, his head wide, fur the muddy brown of an engorged river, growled at Blue. The compactness of his body spoke of strength and survival. When he barked the saliva that shot from his mouth caught a ray of sunlight streaming through the thick foliage around us.

Muddy Water stepped forward, revving his growl like a teenager on a motorbike. The bitch in the brush flanked our left side and when I turned right, two young dogs, their ears still soft from puppyhood, glowered at me.

The owner of the guest house where I lived warned me to take a stick if I planned on running. "Just in case," she'd said with a dip of her head and a flip of her hand. Because of her advice I carried a light but solid piece of bamboo about twice the thickness of my thumb. I tapped it on the ground in front of me as I backed toward Blue, keeping my eyes forward, focused on the alpha but paying close attention to my peripheral vision, watching the dogs to my sides.

When I reached Blue he moved backwards with me, slowly and deliberately. But the dogs started to follow with us. We stopped, and raising the stick over my head, I brought it down hard onto a rock. The loud sound and sudden movement spooked the pups to my right but the alpha male just growled louder.

The two dogs flanking Muddy Waters went crazy barking, the force of their calls lifting their front paws off the ground. The mother and the young ones joined in raising a ruckus that certainly beat mine. Blue, his front paws planted on the road, exposed his teeth and growled, his pitch wavering up and down. He wanted me to tell him it was OK to attack. I could feel his energy bundling up inside him, roiling around, soon I'd have no control.

The alpha charged us, the other two with him following close behind. They weren't coming for me I saw quickly, all they wanted was Blue. It took only an instant for them to cross the space between us. I dropped my stick hard onto the alpha's neck but he ignored my blow, launching himself onto Blue.

Heart pounding I beat at the dogs as they swarmed. The dogs were going for his neck, for the kill. The Mother started to come out of the woods to join in the attack but a quick whack with my stick and she retreated into the trees. It only took a glare at the young ones to cow them into keeping their distance.

Blue was holding his own, but bloody streaks marked all the canines. I kicked one of the street dogs hard in the stomach. It fell on its side and then turned on me, ready to fight. I kept it at the end of my stick. It was missing part of one of its ears. A scar across its muzzle looked fresh and pink. Puncture holes in its neck showed where Blue managed a bite. I didn't want to hurt this dog.

I heard a cry and glancing over saw Blue had the alpha on his back. The other dog backed off. The noises they made were not like anything I'd heard before, almost like a speaker that's been turned on its side, spewing squeaks and squeals of interference. The alpha struggled, kicking his legs in the air, trying to push Blue. But he shook his head hard, knocking the dog under him into submission.

The dog at the end of my stick barked at Blue but didn't move toward him. Blue shook his head again and the alpha male yelped. Blood pooled around Blue's lips. "OK," I said, clapping my hands and getting the rest of the pack's attention. I shooed at them. "Get!" I yelled.

They shuffled away from me.

I stepped forward aggressively, my chest out. "Go!" I

commanded. The dog missing part of his ear jumped out of the road and into the jungle, avoiding putting weight onto his left hindquarter. I stepped to the other who growled at me. I pushed him with my stick and he turned on it, biting through the wood. "Hey!" I yelled, pushing it into his mouth hard. He yelped and stepped back. I came at him and he quickly followed the other dog into the trees.

They watched from a safe distance. Blue wasn't letting go of the alpha and I feared that he would kill him. "Blue," I said. He didn't move, just continued to snarl with his mouth full of Muddy Water's soft neck. "Let's go." He flicked his eyes up to my face. A gash on his neck pumped blood onto his white coat. "Come on," I said, making eye contact. I saw a feral animal looking back at me. There was fear in those eyes, instinct and triumph. The road, I realized, wasn't the only thing that Mother Nature turned to dust here in Goa.

Click here to continue reading
Strings of Glass (A Sydney Rye Mystery, #4).

About the Author

Emily Kimelman is the author of eight Sydney Rye Mysteries, she also co-authors the Romantic Thriller Scorch Series, and is working on a fantasy series due out in 2017. She lives on an airstream with her husband and daughter—they follow the sunshine, great hiking and good food… oh and wifi. Lol!

She shares their adventures on Instagram, Facebook and in her Readers' Group.

Sign up for Emily's Readers' Group to get free books, all her updates and never miss a new title!

If you've read Emily's work and want to get in touch please do! She LOVES hearing from readers.

www.emilykimelman.com
emily@emilykimelman.com

A Note From Emily

Thank you for reading my novel, *Insatiable*. I'm hoping you enjoyed my story. If so, would you please write a review for *Insatiable*? You have no idea how much it warms my heart to get a new review. And this isn't just for me, mind you. Think of all the people out there who need reviews to make decisions. The children who need to be told this book is not for them. And the people about to go away on vacation who could have so much fun reading this on the plane. Consider it an act of kindness to me, to the children, to humanity.

Let people know what you thought about *Insatiable* on your favorite ebook retailer and Goodreads.

Thank you, Emily

Want More?

Visit www.emilykimelman.com for a complete list
of Emily Kimelman titles.

Made in the USA
Monee, IL
16 August 2020

78343732R00204